# Lucky Day

Previously Creative Director at RDF Television, Beth Morrey now writes full time. Her debut novel, *Saving Missy*, was a *Sunday Times* bestseller and longlisted for the Authors' Club First Novel Award.

Beth lives in London with her husband, two sons and two poodles.

𝕏 @BethMorrey

f /BethMorreyWriter

⊡ @bethmorrey

Also by Beth Morrey

*Saving Missy*
*Em & Me*

# BETH MORREY

# Lucky Day

HarperCollins*Publishers*

HarperCollins*Publishers*
1 London Bridge Street
London SE1 9GF

www.harpercollins.co.uk

HarperCollins*Publishers*
Macken House, 39/40 Mayor Street Upper
Dublin 1, D01 C9W8

Published by HarperCollins*Publishers* 2024
1

A catalogue record for this book
is available from the British Library

ISBN: 978-0-00-855526-9 (HB)
ISBN: 978-0-00-855527-6 (TPB)

This novel is entirely a work of fiction.
The names, characters and incidents portrayed in it are the work of
the author's imagination. Any resemblance to actual persons, living or
dead, events or localities is entirely coincidental.

Set in Sabon LT Std by HarperCollins*Publishers* India

Printed and Bound in the UK using 100% Renewable Electricity at
CPI Group (UK) Ltd

*For Polly, who stopped, and for Tom,*
*who kept me going.*

*Finally, I saw that worrying had come to nothing.*
*And gave it up. And took my old body*
*and went out into the morning,*
*and sang.*

**'I Worried', Mary Oliver**

MORNING

# 1

Today started like any other, but then . . . veered off course. It all derailed pretty quickly, to be honest. Little things snowballing, building up to an avalanche. Like that poem about the horseshoe nail: 'For want of a nail . . .' I can't remember it now – God, brain fog again – but it starts small and before you know it a whole kingdom is lost and you're screwed. All for the want of a tiny nail. On Thursday, 16th June, I should have been in my office looking online for nice places in Padstow, but for various reasons I called my boss a prick and had some sort of episode, and here we are.

A headache came on last night, creeping up the side of my face like a dark force, prodding me awake. Ordinary painkillers do nothing, and I've long given up asking the doctor for something stronger. Last time, as I hunched, whimpering, on a vinyl chair that reeked of disinfectant, he suggested I try meditating, and turned away to tap something on his computer. I panicked it would be one of those coded notes medics use, calling me malingering or making sure I didn't get any more sleeping tablets, so I backed out, saying I'd download the Calm app. I did download it, but the sound of rain made me fret that the leak in the loft dormer had opened up again, so it didn't really work.

Unable to get back to sleep, I got up early and pottered round finishing jobs from the night before, folding washing, reloading the machine, blinking as the colours danced in front of my eyes. Scraping dried tomato off the base of the casserole dish, fetching lamb out the freezer for later, mentally adding naan bread to my shopping list, giving Grizelda her breakfast, which she lapped at fastidiously. The fridge door was a seething mass of Post-it note reminders, scrawled by me, ignored by my family: *Cancel milk, Call roofer, Hima's birthday, Jonathan's birthday, Dry-cleaning Tuesday, Cat flea treatment, Ethan inhaler, Order garden waste bags, Book smear, Fix landing light, Pay Lottie, BDD WRAP??* ☹

Those booming capitals reminded me, as they were supposed to. I started checking emails and got sucked into one about the work party later, a viewing of a show we'd made. I had nothing to do with it, didn't want to go, didn't want to be involved, but Vince, my boss, had insisted we all turn up. Now Imogen, Vince's PA, was sending me guest lists and asking me to check in case anyone on it was someone he hated: Clover, You're a Life-Saver!!!! Not even 6 a.m., and I found myself scrolling down a list of names to see if they'd included a commissioner Vince had offended or a former employee with a grudge.

Names, names, mostly unfamiliar, one I recognized

here and there, and then a particular selection of letters seemed to balloon and scatter in front of my eyes until the pain took over and I couldn't look any more. I slapped the laptop shut, pressing my hands to my face to push away the ache, banish it. Who cared who was going to the party, I certainly wasn't, so it didn't matter either way, just forget it, put it out of my mind, none of my business. After pinching the bridge of my nose for a second, trying and failing to do some mindful breathing, I decided to get on with the day, to see if ignoring it would make it go away.

My head was still pounding as I unloaded the dishwasher. Robbie always loads it wrong, fork prongs down, probably to make sure it remains my job. I mean, I pretend I can't understand council tax for the same reason, but the balance of things we both pretend we can't do seems unfairly uneven. When everything was sorted and put away, I rooted about in the ceramic chicken that lives on the windowsill in the kitchen. It's supposed to hold eggs, but who decants eggs? Instead, it's a repository for random tablets – indigestion, constipation, congestion – you name the 'tion' and we've got a tablet for it in the chicken. I like to be ready for any development – steeling myself for disaster, Robbie says.

There they were: two leftover Vicodin pills, the last of a packet he brought back from a work trip to the US where he wrenched his shoulder getting his bag down from an overhead locker. Robbie said they made him high for a week, and he had to stop taking them because he was starting to enjoy it too much. He dropped the last two into the chicken, saying 'These are not to be taken, under any circumstances,' and I said 'Why are you putting them in there then?' and he said 'As insurance against those circumstances.' Like, if they were there, no one would need them. But I did need them, and they were bound to be out of date, so I was doing everyone a favour by getting rid of them. It was basically tidying up, hoovering pharmaceuticals, being useful. But there was also a hint of rebellion there, consuming forbidden fruit – fruit forbidden by my husband, whose loading of the dishwasher should be criminalized. I took them with a swig of tea, and immediately felt better. Well, I felt much the same physically, but had the sated feeling I get after decluttering. Pills, with added jam.

Except . . . what if I was allergic to Vicodin? It's American; they put different substances in stuff over there, like chlorine and pesticides. I pulled up my sleeves to check for hives, the beginnings of anaphylactic shock, then noticed ancient antihistamines nestling at the bottom of the hen – bingo. I took three to finish the blister packet, and chucked it in the bin, figuring that at the very least, this medicinal mix should achieve some degree of numbness. Those letters, that name, still dancing in front of my eyes, stabbing at my skull . . . I needed the drugs to delete them.

That done, I started laying out breakfast things; the cereal library the twins require every morning to get them up and running, a cafetière for Robbie's coffee, which he mainlines as soon as he gets out of bed. I love coffee, but it makes me twitchy as hell so I gave it up in favour of tamer tea-caffeine. Seems lately I react to everything one way or another. Bloated after carbs, queasy after meat, gassy after vegetables. Can't even drink a sip of water without peeing every five minutes. Sometimes I drink wine in the evenings just to dehydrate myself, so I won't be up every hour in the night, heading to the bathroom, quaking in the dark at the sighs and grinds of our creaky old house. But wine gives me a headache. In my twenties, I could sink a bottle and come up smiling the next morning; nowadays I can feel my brow tighten just looking at the glass. An anticipation of undoing. The older you get, the more things stop being fun and just become a chore. Music festivals, flights abroad, wrap parties – someone always has to prepare for eventualities, deal with the mess.

The headache had receded by the time Robbie came down just after seven, in his MAMIL gear, ready to cycle to work. No point in telling him about the drugs, he probably forgot they even existed, it would only cause a fuss. For the same reason, I didn't mention the forks, or the plates thrown in every which way so that they came out flecked with bolognese. My husband began making his coffee with the concentration and precision of a lab technician studying embryos, while I put another tea bag in a cup and picked up my book. I've been reading *The Blind Assassin* for about eleven years and have never got past page 48. Sure enough, as the words blurred before my still-prickling eyes, the washing machine beeped. I got to my feet.

'Don't worry, I'll do it,' said Robbie. He pressed the plunger down slowly, focused on the rolling granules. We both knew he had no intention of emptying the washing machine. I prefer to do it myself, since he once took the wet clothes out and left them in a pile gathering crumbs on the kitchen table, while he went off to fetch the *New European* from the front doormat. He didn't come back.

My husband isn't deliberately unhelpful, or one of those men who thinks it's a woman's job. Just absent-minded, and better – probably deliberately – at other things. He tends to favour building shelves in seventeenth-century nooks, and fixing the constantly-on-the-blink boiler, leaving me to take care of . . . well, everything else. You tend to settle into these roles without either of you meaning to – the school calls the mother when the child is sick, the plumber tells the man the valve is faulty. It can grind you down, but there are bigger battles to fight, like getting Robbie to agree to book a nice cottage in Cornwall for our October half-term holiday, rather than some dodgy Airbnb in Athens so he can visit the Parthenon. On some level, though, the prongs of those forks were needling, reminding me it was my job to put them the right way up so they got properly clean.

After breakfast, the usual hassle of getting everyone up and out, hauling Ethan out of bed, telling Hazel to switch off her GHD irons, wiping down worktops, dashing upstairs to slap on some semblance of a face, despairing at the eye bags, age spots at my temples, thread veins around my nose. Downstairs again, grabbing an overstuffed tote, shouting at everyone to get a move on. Of course, as soon as the front door closed, I had to go back to check the straighteners were off. I have to do this every day – we live in a lovely old farmhouse and I really don't want it to burn down. The ancient wiring worries me enough as it is.

It's the morning dance routine of a million households, we're nothing special. No exceptional circumstances here, unless you count twins, and that's only one in two hundred and fifty. Or is that two in two hundred and fifty? Whatever. The four of us were out of the house by ten past eight, and I was on a train to Bristol by eight-thirty. For a while after we went back to the office, post-pandemic, everyone had staggered starting times, but somehow it all fell away, Vincent began scheduling 9 a.m. meetings again and no one, least of all me, raised any objections. Like the Fire of London. After it razed everything to the ground, they said they were going to rebuild the city better, get rid of that higgledy-piggledy layout and plot big wide streets in grids, but in the end, they just built the roads where they'd always been, same as before. That pretty much went for everything, really. All this talk of making everything better, greener, fairer, came to nothing. Back to how it was, waiting for the next fire to strike.

On the train I was trying to read my book again but felt dozy and distracted, probably because of the pills kicking in, those letters still scrambling under my lids, so let it fall to my lap, as a thousand and one abstract concerns crowded my brain, vying for attention. Shopping lists and guest lists; cleaning tasks and sorting out mess; nails, emails and migraines; eye bags and emotional baggage. So much to do, so many people to placate, circling, jabbing at me like the prongs of the forks. I closed my eyes, then opened them, staring into space, vision swimming and refocusing.

That was when I saw the case. The case with the bomb in it.

# 2

Just to back up a bit here, I have a thing about suspect packages. Like, you know, planes or wasps. Or snakes. I have a thing about all those too, but they're further back in the phobia files. Suspect packages are a more recent fear. You might argue that *everyone* has a thing about them, but it's not true, because I asked my friend Susie and she just looked blank.

'What?'

'Are you ever scared? On public transport?'

'Why would I be?'

'In case, you know, you see something odd. Like, *See it, say it, sorted*, or whatever.'

She shrugged. 'Dunno, I'm just looking at my phone. Probably wouldn't see it.'

So it seemed it was just me. In an average week, I spot at least one questionable item in my carriage and have to react accordingly. I see it, but I don't say it or sort it, just move down the train until I feel like I'm out of the danger zone. Sometimes I get a later, quieter service. Better safe than sorry. Better late than dead. Vince stares at me as I shuffle into morning catch-ups, muttering 'Sorry, sorry, bloody trains,' which is never a lie, because that's my nightmare. One of them. Some people fantasize; I catastrophize. It's extremely time-consuming. My younger sister Maz, who's had extensive therapy, says my phobias are a distraction – i.e. irrational fears divert from the rational. But I'd rather not think about that.

Since our mother refused to pay for driving lessons when we were teenagers and I'm too neurotic to learn now, Robbie is the driver in our family – another reversion to stereotype. But we don't have a car because of the environment, and he likes cycling to work because unlike me he doesn't think getting on a bicycle is a sure-fire shortcut to an early grave. I'm not even sure I can ride a bike, despite learning as a child. They say you don't forget, but I'm definitely more unbalanced now, wobblier with age. Anyway, since I can't drive, it has to be the train. It's only about ten minutes from Keynsham, the market town where we live, to Bristol Temple Meads, where I work, but it's an intense experience.

Why do suspect packages preoccupy me so much when they clearly don't perturb the Susies of this world? It just seems like such an awful way to go. And since this is the thing that worries me the most – more than wasps or planes or snakes – I decided that guaranteed it would happen. Because irony. You're more likely to be crushed by unstable furniture than killed by a bomb, statistically, but in the story of my life, Susie's looking at her phone because there's nothing else to look at, whereas I glance up and see the deadly bag ticking, seconds before the timer hits zero. Susie ends up being killed another way. Falling wardrobe, probably. So I'm always on the alert, as if vigilance can fend it off, and this morning there was a prime candidate, much better than last week's dubious parcel, which turned out to be an empty shoebox.

This was properly suspicious. It was huge, and black, and a very odd shape, propped up against one of the seats. Maybe it was some sort of music case. Really big though; big enough for a cello, or some sort of terrible device. I mean, it was the shape of a cello, but who knew what was really in there? And why was there nobody with it? Who left an expensive instrument just sitting there on its own? I tried to concentrate on my book again, but the words swam in front of my eyes like the names in the email: '*this morning . . . woke . . . dread . . . a feeling . . .*' All my dread focused on this looming receptacle, packing every one of my worries into a black box. If I could just avoid whatever was in there, banish it, run away, then I would be safe.

Looking up, I decided that if no one rejoined the case in the next two minutes, I would have to change carriages, get outside the death radius. Out of sight, out of mind, out of danger. In fact, it was barely thirty seconds before I made my move. I wanted to give the other passengers the impression I was answering the call of nature, rather than being threatened by a cello case, so getting to my feet, I caught the eye of a woman opposite and said 'Are the toilets that way, do you know?' and she said 'Clover? Clover Ashton?!'

'Um, hi! How are you?' It's actually Clover Hendry now, but I didn't like to correct her because there was no way I could take the slightest stab at *her* name.

'Oh, you know, can't complain. It's been ages! You look great!' Did I? I thought I probably looked dishevelled and harassed, and maybe a bit overweight. She looked completely unrecognizable, but I couldn't betray a hint of confusion. Forgetting an acquaintance is the height of rudeness.

'So good to see you! You look fabulous too!' In fact, she was a little overdressed for a commute.

She grimaced. 'I'm tarted up for a work do later. You still in TV?'

'Um, yes. Still at the coal face . . .' I mumbled, desperately trying to recall when we'd met. She'd used my maiden name, so it must have been a very long time ago. Had we worked on a show together? I'd moved about three feet further from the case, but we were still in the blast area, even if I used her as a shield. 'How about you?'

'Same old, same old. I really must move on, but life gets in the way, kids get in the way . . . Have YOU got any little ones?' She put her head on one side, as if she could read my offspring in the lines under my eyes. I often don't mention my kids, because talking about twins always provokes strong reactions from people, inevitably leading to long-winded conversations along the lines of double-trouble, two-for-the-price-of-one, was it IVF, etc. And I didn't have time right now, what with the imminent threat.

'Not that I'm aware of!' I floundered. Denying my own progeny. That definitely destabilized my karma. Now I had two reasons to get away: the bomb, and this woman. Infuriatingly, the train had stopped just outside the station, waiting for a platform. I wondered if I could prise open the doors and pick my way along the track.

'Well, there's still time. Mind you, none of us are getting any younger. And you could get hit by a bus tomorrow!' The stranger tittered merrily and thumped me on the arm.

As if I didn't dwell on that every single day. I already felt like I'd been hit by a bus that morning. The train lurched as it started up again and – horror – the case lurched with it. For a second, it stood unsupported, then toppled to the floor with a crash. I sank with it, one arm over my face, moaning loudly as I anticipated the blow. Finally, it had happened, the thing I'd dreaded and brooded over for so long. It was almost a relief. Blown to smithereens, fears and to-do lists and guest lists obliterated forever . . .

There was no explosion. I remained crouched on the floor of the carriage as the train inched alongside the platform, wondering how to extricate myself from this situation. My forgotten friend gaped down at me in astonishment as I feebly pretended to have something in my shoe, taking it off and shaking a non-existent stone out of it, wishing a sudden detonation would put me out of my misery.

When the train finally stopped, I got to my feet, brushing off my clothes, trying to retain a modicum of dignity.

'Anyway, this is me! Lovely to see you again!'

The strange woman stared at me strangely. Although there wasn't a bomb, I'd basically let off some sort of incendiary device and was now poleaxed by the toxic fug of embarrassment, so it was a good job we'd arrived in Bristol. The doors opened and I jumped off the train, giving thanks to Hermes, protector of travellers. The woman got off as well, giving me a puzzled, tentative wave, and I waved back, watching her go, fuelled by a sense of freedom, and Vicodin. I still couldn't remember who she was, but it was unlikely I'd ever see her again. As commuters surged around me, I turned around, felt a sharp jab at the base of my skull, and everything went black.

# 3

You're statistically more likely to be killed by falling furniture than by a bomb, but I'd hazard a guess there's more chance of you getting blown up than being felled by a businessman's briefcase on a station platform. He was looking at his watch as he got off the train, and the corner connected with my head at a very precise and unlikely point. Maybe I wouldn't have lost consciousnesses at all were it not for the pills, which had already left me fuzzy and disoriented – horseshoe nail territory again. As I lay there, all I could see marching across my eyelids were those letters. Letters in no particular order, or maybe they were, but I didn't want to make sense of them. Like the sliding doors, it was easier to jump out than face what was there.

When I came to, I was still on the platform, my legs propped up on the offending briefcase, a jacket under my sore head.

Obviously, my overwhelming emotion was mortification. All these people having their day derailed, late for work because of me. Maybe they thought I was drunk.

I felt quite drunk, thanks to drugs and head injuries and something else that I couldn't quite explain.

'I'm so sorry,' I said, rearing up. Various hands pressed me back down. 'Truly, I feel absolutely fine.' Taking care to enunciate clearly, not give any evidence of inebriation, I tried to get up again, and this time no one stopped me. They all got out their phones, apart from the businessman.

'Thank God,' he said, picking up his case and jacket. 'I'm a lawyer,' he added, shaking the jacket and frowning at the bloodstain.

'Oh, lovely,' I replied, still feeling dizzy. 'So's my husband.'

He paled and began to back away. 'Intellectual property,' I qualified, to reassure. He shrugged his shoulders and disappeared into the crowds. Hit and run. He could have at least said sorry. Maybe I should have said sorry first, to prompt him. Maybe it was really rude, not offering to dry-clean the jacket. My face began to burn as I considered the faux pas, simultaneously feeling the strange urge to follow him into the hordes and punch him. Another train creaked alongside the platform.

Figuring I'd already diced with death, so was safe to continue my journey, I boarded a bus outside the station, trying not to look at anything. Maybe it was like the tree falling in the forest – if I didn't see it, it wasn't there. As we rumbled along Redcliffe Way, the dizziness receded and was replaced by a vague, out-of-place feeling, like an aura before a migraine. I stared at page 48, not taking anything in. Just dots, join-the-dots, forming a picture I couldn't quite piece together.

Lurching off the bus at Broad Quay, I tried to hold steady, looking up at the blue sky, the waving green trees, orienting myself. Get it together, Clover. I had the sense of things unravelling and in flux, taking in new atoms, cells shifting and regenerating with every shaky breath. Something big was happening, something that I couldn't put my finger on but felt with every fibre. The blue sky. The green trees. The black box. The blue box, the black trees, the green sky. Everything on its axis.

I arrived at Red Eye's offices on King Street shortly after 9 a.m., stumbling into the meeting room mouthing apologies to Vincent, who rolled his eyes and carried on talking about daytime slots. Edging into my seat, I put up a hand to check the back of my neck. It came away sticky with blood, which I wiped on my trousers – regulation black, tailored, paired with a skimming, interesting-print blouse, the work uniform of every woman my age. I still felt odd, dislocated, like I wasn't really there. Was it an out-of-body experience? Had I, in fact, died on the platform?

Contemplating this possibility, I began to feel hot, sweat pooling underneath the silk, threatening to soak through. I licked the beads off my upper lip, eyes darting around the room to see if anyone had noticed. But everyone was staring fixedly at the table as Vince droned on. Petroc, one of my fellow executive producers, was doodling, drawing caricatures of Mr Burns from *The Simpsons*. Vince's nickname is Monty, not because of any physical similarity, but because he has a habit of drawling 'H-excellent' and steepling his fingers whenever a rival company suffers a ratings dive.

I loosened the bow at the neck of my blouse, using the tie to subtly fan myself. My face felt bright red, as red as the blood oozing at my nape. Surely that proved I was still alive? Surely the afterlife was not sitting in a meeting room with managing director Vincent Chapel, pronounced Shap*elle*, as he debated whether or not the 11.45 slot on BBC One was worth chasing? It was a hell of sorts, I supposed. *When* did I die? Was it on the platform, when I was knocked out, or before that? Maybe when I took the tablets, or when I snapped the laptop shut? What was the tiny nail that set it all off?

Time to undo another button. Were there enough vegetables in the fridge for Hazel's curry tonight? Must buy naan bread on the way home, or the twins would moan. Could get it on my way to pick up the dry-cleaning. Cleaning. The compost bin needed washing out, must remember to bleach it later. And do a towel wash. Maybe I could make a list on my phone under the table. Christ, it was hot. Was the air con broken? I glanced around again, but everyone else looked perfectly comfortable, and I didn't like to suggest we open a window. Resting my phone on my lap, I couldn't remember what was on my mind. Was it a to-do list? What did I have to do? Sitting there, thumbs hovering over the screen, I found myself tapping 'BIG BABY'. No idea what that meant.

The headache was creeping back, tingling at my left cheekbone – I cupped my hand against it, to push it away. The room began to whirl around me, but it wasn't entirely unpleasant, a bit like being on a waltzer at the fairground. Or those days when you used to get given gas at the dentist before they banned it. I remember swinging away in the chair as a child, away with the fairies, gorgeous drugs making it all better. What was it? Entonox? Like gas and air for giving birth. When the twins were born, Robbie tried it, got carried away, and ended up high as a kite. High on gas, high on Vicodin; my sober husband was such a junkie. I giggled.

'Something amusing you, Clover?'

Screwing up my eyes, I tried to focus on Vince at the end of the table. 'No, sir.'

What was wrong with me? Everything felt weird, as if I might float away and hover above the table like a drone. It was still hot, but now I was accustomed, it was almost like being in a sauna. Quite comforting heat, really. Maybe I'd have a sleep, wake up when Vince had finished analysing the daytime schedule. I closed my eyes, slid my cupped hand to my chin, and used his nasal tones as a lullaby . . .

It's possible I slept for a while, maybe a few minutes, or an hour – those meetings can last forever. When I resurfaced, Vince was still going.

'What we need,' he was saying. 'Is someone famous and gay. Gay-mous. Ha ha!'

Opening one eye, I saw Flora, one of our assistant producers, wincing. Petroc's pen had stilled, the nib resting on one of Mr Burns' evil eyes.

'Don't be such a prick, Vince.'

Stifling a snort of laughter, I opened my other eye to see who had mouthed off so magnificently. Bitching about Vince behind his back is a common pastime, but saying it to his face is another matter. It took a while for me to appreciate that everyone was staring at me, and it appeared that, in fact, the words had come out of *my* mouth. And it seemed there were more on the way.

'You can't say that sort of thing. It's inappropriate. Pack it in.'

My boss blinked, opened his mouth, and closed it again. Wow. I'd definitely died on the platform. Or before. This wasn't happening. Maybe that meant I could enjoy it? I got to my feet.

'No one has time for this, Vince. We had exactly the same meeting last week, and you said the same things. Petroc's supposed to be prepping for his Astral1 catch-up, Flora's casting, Elspeth's completely overloaded, but you insist on having these unnecessary sit-downs so you can pontificate. Next time, do it in an email.'

My voice didn't even sound like mine. Usually, I end every sentence on an uplift in case anyone disagrees with me, but these new tones were flat, direct, brooking no arguments. Petroc's jaw was somewhere near the floor; Flora gazing at me, eyes wide; Elspeth, the finance director, nodding vigorously. Only Ian, the head of development, seemed oblivious, staring at his phone. He never really left the realm of Reddit. I gathered my own phone, and a pretty little succulent from the middle of the table. The script was right there in my head, and it seemed I had the starring role. Just a question of letting it happen.

'We'll go for the eleven forty-five slot, but we won't do loads of work like last time because the budget's minuscule and they'll likely go in-house anyway. Ian can chuck them a proposal as we discussed, Elspeth can try to push up the tariff, and Flora can sound out a few agents. That's it. If anyone needs me, I'll be in my office.'

I only had a few seconds before Vince blew his top, not that it mattered. Nothing mattered. Nodding to Flora, I walked out, closing the door and leaning against it, taking a deep breath, discharging those atoms. From the meeting room I could hear shuffling and coughing, and then: 'ANYONE WANT TO TELL ME WHAT THE HELL IS GOING ON?'

As the atoms churned, burned and reformed, they pushed me towards the startling realization that I really, *really* didn't give a fuck.

In the toilet, having deposited the plant next to the sink, I stared at my sweating face. There was a smear of blood on my cheek, which I wiped off with a paper towel. Despite a spot brewing on my chin, I thought I looked pretty good.

Maybe it was the nap. Undoing another button on my blouse, I pouted at myself like one of those young things on Instagram. Hot to trot, @Clover_Hendry_TV.

Back in my office, Petroc was leaning against the desk eating a pot of Bircher muesli. I put my newly watered succulent next to the monitor.

'Well, that was unexpected,' he mumbled, waving his spoon at me. 'Are you having some sort of breakdown? Like when you turned forty and started flossing all the time? That's what I told Monty. Everyone's having them, apparently. Delayed fall-out from the pandemic. He'll probably pay for therapy, if you like.'

'I don't need therapy,' I replied, rifling through my drawers. 'I need him to get off my back.' At the bottom of the filing cabinet, there was a sign someone bought me as a Secret Santa Christmas present. Stalking to the door, I hung it outside: 'Piss Off, I'm Working'. That should do it. Except I had no intention of working. Or even being there. I had to get away, right now. It was imperative. I picked up my bag.

'Somewhere you need to be?'

I nodded, getting out an elastic band to tie back my matted hair. 'Going shopping. And for lunch. And maybe an art gallery.' *BIG BABY*. There was an Art Andra exhibition in Clifton, which I'd wanted to see but hadn't. Why hadn't I? I couldn't remember. If I wanted to go, why didn't I just go?

'Seriously, what's going on? You're crazy. You've never done this before.'

'You're right. I've never been to an art gallery during office hours. Vince is always telling us to think outside the box. Maybe I'll have an amazing idea for a show.' I shouldered my bag and gestured for him to get out of the way.

'I'm going to call Robbie and tell him you had a funny turn.'

'Tell him he's making dinner tonight.' I brushed past him, blood thundering in my ears. There's a bit in the *Twilight* series when Bella Swan becomes a vampire – that was the last book I managed to read, before I started *The Blind Assassin* – where everything feels heightened to her, like nothing in the past was real and this was the first true moment of existence. Something electric flowing through my veins, out the tips of my fingers, charging me. My head doesn't hurt, I'm not tired, or anxious, or embarrassed, or vaguely melancholy. I don't feel the urge to make a to-do list. I just want to eat a burrito, and see a sculpture of a massive fibreglass baby. If anyone tries to stop me, there'll be hell to pay.

I feel fine. I feel like a vampire. Invincible. Deadly.

# 4

Before today, my chief aim in life was to avoid a scene, at all costs. I've always been frightened of them. Of confrontation, fuss, unpleasantness. My wedding day, for example.

Robbie proposed in a lackadaisical way, seventeen years ago, in the bathroom of a Travelodge near Milton Keynes. I was washing out the toothbrush holder because it was made of glass, and I figured we could put wine in it, even though it was more of a thimble. There was a bottle chilling on the window ledge outside – it was impossible to get through an evening in that bleak limbo of a room without sustenance of some kind. We were in the Travelodge because I was doing some godawful job in Bletchley Park, and Robbie thought he'd come along for the ride as there was a Roman villa near there he wanted to visit. He was excited about his impending trip, and probably got carried away.

'I thought we might get married,' he said mildly, idling in the doorway watching me scratch at the limescale on the bottom of the glass.

I was so surprised I nearly dropped it. And then instantly worried, as is my wont.

'Has Rose put you up to this?'

He raised his eyebrows. 'No, were you expecting her to?'

I rinsed, mulling. The last time I'd seen my mother, she'd told me to dye my roots and then quoted some study about women's fertility dropping off a cliff edge at thirty-five. Given I was still in my twenties at that point, this seemed precipitous in every sense. It wasn't that she particularly liked Robbie; she just thought he was suitable husband material in the same way she believed any man on the street would make a fine spouse for a desperate case like me. Odd that my mother, a bitter divorcee, would still be such an ardent proponent of marriage when her own floundered so spectacularly, my father running off to Spain with a woman he met at a conference on wind engineering. Yet she retained her faith in the institution, in what it would provide for me. I suppose it was a compliment, in a way, that she thought it was still a possibility. She'd already given up on my sister Maz, who's three years younger than me, because she'd decided to go to agricultural college, which my mother considered akin to entering a nunnery in terms of marriage prospects.

Thinking about my mother distracted me from this, my first proposal. And last, I assumed, because I figured I was going to say yes, or this mini-break could turn really awkward. Of course, we might divorce, and I might get another proposal at a later date, so technically it might not be my last proposal, although I couldn't imagine anyone wanting to marry me with a failed marriage under my belt, possibly with kids in tow, not to mention my bristling mama Rose.

'Do you need some more time?' Robbie had a quizzical expression; he knew me well enough by that point to guess my thought processes.

'Sorry,' I said, dashing the image of me as a not-dashing divorcee. 'I was just thinking it through.'

'And?'

'Yes, please,' I said, and he gave me his grandmother's ring, which was an emerald set between two diamonds. The emerald was rectangular cut, which is called an emerald cut, so it was an emerald emerald. When Robbie told me that I tittered, which isn't really the correct response to being presented with an engagement ring. Afterwards, I found out rectangular is cheaper than round, and though I don't want to cast aspersions on Robbie's grandfather's generosity as a suitor, it wasn't quite what I would have chosen. But as an heirloom it was free, which was good because we were saving for a flat and I didn't want him spending our deposit at Tiffany's. Or, knowing Robbie, bidding for some artefact at Sotheby's. I did – *do* – love him a lot because he was – *is* – the opposite of me, which balances things out. I need a lot of balancing; he's a heavyweight in husband terms.

Anyway, as proposals go it was fine, and we drank the bottle chilling on the ledge, passing the toothbrush holder between us as we tipsily planned our wedding. He wanted to get married in the ruins of a priory in North Yorkshire; I wanted an Indian buffet; he wanted a Celtic theme; I wanted a cheese wedding cake; he wanted to source some nice champagne from a French supplier he knew; I liked the idea of a green dress with a bustle. We both wanted to keep it low-key, for us.

But it turned out it didn't matter what we wanted, because my mother wanted something else. And what she wanted, she got, which was a church near Taunton and a reception at a spa hotel down the road; me trussed up in a meringue with Maz as the world's most vacant (drunk) bridesmaid. Rose even arranged for a flower girl in a sequined cape – I didn't know any little girls at that point, being a twenty-something-about-town whose fertility was nonetheless approaching a cliff edge, but she roped in her friend Ginny's daughter . . . what was her name? Venetia! Sulky little madam, with blonde ringlets straight out of a Boden catalogue.

To be honest, I didn't really mind any of it, because having decided I wanted to marry Robbie, I was keen to get it done so we could move into the flat we'd found in Essex Road – a fixer-upper with a roof terrace – but when it came to it, I *did* want to have a nice day. You know, just relax, enjoy the ceremony and then drink the hotel's inferior fizz. But it went wrong from the very beginning.

# Lucky Day

On the morning of the wedding, we – Maz, my mother and I – met the vicar for a quick run-through of logistics. Father Stephen was an impatient man of the cloth, anxious to get shot of us so he could fit in a round of golf before the ceremony. My mother was fussing about the flowers – she'd ordered roses with glitter-fringed petals that had made Maz retch behind a pillar – Father Stephen kept checking his watch, and saying, 'Mrs Ashton, if we could . . .' and I just wanted it to be over so I could have a hot bath and fret about fitting into my not-chosen-by-me dress. But gradually I became aware of a buzzing above my head, the heralding of the disaster. And I could see then and there how the ceremony would pan out; how it would be mortifying and panic-inducing and protracted, but ultimately just, somehow . . . bloodless. No one would listen to me, and I would just bear it, get on with it, carry on. Sometimes I look down at that clunky oblong on my finger and think: what if I'd kicked up a fuss? What if I'd just stopped it all? Did it the way I wanted, with my Indian buffet and cheese cake and Robbie's French champagne in the ruined priory? But I never did. I didn't want to make a scene. Didn't want to upset anyone. Didn't want to say no.

\* \* \*

So here we are. Today I'm a vampire, but rather than blood, what I really lust after is some time out. I just want to escape, cut loose, chill. With my newfound powers, I make it out of the office without getting sucked into another pointless meeting about profit margins or compliance. This involves standing behind an enormous yucca to avoid our finance director Elspeth, who wants to cut the editing budget of my show. It's a £1.2 million pound commission, and we need every penny of it, but she wants to pinch them. Elspeth's fantasy is that people start working for free; that Red Eye Productions, the company we work for, somehow achieves charitable status, and all our employees are trust fund babies who live in Daddy's spare flat in Chelsea. A vision shared and fostered by Vince, who once tried to persuade an employee to take a pay cut because her youngest kid had started school and 'You're saving loads in childcare.' He still doesn't understand why that was unreasonable. The yucca also shields me from Imogen, Vince's PA, who is wandering around holding a piece of paper. That fucking guest list. I don't want to know.

Another executive producer, Oswald Phillips, is also on the warpath because he thinks I poached one of his researchers. I didn't; she just came to me crying because she was sick of him making her stand in a tank of water to test the challenges they were devising for their new gameshow *Gamesh-Ow!* Because her salary is so low, she's working in a bar in the evenings to make up the shortfall in her rent, but the manager didn't like her turning up with wet hair. I referred her to HR, who shifted her onto my production, *More Than They Can Chew*, which she's really happy with because she's going to get to hang out with beautiful people

31

in a beautiful vineyard in Somerset and have her share of the £1.2 million. But Oswald is *not* happy.

I step out from behind the yucca and hold up my index finger as he approaches. He stalls, confused.

'Get lost, Oz,' I say. 'Quick sharp.'

I'm aware my behaviour is unusual, but it's like being in a dream where you just go with it. I have a recurring nightmare where there's an intruder in the vast house I'm staying in, because I forgot to close one of its many windows. I have to go round frantically shutting windows to keep him out, but never question where the hell I am and who put in all those entry points. For the seven years I've worked at Red Eye, I've been very patient with its most unpleasant and untalented executive. But now, looking back, I can't quite see why. What did it achieve? It just made him ride roughshod over me, and wasted my time. Now I'm going to close the window in his stupid face.

'Whatever you're about to say, save it. Or better still, swallow it. And get out of my way.'

Oz mouths like a fish, and I stalk past, looking for a window to escape from.

'But . . . but . . .' he stammers, his face purpling like an aubergine.

'Button it,' I say, and make for the lift. Inside, there's a brief moment of perfect stillness and solitude, before the doors ping open, and I'm faced with one of Red Eye's lawyers, come to nitpick about some contractual issue.

'Ah! Just the person I was hoping to . . .'

But the exit is right there – freedom and space and no one bothering me, just fibreglass babies and burritos and maybe a walk in the park. I put the flat of my palm over his hopeful face and push him aside, and then I'm through the sliding doors into Thunderbolt Square, blinking in summer sunshine, gone.

# 5

Obviously, I've never played hooky before. Never thrown a sickie, had a duvet day, or even stretched out my lunch hour. I don't even *take* my lunch hour; it feels like an imposition. Years ago, I took two days off when I had proper flu, dragged myself into work before I was well, and as a result developed a lung infection. My GP grudgingly gave me antibiotics and I struggled on, hacking my way through meetings, discreetly coughing phlegm into a tissue. Red Eye gives its employees twenty days' holiday a year, plus a day for every year you've worked there, but they cap that at five extra days, so I have twenty-five holiday days, which HR keep tabs on like soldiers patrolling Guantánamo. The last day off I booked was to take Grizelda, our cat, to the vet – it's near a Co-op, so I treated myself to a browse and bought some AA batteries.

What to do with *this* blessed, beautiful day? The exhibition, obviously, but time stretches ahead invitingly, loaded with possibility. I want delicious food, and delicious free time, and delicious me-time. I want to stare at art, and a beautiful dress in a shop window, and the blue sky, and I want to move slowly, like I'm wading through glue. I want to breathe, and not think, and feel, but not too much. I want to *stop*. I want to just *be*.

There will be no picking up groceries, or collecting dry-cleaning, or going to the post office or queueing at the pharmacy. I want to do nothing, and then something gently illuminating, and then nothing again, and then rest. I want to be left alone, maybe see someone I love, briefly, and then be on my own again, just blinking and being. I want that taxi I see ahead, because it can take me someplace else, and I can sit watching the world go by, not engaging in any of it. As I step forwards holding out my hand, the driver sees me and nods, slowing and swerving to the kerbside. I smile and salute him, ready to begin my adventure. Off we go, into the unknown—

I'm shoved aside abruptly, as two smartly dressed men barge past, one of them opening the door while the other barks at the driver: 'Victoria Square.' I blink, but not in a good way. This has happened to me before; in fact, last week, a group of office workers hijacked my hailing and I was left standing at the roadside, speechless, stock-still and drenched in pavement juice as another taxi sped past ignoring me. What to do in this situation? Old Clover would retreat in defeat but New Clover's pulsing atoms push her forward. Having missed my opportunity to wrestle for the cab on the kerb, I hop in after them.

'I said to Samsy, you got lucky scalping some before earnings . . .'

'Feed those gift horses, get reloaded, baby, it's bang time!'

Fnarr fnarr, etc. They're both dressed in well-cut grey suits, that kind of expensive floppy material that drapes nicely. Turnbull & Asser shirts dry-cleaned by their secretaries, ties that will be loosened during long lunches, along with their tongues. So busy with their business, it takes them a while to clock me, but when they do, their double-takes are pleasingly – well, double. They're like a FTSE Tweedledum and Tweedledee. And I'm their monstrous crow.

'What on earth . . .?'

I hold out my hand to the one who spoke, which he stares at as if it's an alien cadaver on a slab. 'Pleased to meet you.' *Pleased* is obviously an overshoot, but one must maintain niceties, particularly with such dapper gentlemen.

The other one (Dee) shakes his head. 'What are you doing here?'

My eyes rove around the cab. 'I'm hitching a ride.'

'But it's our taxi!'

'Well, no, technically, it's *his* taxi.' I indicate the driver.

'But we . . .' Dum trails off, confused.

'Yes,' I appreciate their predicament. 'You were about to say you flagged it, but you didn't, did you? *I* did. You appropriated my hailing. Normally, I would overlook it, but today is not a normal day, and also, I just happen to be going to Clifton myself. So, we'll go together.'

Dee's eyes widen in alarm. 'I . . . we can't!'

'Why not?'

'We don't know each other!' He produces this triumphantly, as if that will be the end of the matter. It won't be, though. Not today.

I settle myself more comfortably, shifting my bag off my shoulder. 'You're quite right. Allow me to introduce myself. I'm Clover Hendry, and I work in television as an executive producer. No, you probably haven't watched anything I've made. I have two children, twins aged sixteen, and a husband – he's a lawyer who could probably sue you for assaulting me on that pavement. Your turn.'

Dum begins to fumble in his pocket, as Dee gets on his phone, maybe to offload some shares before the world order collapses entirely. 'This is really not on. I don't see how . . .' He looks up at the driver. 'Hey, can you stop, so that she can get out?'

I get out my own phone, to google the gallery. 'That's a shame, when we're just getting to know each other. Anyway, I'm not getting out. You guys can get out if you like.'

'We're not getting out. It's our taxi.'

'We've already established it's *his* taxi, and my hailing.'

'We're not getting out.'

'Well, then, we'll have a lovely cosy journey together, won't we. Tell me about yourselves. I bet you've had all sorts of banking adventures.'

Dum and Dee hastily call a board meeting, conferring in vexed whispers as I do my research. The art gallery is near a club I'm a member of, not because I want to be, but because Vince paid for me to join so we could have meetings there to look cool. Avon House is the poshest members' club in Bristol, with a rooftop pool, two restaurants and numerous luxurious lounges. I'm sure no one really cares about sitting next to a swimming pool to chat about access-primetime opportunities – it doesn't really aid the process – but Vince loves schmoozing people in bars, so more often than not I've found myself perched on a sunlounger, earnestly pitching an unlikely celebrity journey to a disinterested commissioner, ducking every time a wasp flies past. Now though, I'm thinking I could idle away some time, maybe even have a swim, wash off the blood. Why not?

'We can't do this.' Dee is sweating. 'You've got to get out. It's not right.'

'What? We're not having an affair, just sharing a cab. It's good for the planet, if you think about it.'

'But . . .' He pulls at his tie. 'It's weird.'

I sigh. 'No, what's weird is you two shoving me out of the way to muscle in on the taxi I waved down. Like you don't give a shit about anyone. *That's* weird. This is just . . . convenient.'

I hear what sounds like a snort of amusement from the driving seat behind me.

Dum intervenes. 'We're . . . whatever . . . sorry about that, OK? You've made your point. Could you just get out?'

There's an exhibition viewing slot in an hour. Perfect. 'If

you're sorry about that, then you acknowledge it was your mistake, therefore *you* should get out.'

'You're a psycho. Driver, stop. Make her get out, she's insane.'

I chuckle as I book my ticket. 'It's not 1843; you can't have me committed to Bedlam for being in the right. Just sit back and relax, we'll be there in no time.'

The driver now feigns deafness, mercifully ignoring this nonsense, his eyes on the traffic. Dum and Dee sit back, brows creased, fingers drumming, their own axis shifted. This is a very beneficial little episode for them, and I'm glad we could have this chat. I wonder if Susie would be free to join me for a swim, and text her, suggesting a meet-up, as she's working round here today.

My best friend Susie has a very interesting and flexible job, which I'm often envious of. She runs a company called SOjourn. They take rich people's unoccupied houses and turn them into hotels for high-class house-sitters, who pay to stay there and keep burglars away. It's like a private members' club, but for property. As part of her job, Susie sources the houses and writes the copy for them: 'This Canynge Square residence dazzles in its deep dive into grandeur. With a wine cellar and cinema room, you'll be all sorted for entertainment!' She travels to these amazing homes so that she can 'get a feel' for the place and convey its splendour. Once, she stayed in a sultan's mansion in Hyde Park for free, so she could wax lyrical about his mega-basement – she tried to make me go with her, but

I was worried he'd have CCTV and his security guards would come and cart me off. Now I regret it; I wonder if it's still unoccupied and we could go and roll around in his subterranean playroom. She said he had an indoor fire pit like a Bond villain. Bristol is a rich hunting ground for SOjourn, with numerous elegant Georgian townhouses, spacious villas and converted warehouse apartments to choose from. Only an hour and a half by train from London, surrounded by stunning Somerset countryside, the city has a lovely waterfront, superb restaurants, independent shops and a bustling arts scene . . . I've read too many of Susie's blurbs. She's very good at her job.

'*Please* get out,' Dee is saying. He appears to have tears in his eyes. 'I just can't . . . have this . . . proximity.'

'Take this.' Dum holds out a twenty-pound note, his fingers shaking.

It's like the opposite of prostitution – they're paying me to go away, and we're nearly at the club anyway.

'Very well.' I take the money and shoulder my bag. 'But next time, remember your place in the queue. And don't be such selfish bellends.'

This is all very liberating. I have no idea where it's coming from, but it's extremely useful to be able to tell it like it is, without worrying about the consequences. I should really phone our useless roofer, give him a piece of my mind. Both boys dip their heads, chastened; the driver stops, and I get out, giving him a thumbs up as I slam the door and wave them off. I bet they wear salmon-pink chinos at the weekend and go round to each other's houses to have barbecues and eye up each other's wives. Pair of planks.

As the cab pulls away, Dee or Dum, I really don't know which, leans out the window and yells 'Slapper!' which is totally unoriginal and childish. So I yell 'Wall Street wanker,' with the appropriate accompanying hand gesture, shrugging as a passing pedestrian tuts in disapproval. Normally an altercation like this would leave me trembling, with weak legs and palpitations. But now I feel strangely energized by the encounter. This is going to be a great day.

I cut through Birdcage Walk, a lovely arboreal tunnel that leads to Clifton Hill, the curved branches shading me from the sun. Clifton is so chichi; I wish we could afford to live here but we'd have to be richer than Jeff Bezos. Or Oswald Phillips. Mind you, according to local legend, the highly desirable properties round these parts were likely built with the dubious profits of some very dodgy traders, so maybe we're better off in our tumbledown Keynsham farmhouse which at least has a more innocent history. I tell myself that when I feel the urge to get on Rightmove.

Arriving at the club, I can see Susie down the road, getting distracted by estate agents' windows. At nearly six foot, with a mane of ginger hair, pale freckled skin and black lashes she has dyed at a salon in Swindon called Glamour Puss, she's the shire horse to my pit pony. With my mousy-brown locks and slightly sallow complexion, I always feel distinctly beige around her, but I have straighter teeth so it's not all bad. We're both around a 7, but if you put us together – the best bits – we'd be a 10. I mean, technically, we'd be a 14 but you can't have a 14 out of 10, can you? Not unless you're on WeRateDogs. The point is, together we kick ass.

When she finally reaches me, Susie puts her hands on her hips, eyes narrowed suspiciously. 'What's this about?'

'Just fancied a swim.'

'In there?' She jerks her head towards the entrance. 'I thought it was a knob magnet?'

'It is, but the pool is nice.'

Avon House is an old hospital that a very rich and mysterious businessman bought at a knockdown price because after years of neglect everyone said it was haunted. It's funny how an extremely expensive refurb can banish ghostly presences, almost like spooks prefer to live in squalid, empty ruins. If I was dead, I'd hang round in busy upmarket establishments, throwing valuable items and unnerving the well-off. I'd be a ghost with a taste for the finer things in life. Imagining myself as a naughty phantom makes me think of how Susie and I first met, and I smile at the memory.

As we get the lift up, Susie scrutinizes me. 'I'm sensing something different about you.'

'Hmm.' Staring at my grinning reflection in the mirrored wall, I do look different. Ironed out. Thinner. 'Just for today.' Our eyes meet in the mirror. Susie knows me, knows everything. She's known me since we worked on our first show together – before Red Eye, before Robbie, before anything. I was in my first year out of university, living in a basement flat near Earl's Court that was riddled with silverfish. My room was officially the living room, and whenever the landlord came round, I had to turn my bed into a sofa and pretend I was just visiting. It was miserable there of course, because anyone in their early twenties with no money in London is quietly or loudly having a devastating quarter-life crisis. Susie was my salvation.

We met when I was a junior researcher on a show called *Ghostly Goings On.* My job was to visit owners who said their homes were haunted, to ascertain whether or not it was true . . . Like the window-dream, I didn't really question it, just dutifully took myself round the houses to 'get a feel' for them, much like Susie does now, but with an EMF meter. When Susie joined the production team, she started coming with me and we clicked. Location-scouting immediately became much more fun. In many ways, it was the best job I ever had, even though salary-wise, 'hobby' would have been a better description. We found a poltergeist terrorizing a semi in Basingstoke, a grey lady in a cottage near Deal, strange knocking from the attic of a terraced house on the Welsh border, and a phantom dog on a farm in the Peak District. We measured the electromagnetic field of every pub in the vicinity.

When I say 'found', of course I mean that in a TV sense, in that none of it was real or happened, but we somehow got a show out of it. Quite a good, successful show, which meant that we both got offered other jobs, and that was how we started out in showbiz. Susie doesn't work in telly any more but, while our careers diverged, our friendship stayed on the same track. The track that means when she looks at me today, she sees something she's never seen before, that she doesn't recognize. Even I don't know what it is, but I know that I want her here, briefly, to dip her toe in the water with this New Me. Like a baptism, after the event. I think of Father Stephen running down the aisle at my wedding, cassock flapping, as tears rolled down little Venetia's cheeks, and then exorcise the image, in the same way I got rid of the woman on the train. In the same way I got rid of the jumbled letters. Run away from the box, don't look inside.

'What have you got on today?' Susie is on a SOjourn jaunt. It'll be some humongous pad with sixty-seven bedrooms and a palatial annexe for the au pair.

Susie smirks. 'Mansion on Cheltenham Avenue, some art collector dude with a basement garage for his Ferraris.'

'Right, we'd best get on so you can go and see his etchings.'

The lift doors open and we step out, ready to dive in.

# 6

On some level, there's a constant reverberation in my brain, a warning demon whispering 'What if . . .?' Specifically, 'What if something goes wrong?' What if you do this, and this happens? What's the *worst* that can happen? What if you step out into the road and there's a car coming right for you? What if that headache is an aneurysm? What if you don't cut up that grape? What if you open the box? The lost nail *always* leads to the lost kingdom.

My life is a litany of potential disaster scenarios, some of which are unlikely to the point of impossible. Once, before a meeting at ITV, I went to the toilet and became so distracted by the idea of a theoretical terrorist incident that I forgot to close the door of the cubicle and absent-mindedly pulled down my knickers before I realized an entertainment commissioner was washing her hands and staring at me bemusedly in the mirror. Worried about one catastrophic outcome, I'd generated another. From 'What if a gunman suddenly burst in?' to 'What if I put my foo-foo on display in a professional environment?' Hastily kicking the door shut with my foot, it struck me I'd almost rather the shoot-out, because at least I'd prepared for that, mentally, and it wasn't my fault. Of my twin fears, embarrassment and death, the former is perhaps the most excruciating to contemplate.

Today that voice is still there, but he's more of a mischievous imp. 'What if . . .?' becomes laced with possibility and innovation. The consequences could be intriguing, adventurous, fun. What if I leave the office? What if I get in the taxi? What if I go for a swim? What will happen next? Instead of quaking, I'm rubbing my hands.

Like the rest of the sprawling complex, the Avon House roof terrace has been extensively and expensively refurbished for its superior clientele. Susie would say it's 'a model of urban regeneration'. When we arrive, it's fairly quiet, just a few people having cocktails on the sunloungers. A DJ is playing music that sounds like a gong bath. As usual, the pool is empty. Great, we have it to ourselves.

'We can get changed in the toilets.'

'Dammit, I didn't think about a swimsuit. Have you got yours?'

'We can just go in our undies.'

Her eyes narrow again. 'You *are* different. What's up?'

'Nothing. I just want to have a swim.'

That's all I want. To swim in the open air, inhale the faint scent of chlorine, maybe have a coffee after. Is that too much to ask? It appears it is, because when we emerge from the toilets, two of the staff are barring our way to the pool. For Old Me, this would have sent me into immediate panic mode, stuttering sorrys and backtracking to the bogs. But New Me is fired up. This skirmish is going to make my swim all the sweeter.

'Are you members?'

'I am. She's my guest.' I indicate Susie, who is vaguely attempting to cover her blue pants and crop top with her hands. I have no urge to conceal my dimpled flesh, not because I want to flaunt myself, but because it seems staggeringly irrelevant to be concerned by it. Who cares?

'Is that a swimsuit?' The female staff member points accusingly at my fraying black bra and big knickers, which I'm quite pleased with, because at least they match.

'Yes.' I give them a winning smile. 'It's my favourite bikini.'

'It looks like underwear. We have a policy against customers wearing underwear.'

'In the pool, or generally?'

Her lips twist. Susie starts to hum with anxiety. I'm quite intrigued as to where this conversation is going, but also keen to get on, because I have another booking at eleven.

'We just want to have a swim.' Reaching past the male staff member, who jumps back in alarm, I grab one of the striped towels from the pile on a shelf behind them.

'You can't use those.' It's her again, looking down her nose.

'Why not?'

'They're not for . . . customer use.'

'What are they for then? They're towels, next to a pool. It's not a huge leap to assume they might be for . . . customer use.' I wrap one around my chic bikini, passing another to Susie.

'You're not actually supposed to use the pool at this particular time.' Anti-Underwear crosses her arms.

'Seems like a terrible waste,' I say. 'When it's right there, looking very tempting.'

'Let's just go,' says Susie, her teeth chattering despite the warmth of the day.

'No way,' I say, taking her arm. 'I want to get my lengths in.'

Watched by the disapproving staff, I sit on the side and dangle my legs in the water. It's lovely. A wasp lands on the wet tile next to me, stopping for a paddle. Usually that would send me into a frenzy of hysterical flapping, but now I find his presence simply intrigues me. I wonder why I was afraid before; what was the worst that could happen? A sting? Nothing.

'If you carry on, I'll have to call the manager,' calls Anti-Underwear.

'Off you go, then,' I say, and slide in. 'And you . . .' I beckon the male staff member, who looks all at sea. 'Could you get me a sparkling water? With ice.'

They both disappear, and Susie hastily plunges in. 'Everyone's staring at us,' she murmurs, as we settle into a steady breaststroke. I glance around. The drinkers on the sunloungers have stopped chatting, and are watching us like they're on safari. 'What's going to happen?'

I raise my hand to a hipster who's filming me on his phone. 'I don't know. It'll be interesting to see how it pans out.'

'What's gotten into you? Are you on drugs?'

'No. Oh, I suppose I am. But not very strong ones. Maybe I should top myself up.'

I flip over onto my back and float like a dead starfish, staring up at the sky. It's the deep blue of early summer, with a few wispy clouds floating by. My hearing is deadened by the water, my body cushioned by it; buoyant, unencumbered, undulating. I can feel the warmth of the sun on my face, water lapping delicately at my cheeks, my mermaid hair streaming out, the dried blood loosening and dissolving like smoke. This feeling is so unfamiliar, out-of-body – the weightlessness, stillness, carelessness, in-the-momentness. What if I just floated here forever? I don't need drugs; I just need to drift.

How many times in my life have I indulged this urge? I could count them on one hand. Once, long ago, Robbie and I went to Granada on mini-break – back when weekends represented actual free time, rather than ferrying kids to various activities, appointments and parties. Aside from visiting the Alhambra and drinking ourselves into a stupor, the main thing I recall about that trip was we visited a hammam, a kind of Arabian spa. It was a beautiful crypt lined with gorgeous Moroccan tiles, and various baths you could dunk yourselves in. After a massage, we dangled, steamy and replete, in one of the small pools, and I remember staring at my feet, pearly in the water, just watching my splayed toes. We stayed there until our skin wrinkled like raisins, and afterwards my chin came out in horrendous spots from the steam, the white-knuckled flight home, and all the shite we ate and drank. But I kept thinking about my immersed feet, bleached and flexing, the sublime purposelessness of the moment. Usually, life is just an endless treadmill of toil and transport and catering, interspersed with the toss and turn of sleep. Pausing long enough to appreciate your own shrivelling toes is a rare privilege.

Gradually, I become aware of a dull probing at my eardrum. 'DUM-DUM. DUM-DUM. DUM-DUM.' Go away.

'Madam. Madam. MADAM.'

I open one eye. A man is leaning over the pool, looking stern. This must be the manager who Anti-Underwear threatened me with. Sighing, I flip round again and stroke slowly towards the edge of the pool.

'Yes?'

He squats at the side. 'I believe you were made aware of the circumstances.'

'Why don't you explain them again? I enjoyed it first time round.'

His nostrils flare. 'My colleague, Ms Adams, informed you that the pool is not in use at this particular time.'

I rest my arms on the edge and kick my legs gently. 'But why not? Is there a health and safety issue? Has it been contaminated? There's no sign.'

'There's nothing wrong with the pool. We, ah, just prefer it if guests don't use it at certain times.'

'What's the point of having a swimming pool you don't use?'

He clears his throat. 'At the moment, it's more of a . . . viewing benefit. And you and your friend are . . . ruining the view.'

At this point, the male staff member brings over my drink, setting it poolside, with nervous side-eyes at his boss.

'Thank you so much . . .?'

'J-J-Jeremy.' He backs away.

'Jeremy. Nice boy.' I nod towards him. 'Excellent service.'

'You can't drink that, and you can't swim here.'

'Yes, you said we're ruining the view by swimming in the swimming pool. But I can't help noticing it's heated. What's the point of heating a pool that no one can swim in? It's terribly unecological. Particularly on a hot day like this.'

He's starting to get the same sweaty look that Tweedledee got in the taxi. I sip my water, which is very refreshing.

'It's not that . . . *no one* can swim in it, ever. But you can't, now.'

'It's all very complicated, isn't it? There's a pool and some people can swim in it, but not us and not now. I don't remember anyone telling me this when I joined. I feel like it's something you should warn us about.'

'The members' contract clearly states that swimming is permitted at the discretion of the management. And *I* am the management.' Bashing his chest, he inflates like a big rubber ring.

'So who *can* swim in it, and when? Do you all jump in at the end of the day, like the pool party in *It's a Wonderful Life*?'

'No, of course not.' He sounds exasperated. 'At certain times, we ask selected guests if they would like to . . . enjoy a special privilege.'

'Well, why can't we enjoy a special privilege? What have they got that we haven't?'

I turn and gesture towards Susie, who is paddling up and down, panting, hair scraped into a topknot, her face scarlet with the effort, or maybe the manager's presence. As a TV producer who's done my fair share of casting, I can see exactly where this is headed, and I'm going to make him say it.

'They are usually . . . they are there, in the evening, for more . . . *decorative* purposes.'

'What, like . . . water baubles?'

He allows himself a small, tight smile. 'If you like.'

'You mean, not a couple of middle-aged lard-arses here for a dip during the day.'

He holds up my towel. 'I wouldn't put it like that. But if you don't mind . . .'

I launch myself back into the middle of the pool with a whoosh. 'Oh, but I do mind. Now that we've violated your viewing benefit, we might as well enjoy our special privilege.'

He stands, his expression hardening. 'If you don't get out, I will be forced to call security.'

Why can't he just let it go? Why does it matter so much that we haven't followed orders? I've always been a rule-taker; now it seems I'm breaking my own, and theirs too. Like him, I'm not ready to back down – not today. And so, I snatch his smile, staring back up at the sky. 'Go ahead. It'll give me an extra five minutes.'

In fact, it takes security at least ten minutes to get up here, by which time Susie has flopped out and rushed off to the toilets. I stay, idly bobbing around, admiring the feathery cirrus clouds, enjoying the feeling of silky water on my skin. For so many years, going swimming was such a chore – hoiking the twins into their suits, shivering in the shallow end watching plasters bobbing by, apologizing to ploughing front crawlers who crashed into my splashing kids, wrestling clothes on wriggling, whingeing wet bodies while my own damp skin prickled in the chill. With the introduction of children, swimming went from a fun, relaxing pastime to a teeth-grinding trial. Much like Christmas, and adult conversation. I feel extremely serene, even though I'm apparently about to be escorted off the premises by some bouncers.

When they arrive, I have to stifle a giggle, as they're

straight out of Casting Central, biceps squeezed into their suits, earpieces in place, ranging round the pool like Men in Black. Susie comes back from the toilets, fully dressed. The manager and Ms Adams also return, ready to nod approvingly as I'm borne away. The hipster is filming again. May as well put on a show.

'I'm doing my best to be a water bauble,' I say to the manager. 'Would it help if I did some artistic swimming, like in the Olympics?'

'You need to get out now,' he replies, a muscle flickering in his cheek.

'I'm shy. Everyone's looking.'

One of the bouncers holds up a towel, which is actually rather gentlemanly. I have no beef with him, even though he is very beefy. I shake my head, while maintaining an elegant support scull to keep myself afloat.

'Come and get me,' I say, and attempt a flamingo position quite creditably.

This, predictably, causes some consternation. Security are unwilling to get in the pool, feeling it will compromise their authority. Ms Adams also flat-out refuses. The manager is reluctant but determined, and actually starts taking his shoes off, when he spots poor Jeremy walking past with a tray. Jeremy is dispatched to fetch me out. Susie is now on a lounger, wearing sunglasses, watching us from behind her Jilly Cooper. Her mouth drops open as Jeremy takes his shirt off. Topless, in his underpants, he's not very decorative.

'Just get in,' snaps the manager.

Jeremy eyes the lapping water like it's lava. Miserably, he jumps in, and I'm propelled backwards by the subsequent wave. He starts to wade towards me. I'm ready to wind this up now, but can't resist flicking him with water and swimming away. It's all so silly, and still feels unreal, like the phantom dog on the farm. None of it matters. Some things matter, but this doesn't. I don't know why I never realized that until now.

'Please, miss,' says Jeremy, holding out his hand. I do feel sorry for him. But he's a dolt. I dive under the water, can see him groping around, flailing as I slither by. There's the dull sound of a music beat, and when I emerge at the other end, the DJ has upped the ante and is playing 'Move Bitch' by Ludacris. It's a banger – we tried to use it on a Red Eye show about training unruly dogs, but couldn't get the clearance.

Dashing water from my eyes, I catch sight of a big clock on the far wall. It's nearly 11 a.m. Shit. My booking. I haul myself out of the pool, saluting the DJ, who sticks out his pierced tongue. The hipster whoops.

'A wise choice, madam,' says the manager, trying to disguise his relief. 'You need to leave now.'

'Don't be ridiculous,' I reply, taking the towel from the bouncer. 'I need to get dry and dressed. Do you want me dripping through your dining room?'

Once again, there's a brief moment of confusion, before the manager gestures me towards the toilets.

'Please be quick,' he says, and I'm satisfied he's sufficiently broken.

As I pass Susie, I reach into her bag, fish out her purse, and produce a tenner. 'This is for Jeremy, and Jeremy only,' I say, handing it to the manager, who bows, receiving it between finger and thumb.

'Oi,' says Susie. I smile down at her and we high five. No – not really; we're not in a movie. Instead, she leans forwards and hisses, 'I'm going to fucking kill you! We could have been arrested! I'm so embarrassed I could die!' She follows me to the toilets, haranguing me as I rub myself dry.

'This is so out of character,' she continues, as I take off my stylish but sodden bikini. 'What's gotten into you? Have you had a row with Robbie? Why are you just standing there naked like you don't give a toss?'

'I took some Vicodin this morning.' I ponder, waving my underwear under the hand dryer.

'What?'

'I had a headache, a really bad one. And I took some other tablets. And then I got knocked out at the train station.'

'*What?*'

'Only for a second. Anyway . . .' I put on my damp knickers. 'I don't think it's any of that.' It's the atoms, regenerating me. Where they came from, I don't know. I could guess, but I'm not sure I'm ready yet. I just want to drift, for now.

'Then what is it?' She helps me fasten my bra. 'Christ, look at your toenails.'

'I know, I haven't had time.'

'What's going on?'

Squeezing out my hair under the dryer, I attempt to define it. 'I want to have a nice day. Just . . . do what I want.' *What if I did what I wanted?*

'And you want to get arrested.'

'For swimming? No, I want to slow down. You know, like that TV show where the reindeer just plods through the snow? I want everything to be . . . leisurely and simple. I want a leisurely, simple day. Just for a change.'

'It's going well so far.'

'It is,' I say, pulling on my trousers. 'It really is.'

On the way out, the hipster stops me, holding up his phone. 'Filmed it, bruh,' he says. 'You mind it on the Gram?'

'Sure,' I say, blowing the scowling manager a kiss. 'What's the worst that can happen?'

# 7

My two favourite people, apart from my children, are Susie and Robbie. Quirks of fate in the meeting of both. I met Robbie when I was a floundering twenty-seven-year-old, a newly promoted assistant producer who'd graduated to a flat above ground level and was struggling to meet the astronomical rent. I was recceing a ruined priory outside Northallerton to check out the monks' cells, and he'd gone there to scratch his antiquity itch. Robbie really loves relics and is never happier than when he's poking at some old rubble in his spare time, imagining the ancients who inhabited it. I didn't know that then, of course, just wondered why this odd bloke was following me round. I was a bit of a ruin at that time myself, so maybe he sensed it. After tailing me along a ditch for a while, he pointed at it and said:

'That's an old sewage system.'

I looked at the trench, picturing the effluence that must have run down it long ago. 'Oh right.'

'The monks were very hygienic. Well, by their contemporaries' standards, at least.' He toed a rock that was probably once part of a priory privy. 'Are you interested in the Dissolution?'

I wasn't, particularly, but didn't want to seem rude, and also, he was tall, dark and handsome – elegant, like a Tudor courtier. 'I love it.'

He frowned, so I hastily clarified. 'I mean, it's such an interesting period. All that . . . reforming.' Faced with a proper history-nerd, my flimsy grasp of sixteenth-century religion and politics crumbled like centuries-old mortar. Desperately, I groped for a detail. 'All for Anne . . .' Was it 'Boleyn' or 'of Cleves'? 'The six-fingered witch.'

He laughed. 'The Cromwellian take on Nan Bullen!'

I laughed too though I had no idea what he meant, just knew that I liked him very much because his eyes were so kind, and he'd assumed I was making a knowing joke when in fact I was a fool.

'I'm actually here for work.'

I said it to make myself seem more important, and his whole face lit up. It was clear he'd decided I was some sort of archaeologist with an interest in the suppression of the monasteries, and therefore his ideal woman, rather than an idiot-box idiot who wanted to see if there was a suitable place where Richard Madeley could do a sleepover so he could find out what it was like being a Carthusian monk. I decided he must never find out my true profession; I would just have to fake it as a dedicated antiquarian until he was too in love with me to care.

'I'm Robbie,' he said, holding out his hand. It seemed

like a very old-fashioned thing for him to do, but when I took it, it felt like a consecration. There we were, kindred spirits meeting on sacred ground.

'I'm Clover.' We beamed at each other, not letting go.

'My day job is at a law firm, but by night I'm an amateur archaeologist. Like Indiana Jones, but without all the fighting and Nazis.' He tipped an imaginary hat to me and my legs felt weak.

'Did you find the Headpiece to the Staff of Ra in Nepal?'

'No, but I once found a Bronze Age bead on the Isle of Man.'

'Sexy.'

We went to the cell to have a look around, and he told me about the monks being hermits, and mostly silent except for singing, and I said that didn't sound like much fun, and he said very little *was* in those days, unless you were a king, and even that soured in the end. He described Henry's ulcer, how putrid it was, and then we talked about the plague, and pus-filled boils, and smallpox, and it was the sweetest, most romantic conversation of my life. I was a crumbling ruin, bearing the scars and pockmarks of my previous encounters, but here he was, applying a compress, taking away my pain with a posset of herbs.

We went to the little café and had a pot of tea and, again, it felt gloriously quaint, like two wartime lovers canoodling. This was before the days of Tinder, but most of my friends were meeting guys in clubs, yelling their flirtations over the relentless thump of 'Luv 4 Luv', which really didn't feel like a desirable way to conduct a courtship. Instead, we sat across a dinky round table, earnestly discussing sixteenth-century maladies, our eyes telling a different story. I wanted to stay there forever, letting empires and dynasties disintegrate around us.

After over an hour of pus-chat, he looked at his watch and said he'd have to get the train back as he'd taken the day off to come up from London. I said I was staying in a B&B in town, but would be travelling back to Herne Hill in South London tomorrow, then looked at him, trying not to let the hope show on my face.

'I'm in London too,' he said. 'West Hampstead, north of the river. But I could get the train down and we could go for a drink when you're back. Or not, if you don't want to.'

The strength and simplicity of those words were breathtaking. It was up to me, my choice, my say-so. He didn't know it, but he was tearing down edifices and rebuilding them right before my eyes. I couldn't tell him then because it was too much to load on one young man of slender acquaintance. But I said I'd like to meet him for a drink, he took my number, and the rest, as they say, is history.

I never told Robbie, but I find ruins quite depressing. To me, they represent something not working out, a failure left to fester. If it was worth it, you'd make the effort on the upkeep, wouldn't you? Or repurpose it, like the abandoned hospitals and tobacco factories in Bristol. I feel sad for buildings that fall into disrepair, reclaimed by nature because they're irrelevant, past it, no longer useful. Maybe because, nowadays, I tend to feel like that myself. The priory had a certain decaying beauty, but I couldn't help thinking it would have looked better in its former glory, gaping holes filled in, repointed and resplendent, young once more. But I kept that to myself. After Robbie left, I went round the whole place again with my camera, doing the recce. It was nearly dark when I finished and then I had to wait forty minutes for a cab to turn up to take me back to Northallerton. The show didn't get made, of course – they almost never do. But I think the trip was worth it, all the same. Something beautiful emerging from the rubble, banishing the ghosts.

# 8

The art exhibition is in some sort of big disused garage down a quiet lane off Clifton Hill. Bristol is really arty, maybe because of Banksy, one of its most famous citizens, or maybe because there are a lot of old factories and warehouses that can be converted to display installations. As I go in, there's a neon sign above the door that says 'IS IT ART?', which bodes well.

I love this stuff. When I was having my quarter-life crisis, I used to go to London's Portrait Gallery to visit a painting of Germaine Greer. She's doing a sort of squatting sit with her head on one side, like a therapist, so I used to tell her my problems, even though in real life she'd probably be really brutal and tell me to get a grip. But I started to associate looking at paintings with some sort of soothing, unburdening process – when I see the Leonardo da Vincis in the National Gallery I well up and spill over in blessed release, and there are Rembrandts that give me a sore throat from trying not to cry. Sometimes I wonder if I have Stendhal syndrome, a condition where you become highly emotional and panicky in the presence of great art. Or possibly I was just reacting to life generally.

We used to try to take the kids to galleries, but they only wanted to go to the shop and argue about whether to buy a fridge magnet or a pin brooch. Once, at the Bristol Museum, Hazel gazed around disdainfully before loudly announcing 'ALL THE PEOPLE HERE ARE DEAD,' as Ethan tried to wipe one of his bogeys on Alfred the Gorilla's glass case. Children are philistines, so I stopped trying to educate them, missed all the showcases and light installations and masterpieces I wanted to see. Now I intend to walk round incredibly slowly, reading all the little cards, then walk round again and maybe even listen to an audio tour. I want to steep myself. I want to be one with the art. Then I'm going to have a lovely lunch.

The first room is large and very bright, painted white, even the concrete floors, which are lightly caked in the summer dust of a thousand shoes. *Is it art?* First up is a sculpture of a vast beach ball resting on a bed of sand. I don't know what I think about it at all, and I like that; to look at something and think . . . nothing. My head is empty, which is what I crave. Having banished the usual hubbub of my brain, I'm enjoying the peace and quiet. Walking around the ball, I find a card that says 'All A Round'. Marvellous. The room is hushed apart from footsteps, the rustle of leaflets, murmuring. I move on to a giant shell. Another card encourages you to walk inside the shell, so I do, and there's the sound of the sea, which has been piped in somehow. It's Thursday morning and I'm standing inside a fibreglass conch listening to artificial waves – it really couldn't be better.

The next piece in the room is an enormous deck chair with a book splayed open on it. It's an upsized edition of *Crime and Punishment*, which seems a bit unlikely. By no stretch of the imagination could it be described as a beach read. The card at the side reads 'Culture Clash'. Ah, I see. Someone who sits on a deck chair wouldn't read Dostoevsky. Now, despite my own judgement, I'm irked, which gives me a pleasurable frisson. Thursday morning, and I'm being kindled by a sculpture. I'm not sitting in a meeting room listening to someone drone on about the problems of an online edit, or telling a presenter they can't send the cameraman on a coffee run, or getting a call from my kids' school during a shoot because Ethan lost his three-in-one booster form. I am free; free to be culturally irked.

Just as I'm breathing in the heady fumes of personal liberty, my viewing benefit is violated by a small boy who squeezes in front of me, picks up the huge book and staggers off with it. Is this art too? I look around for a parent but can't see anyone looking remotely responsible or bothered. Deciding to ignore him, I move on to the next seashore offering, which is a massive dead jellyfish, splayed on the floor like a transparent rug. Reaching out a tentative finger, I prod it, and it judders satisfyingly. It's very clever. As I'm studying the watery corpse, the boy scampers across it, his trainers leaving a huge dent in its glutinous centre. This is an interactive exhibition, but not *that* interactive. I wish it had stung him.

'Hey, you!'

There's now a cross-looking woman bearing down on me. She's wearing a lanyard so I guess she works here.

'Hello?'

'Can you control your child, please? He's just tried to kick the beach ball.'

'He's not my child.'

But I'm drowned out by the child himself, who tears between us, shrieking, holding a handful of sand, which he flings over the man o' war. He must be about four years old and clearly has the devil's light in his eye. I've seen this light many a time, on dreaded playdates when Ethan would bring home one of his class's chief marauders. These monsters live to destroy, to create chaos and havoc, to piss you off and terrify you. And you have to accept it meekly, because other parents can be funny about you disciplining their darlings, and you don't want little Archie sobbing and yelping 'She shouted at me!' as he's led away. I once hid in the bathroom during a particularly noisy and destructive afternoon which resulted in our Christmas tree being knocked over and excrement being liberally rubbed into the landing rug. When the mother arrived to pick him up, I just avoided her eyes and said 'Yes, fine!' But I learned to recognize that martial light, and move heaven and earth to make sure it didn't cross our threshold.

'I'm not your mummy,' I say to the demon child, feeling like I have to say it for the benefit of the woman with the lanyard, who seems to be conferring parental responsibility on me.

'Mummy,' he says, wiping his hands on his top and twinkling evilly. I resist the urge to kick him like he kicked the beach ball – a feat of inner strength that might not last for much longer. Tutting, lanyard woman picks up the big book and takes it back to the deck chair while I look around in search of his true parent. There's literally no one else here apart from a teenage girl with pink hair who's dancing in the entrance to the shell.

'What's your name?' I ask, even though I don't care.

'Lucifer,' he says. He doesn't; he says 'Lucas,' which is near as dammit.

'Is that your . . . nanny?' I point at the pink-haired girl and he shakes his head.

Five minutes ago, I was having a fanciful, fancy-free artistic moment; now I'm in charge of a demonic child. Indulging in my own tut, I take his hand.

'Where is your mummy or daddy?'

He jerks his head towards the next room, and together we go onwards. His palm is sand-rough and disgustingly sticky, covered in a substance I don't want to think about. It's definitely not art. The second room is so dimly lit it takes my eyes a while to adjust, peering in the gloom. There are paintings on the walls, but the images aren't distinguishable, and a rope prevents onlookers getting up close. Five minutes ago, I would have enjoyed this hugely, but now it's not ideal, groping my way through the dark with a small child in tow. There's a sort of lump in the middle of the room, possibly another artwork, but as we get nearer, the boy points down.

'Daddy,' he says, dropping my hand.

Up close, the lump is a man lying prone on the floor, with headphones on. He must be listening to one of the audio descriptions. As I gaze down at him lying there without a care in the world, I feel a rising . . . what is it? Whatever it is, it's dampened down, like the sounds in the swimming pool. Hiding from Ethan's friend Archie in the bathroom, I'd felt angry, but it was a hopeless, impotent fury. There was nothing I could do – or at least, it felt that way at the time. But now I feel more purposeful and . . . enterprising. Lucifer's daddy is otherwise engaged; he expects his son to be contained and entertained elsewhere. And I remember the picture I saw in the paper when I was reading about this exhibition – the photo of a huge fibreglass baby, and beyond, a whole playroom. Just what this little Prince of Darkness needs.

'Come with me,' I say, taking his hand again.

In the next room, the giant baby dominates, and I pause by the enormous screwed-up face. There's some sort of liquid drooling out of its mouth, and the eyes are squeezed shut, but not in sleep. I take a moment to remember that phase of my life – two angry, spewing newborns, sucking me dry. It's not a stage I would care to revisit. There were nights when I would have to put a wash on at two in the morning because we'd run out of muslins. Days I would spend in a kind of despairing stasis, jerking awake to feed every forty minutes and then slipping back into an uneasy twilight, a body nestled into each elbow. When Robbie came home at the end of the day, I would hand them to him wordlessly and head upstairs to sink, sink, sink into bed. I couldn't sink far enough, would have let it swallow me whole if I could. That time broke me, though of course, in many ways, I was already broken. So many people to satisfy. Was I ever really fixed?

'Bored,' whines the boy.

'Only boring people are bored,' I reply, echoing my mother, and pull him onwards. The baby is just the beginning. There's also an enormous rattle, and a big giraffe teether. It makes me feel as though I've been shrunk, belittled by this massive infant and its detritus. Which is effective, definitely art. But we're heading to the corner, the biggest structure in the room looming ahead. It's a gigantic playpen, its mesh walls as high as my shoulders. Inside are various enlarged toys – wooden blocks, a bulky xylophone, a blankie the size of a duvet. It's perfect. Heaving the boy up, I propel him in. He lands with a little bounce on the blankie, and looks up at me, devil eyes alight with mischief.

'Knock yourself out, kiddo.' He launches himself at the xylophone.

Wandering to the next room, I congratulate myself. I've created more art out of art – possibly ruined it, but Robbie would say that ruins are often more interesting than the original. In the final room, I sit for ten minutes looking at a video loop of bees mating, watching the drone die over and over again. Then my tummy rumbles, reminding me of the next thing on my list. My delicious burrito. But as I exit the gallery, shading my eyes against the sun, there's someone waiting for me outside.

# 9

'What in John Logie Baird's name are you doing?' Petroc says.

My colleague and fellow executive producer at Red Eye. He's holding his cockapoo, Lafayette, the world's worst dog. A vicious, yapping minibeast with separation anxiety, Lafayette is a lockdown pet who, having finally been introduced to the world, decided he hated it. I have some sympathy with this, but he's a pain in the arse. Petroc has to bring him into work, and he craps everywhere, glaring at you with his mean little coal eyes. In many ways, he reminds me of Vince.

'Why are you here?'

Petroc sets the dog down on the pavement; he immediately starts yapping in a frenzy. Petroc picks him up again.

'Why do you think I'm here? Looking for you! Monty's gone crazy, says if you don't come back to the office, he's going to have you killed.'

'He'll have to call in the hitmen then. How did you find me?'

He smooths one eyebrow with a finger. 'I've had Finian the runner following you since you left the office.'

'Isn't that a misappropriation of company resources?'

'I had reason to fear for your health and safety.'

'I'm fine. I'm just going for a burrito.'

'Like that?'

'Like what?' I look down at myself. I look great.

He spins me round, and marches me back up the hill, pushing me towards a shop window. Reflected in it is a blurred version of me, and for a second it's clear what the problem is. I catch sight of it; a glimpse of what's really going on inside that tousled head . . . Nails leading to lost kingdoms, a candle burned at both ends until it's just a pool of wax on the floor like the dead jellyfish, an endless to-do list that morphs into a guest list, names scrolling and scrolling in a crazed credit sequence. But then it's gone, the water is smooth again and I can only see the outside of me. There's nothing wrong.

'I look incredible.'

'No, you don't. What's with these rats' tails?' He lifts crisp sections of my chlorine-desiccated hair.

'Went for a swim.' My bra is still damp, making patches on my shirt, but who cares?

'I know you did. It's on Instagram. Finian showed me. I tagged you, you'll be viral by lunchtime.'

'Fame at last.' Getting out my phone to have a look, I see I have thirty-four missed calls. Mostly Vince. I can't be bothered with that, so put it away again.

'Come with me,' says Petroc. 'If we're bunking off, we may as well do it properly.'

'Where are we going? I want my lunch.'

'It's not even quarter to twelve, greedy-guts. Plenty of time.'

'What for?'

'Sorting you out.'

He heads up the hill towards Regent Street, dragging me with him, and I follow because I don't really care, as long as he's not going towards the office and Vince and emails and lists.

'You're walking really fast. I'm not doing fast today.'

'There's a Great Dane behind us. If Lafayette sees it, he'll try to fight it.'

Two minutes of outrunning the Dane later, we're there, wherever it is – the sign above the shop says 'Locks Are Everything'. Petroc pushes me inside, singing 'Ta-da!' as I study the row of chairs and mirrors. Annoyed at him for derailing my day, I now wonder if this isn't exactly what I need. Stillness and abstraction were my primary aims; where better to find them than a hairdressing salon, a temple of tranquillity?

Whenever I go to the hairdressers, I'm often exhausted by the inane chat – 'Going anywhere nice on your holidays?' – then vaguely appalled by the finished result, which inevitably leads me to over-tip out of confusion and embarrassment, but today will be different. Today, I will sit in silence, majestic like a Sphinx, while someone makes me beautiful.

'Sasha, darling, are you free? I've got a challenge for you.'

Of course, Petroc knows her; he knows everyone. He's always chatting to people in case they'd make good TV. This Sasha might make good TV but she doesn't look like she wants to. She's quite forbidding, and shaven-headed, which isn't a great advert for a hairdresser, as if she attempted a self-style that went wrong, and had to start again.

Sasha looks at her watch. 'I've only got half an hour before my next client.'

'That'll have to do. Make her look half-decent so we can go for lunch.'

She sits me down in one of the chairs and dead-eyes me in the mirror. 'What'll it be?'

Usually cowed by hairdressers, their superior knowledge of undercuts and feathering, I tend to resist asking for what I really want, leaving them to make the style choices for me. Gearing up to keep it simple – 'Just a wash and blow-dry please' – my gaze is snagged by a photo on the wall behind me. 'That,' I say, pointing. That's what I really want.

For years, as long as I can remember, ever since my mother started needling about my roots, I've hated my hair. A really visceral, resentful loathing of my own follicles, which continually let me down. Firstly, of course, it's grey. There are some people – striking, dramatic people – who can carry off grey hair, but I'm not one of them. I'd look like Miss Marple. I have to dye it. There's no way I have time to spend four hours in a salon every six weeks, so it has to be a packet-job in the bathroom at home – as a result, all our tiles are flecked with Nice'n Easy Light Ash Brown. Is there a more depressing colour than ash brown? I'd love a more interesting hue, but red makes my skin look yellow, black makes my skin look dead, and blonde makes me look like a randy divorcee. Lastly though, what I really hate about my hair is its flatness. It does nothing, just dangles. Locks *are* everything, and I have always lamented mine's lack of ambition – where other tresses wave or curl or spiral or bounce, mine just hang limply, like a basset hound's ears. Of course, it's my dad's hair, which is why my mother despises it. In conclusion, my dream hairdo, in terms of dimension and vibrancy, is probably Marge Simpson's, but in the meantime, the woman in the picture behind me looks pretty good. Different from me, which is key. The difference I'm feeling on the inside must be reflected externally. Time to change the DNA of my hair.

'That,' I say, again. That wonderful woman in the photo. She has wild, untameable ringlets sticking out in a halo around her head. Marvellous.

Petroc surveys me scornfully. 'Seriously? It's quite a style departure for you. Style exiting the building, in fact.'

'That's what I want.' Catching Sasha's eye in the mirror, I point at my lank, crisp thatch. 'Can you do it?'

'Sure.' She shrugs. 'But it'll wash out.'

'Just for today.' I sit back, satisfied. 'Don't talk to me,' I tell them. 'Pretend I'm not here.'

So Petroc and Sasha start talking to each other as she washes my hair, about another hairdresser in the salon who Petroc dated who is now dating someone famous, which Petroc is livid about, and then I'm away, not listening any more, just drifting, as Sasha tugs and pulls with the tongs. Thoughts float across my brain like bubbles, ready to be blown away or popped. I think about my kids, safely tucked away at school, how I love school, taking care of them, for free, educating them and enriching them so that I don't have to. I think about Robbie, in his office in Finzels Reach, managing portfolios and dealing with IP infringement or whatever it is he does. He rarely talks about work, rarely talks about anything really, except his passion for ruins, and sometimes the rugby. Unlike Petroc, who's dated everyone, I have only had four boyfriends, and three of them were unremarkable. I was never one of those girls who went for the dangerous type; never understood the attraction. I didn't go for dangerous *anything*. There was already enough to worry about without aligning yourself to romantic peril. And then another bubble sails past that looks like a suspect package, and I pop it quickly before it can open or explode, but it's followed by another – the emailed guest list resurfacing, names, names, names – and I start to get hot again, like I was in the office earlier, but it's probably just the curling tongs, which have a lot of work to do, and with a bit of slow and even breathing I'm all right again, and bubble-free.

76

When Sasha finally steps back, I refocus and study my reflection. It's very, very curly.

'I look amazing.'

Petroc wrinkles his nose. 'You look weird. No offence to Sash.'

'I look like Lady Marian in *Robin Hood Prince of Thieves*.'

'But less attractive,' notes Petroc, scrupulously.

'It'll wash out,' repeats Sasha, as she whips off my robe.

'I'll never wash it again,' I assure her, as I pay her thirty pounds. She looks completely indifferent, and I think I might be in love with her. Petroc drags me away, just as I'm wondering whether to book in another appointment at the weekend to get my head shaved just like hers.

'Lunch,' he says.

'Aren't you supposed to be meeting that Astral1 commissioner?' Astral1 is a new channel with big ambitions and entirely unrealistic ideas about budgets.

Petroc smiles, hugging Lafayette, who snarls. 'He cancelled! When it came to it, he couldn't face trekking over to Bristol. The advantage of being out in the sticks!'

'Did you tell Vince?'

'Of course not. I'm going to tell him it went really well and that I got some excellent intel.'

Originally, I imagined I would have lunch on my own, because I didn't want anyone seeing how quickly and inelegantly I can cram a burrito into my mouth, but I guess if I'm going to dine with anyone, it may as well be

Petroc, who I'm fond of despite his terrible lockdown life choices. Not only did he get Lafayette, but he decided he'd had enough of the city and bought a derelict church in Batheaston that's been a total headache – he should have stayed in his lovely Georgian flat in Montpelier. However, he's certainly the most likeable of my fellow executive producers at Red Eye. Better than Oswald, the other exec, who's bone-idle, bullies underlings and yet somehow has a bonus package that would pay for an evil trader's house in Clifton.

'I want to go to Little Donkey.' Bristol is full of lovely little cafés and restaurants, and today is a day to take advantage of them.

'You're so unsophisticated.'

I toss my ringlets. 'I actually like food. Come on, it's not far. We can discuss your imaginary Astral1 meeting en route.'

He takes my arm, then releases it as Lafayette snaps in outrage. 'Lead the way.'

# 10

Petroc and I go way back – seven years, to be precise. I got my job at Red Eye aged thirty-nine, working on a new commission they'd just secured called *Massive House, Micro House*. The idea was that you'd take people who lived in huge houses, and people who lived in tiny houses and . . . swap them. I have no idea why. At least, I suppose the people who owned the huge houses would return home appreciating the extra space, but what was in it for the tiny house owners? It made no sense but I guess it was just a way of repackaging property porn. Anyway, it was a six-ep series, they wanted me to oversee it and it was my first executive producer role so I would probably have said yes even if it was called *Murder House, Morgue House*.

I spent the majority of pre-production trying to make sure most of the properties were in the West Country so I didn't have to travel far. Vince kept putting his oar in because he wanted a Scottish laird to swap his Highland castle for a grotty Tottenham bedsit and I regularly had to explain his own format to him: the small houses weren't necessarily shit, they were just small. We'd found a gorgeous beach-hut in Dorset that I wanted to move into myself.

Red Eye seemed pretty similar to many of the other production companies I'd worked at – a load of overpaid cynical white people at the top, and a smaller, more diverse team of underpaid minions doing the actual grind. As an executive producer, you'd think I was near the top, but in fact I'm more upper-middle. There are endless echelons of MDs and CEOs, CFOs and presidents and global heads and elusive chairmen of parent corporations above me, and what unites them is that they love meetings. They live for meetings. The more obscure the point of the meeting, the better. Utterly pointless is by far the best. I've lost count of the number of 'catch-ups' I've been invited to, where the subject line of the email was something like 'Redefining Group Collective Strategy in the Post-Linear Era'. I'd be assured attendance was obligatory, sit through three hours of a PowerPoint presentation full of pie charts, and come out to discover that my entire production had fallen apart in my absence, requiring major firefighting to rescue it. Just as I'd finished picking up the pieces, another email would arrive: 'Understanding the Creative Process through Team Building'. Frequently, I'd find myself invited to two different meetings at the same time – when I asked Imogen, Vince's PA and general office assistant, what we were expected to do in these circumstances, she simply reorganized them so they were back-to-back. I'd often spend six hours of my day watching PowerPoint slides, and then hustle out to do my actual job. It made me so mad I wanted to scream.

But, of course, I didn't scream. I just got on with it, staying late, starting early, bringing in doughnuts for everyone to curry favour. *Massive House, Micro House* got made; it managed nearly two million viewers which everyone thought was pretty good; the *Guardian* said it was 'televisual baby purée', which made Vince spit until Petroc reminded him that all publicity is good publicity. The channel recommissioned the series and Vince asked me to stay on to make it, which was a tacit admission that I'd done a good job.

However, second time round, he said that since it was an 'up-and-running show' I'd have more time on my hands, so he was giving me responsibility for his development team, a motley crew of misfits who'd been mismanaged for months. Development teams are the engine room of a TV company, responsible for coming up with the ideas for shows that the producers then make. It's a very specific skill, and driving a team like that is a full-time job. I already *had* a full-time job producing shows and didn't have time to come up with them too. But Vince said it like he was conferring a huge honour on me, so rather than refuse point-blank, I said thank you. Now I essentially had two roles, but since Vince didn't believe in remunerating his staff adequately, I was never offered a salary increase or any other kind of perk. And since I was chronically incapable of standing up for myself, once again I just had to get on with it. My window intruder dream started up again which, on top of everything else, made me constantly teary, exhausted and on edge.

Three weeks in, Petroc found me crying in my new office. I wasn't making a noise or anything, just silently weeping while I emailed the series commissioner of *MHMH* to tell her we'd found a fortified manor house in Fife and a gypsy caravan in Pembrokeshire. He caught me unawares, tears rolling down my face as I typed, and there was nothing I could do but hastily rub my cheeks with my sleeve.

'I feel that way whenever I email Channel Four,' was all he said. He'd come to ask if I knew a particular producer he was thinking of hiring, so we had a brief but enjoyable bitch about various people we'd worked with, and then he asked if I wanted to go for a 'snifter' later. During a marathon drinking session in the pub around the corner, he provided eye-opening details of some of the sexual encounters and punch-ups at previous Red Eye parties, including a Christmas lunch that ended in arson, gave me the lowdown on company finances ('completely shot') and told me off for the doughnuts.

'You'll get a reputation,' he warned, signalling to the barmaid.

'As what?' I mumbled, through a packet of salt and vinegar crisps.

'A crowd-pleaser,' he replied.

'Isn't that a good thing? To please a crowd? Like, Lady Gaga or Beyoncé?'

'More like Vera Lynn putting out for the armed forces,' he said. 'You want to sharpen up your act.'

Drunkenly, I confessed about my new appointment, which Vince had never announced because he knew it was a dubious management decision, and I'd never mentioned, because I was too embarrassed to admit I'd been coerced into doing two jobs for the price of one. As he listened, Petroc's lip curled, making me more ashamed than ever, but all he said was 'Leave it with me.'

I thought no more of it, mainly because my memories of the evening were hazy, but the next day, Vincent came to my office and said he'd had a rethink, and that he'd decided to hire a proper head of development instead. In fact, he asked me to do the hiring for him, which was another thing on my plate, but this was more of a swiftly dispatched amuse-bouche instead of the hellish feast with a long spoon I'd previously been condemned to endure. I went for a woman called Naomi Horowitz, who was terrifyingly clever with a finger so on the pulse it was pretty much tapping directly into the vein. But, of course, she was very much in demand, and decided to take another job at the BBC, so instead we ended up with Ian Gittings, whose finger is pretty much circling his own arse crack, but at least he's nominally in charge and I'm left to get on with my actual job, which is making programmes and watching PowerPoint slides.

A few weeks later, during another post-work drinking session, I plucked up the courage to ask Petroc if he'd had anything to do with Vince's change of heart. He grinned and tapped the side of his nose.

'I told him I'd heard on the grapevine that Light Fantastic were looking for a new head of development.'

I squinted into my drink, puzzled. Light Fantastic was a hot new indie run by an ex-ITV commissioner who specialized in big-budget entertainment shows. 'Why did that make him change his mind?'

'Because to find a new head of development, standard procedure is to go round all the other indies finding out who *their* HoD is. Which means that eventually they would have come to you.'

For a long time, I didn't say anything, just ran my finger around the rim of my glass. 'Thank you,' I said eventually. 'I owe you one.'

'Don't worry,' he said. 'One day I'll call it in, and you can repay the favour.'

I didn't forget what I learned that night. First, Vincent didn't want to lose me, and second, there's more than one way to skin a cat. I assumed that to get what I wanted, I'd have to storm around, making a scene, chucking my toys out the pram. And because I couldn't do that, I thought I was stuck. But sometimes, you just have to know what buttons to push. Quietly, in a darkened room, flicking a switch here and there, to get the precise cut you want.

# 11

Little Donkey is the best burrito joint in the world because they have a long bar with about four hundred and eighty-three different fillings, and you can put them all in a tortilla which they roll up really tight so it fits everything in. They can *always* fit it in. Usually, I don't allow myself to go there because, firstly, lunch breaks don't exist at Red Eye – you eat a limp canteen sandwich at your desk, spilling crumbs between the keys of your computer, or fight over a warm tray of sushi in a meeting. Secondly, I suspect the calorie content of their burritos is verging on bacchanalian, and despite the fact that I adore eating and am really good at it, I started restricting myself when I hit forty. It's just something I felt I had to do (because my mother told me to), like waxing my chin and applying anti-ageing hand cream before bed. But not today. Today is outside the normal rules; today nothing counts; today I will have my fill.

We queue up. I order a Stuffed Donkey Special, which makes Petroc massage his temples when he sees how much is packed in there. He orders a salad, which is a total waste. We sit outside because of Lafayette, who insists on perching on Petroc's knees. I look at my burrito nestling in its wicker basket and sigh in anticipation. I might actually start dribbling if I don't eat this immediately. An al fresco lunch! How decadent. We're next to Clifton Arcade, a pretty, bustling row of shops with a great vibe. I'm bringing my own great vibe, it's all groovy.

Shaking out my napkin, I lay it carefully across my trousers before taking my first bite. God, it's wonderful. Chewy and umami, morsels loitering around my tastebuds, caressing them with their beautiful rich flavours. I am going to eat the hell out of this. Might have another one after, like a burrito chaser. The second mouthful is even better than the first, building on the salty, piquant tang – I cup my hand under my chin to catch the falling fragments and cram them back in. Yum *yum*.

'Shhno. Wut zzzz yoo dup shnul frintl?'

Petroc pauses with a piece of lettuce speared on his fork. 'I'm afraid I didn't catch that. Your diction leaves a great deal to be desired.'

'Sorry.' I swallow. 'So, what's your made-up Astral1 intel? What do the big streamers want?'

He lances an olive pensively. 'They want stuff that's bold? Ground-breaking?'

'Empowering? Candid? Raw?'

'Good, good. Keep it coming, I'll take notes.'

'Bring us the ideas you wouldn't take to anyone else,

because they're too chicken-shit. Let's blow up the moon. Get Ricky Gervais to push the button.'

'Think bigger. What about Jupiter, and James Corden?'

'Nice. Can you put in a call? We'll pay thirty K per hour.'

We're sniggering but it's not funny at all because we have actual conversations like this, meetings where by the end of the hour you have a page of scribbled notes that say things like 'Would Dame Judi Dench jump from space?' and you feel tearfully despairing at the prospect of making an unmakeable big budget entertainment show with a national treasure for the price of an online short. Commissioners also have the 'what if . . .' devil at their shoulder, but he's more of a sadistic puck who says things like *'What if we made a scale model of the Eiffel Tower, but with cheese? And what if we made Joanna Lumley eat it? Or Nigella put it in a fondue? Come on, I'm just riffing.'*

'Humph!'

I'm laughing and chewing, and when the noise cuts through our chat, initially I don't hear it, or it doesn't register.

'Give me a life-endangering celebrity journey! Someone world-famous who's never been on telly before. Must have a regional accent, and travel by camel.'

'Just sitting there!'

'I want Prince Harry to parachute into a volcano.' Petroc's still going, but there's a robotic tone to his voice now, as he tunes in.

'Butter wouldn't melt!'

Still holding my Special like a priceless artefact, albeit one I'm in the process of destroying, I turn towards the voice. It's coming from an old woman sitting next to us. Wearing too many layers for a summer's day, she's the shape of a slowly deflating balloon, and she's glaring at us like we just gobbed in her soup. She definitely does not have a great vibe. For a second, I fret about what this means; maybe I've somehow offended her, she considers my unparalleled greed a disgrace. But then I realize her little jackdaw eyes are directed towards Petroc. What's wrong with him? The salad is a disappointing choice, certainly, and I guess eating with a dog in your face might be considered unsavoury. But I can't really see what that has to do with her. Picking at his leaves, Petroc now has a pink tinge to his cheeks as the woman rambles on.

'Shoving his politics in our faces!'

I put down my burrito and lean forwards. 'Sorry, what's wrong?'

'Leave it,' murmurs Petroc, determinedly jabbing at his meal.

She sniffs. 'Him and his rainbow.'

Glancing back at my colleague's reddening face, I notice the Pride pin on his lapel. He may be a disastrous judge of the property market, but Petroc has an incredibly individual and elegant sartorial style – he always looks beautifully put together and highly original, whereas I manage to make a mess of trying to look like everyone else.

Today he's wearing a checked purple suit, which somehow manages to be both outrageous and understated at the same time. It's really quite a skill.

'You object to rainbows, do you? I think they're very pretty.'

'Don't,' says Petroc, rubbing Lafayette, who growls.

'We all know what it means,' she sneers.

I was at a bus stop in Stroud last year, on my way to the train station after visiting my mother. Waiting next to me was a young man wearing one of those 'La!' T-shirts inspired by a TV drama about the AIDS crisis. Another group of lads were jostling past, and one of them called out 'Fag!' The young man didn't say anything, just stared at his pristine leather sneakers with the same shamed flush Petroc now sports. And I didn't say anything either, because I was scared of what they might do to me, and besides, I didn't know what to say. But now I do, and I'm not scared.

'I know what it means. I don't think you know what it means.'

The balloon rapidly inflates. 'How dare you?'

'It's an interesting question. I might ask you the same thing.'

'Please,' murmurs Petroc. He's gone pale now, but I can't really stem this flow because I don't know where it's coming from, or where it's going. I just know that, like the rolling credits, it's going to carry on.

'I'll say what I want, it's a free country!'

I take another bite of my burrito. It's so delicious. 'And what exactly do you want to say?'

There's a pause as she works out how to put it. 'Great Britain's not what it was.'

Chewing, I nod. 'There we can definitely agree. There used to be slums, and people dying of scurvy and TB. Women couldn't vote, and there were only three channels on TV.'

'That's not what I mean.'

'Then what *do* you mean?'

'Clover, stop.'

With an eyeroll at Petroc's interjection, there's another inflation. 'This used to be a God-fearing country.'

'Again, I agree. Witches were burned at the stake. You'd have been toast.'

She bristles; she's very bristly, in all senses of the word. 'We used to have standards. There were rules. People knew what was what. Young folk looked up to old folk. They didn't go off . . .' She eyes Petroc. 'Doing whatever they like, with whoever they like. No standards.'

'What on *earth* do you mean?' She's speaking a language only Lafayette can hear. 'Try talking in the Queen's English. I bet you're a fan.'

'Clover, *please*.'

But Petroc has faded into the background; it's just me and this gouty old cow, staring each other down, willing each other to concede. So many times I've stayed mute, chickened out, but today I'm putting my head over the parapet and aiming fire. She swells once more, peg-teeth bared, goaded into breaking cover.

'It used to be illegal,' she spits.

'*What* did?'

She leans forwards, beady little eyes gleaming. 'Sodomy,' she breathes, jerking her head towards my friend.

I take one more bite, then find my hands are moving of their own accord, lifting the burrito again, not to my lips but across the gap between our tables. I unroll it, emptying pulled pork, Mexican rice, chopped tomatoes, refried beans, grated cheese, shredded lettuce, guacamole, and a dollop of sour cream into her sagging lap. They really do pack in a *lot* of fillings.

'No,' moans Petroc softly, burying his head in Lafayette's fur.

'You!' shrieks the old woman, hauling herself to her feet, jabbing with her finger like a witch cursing a wedding. 'YOU . . . FAG HAG.'

I start to laugh. 'I think of myself as more of a gay icon.'

She looks so ridiculous, dripping burrito fillings, that I can't stop giggling, which makes her even more incensed, huffing and exclaiming as she shakes shards of meat off her dress. Passers-by are stopping to look, and one of the Little Donkey bar staff rushes out to see what's going on. Petroc is rocking and moaning, clutching his dog, the old woman is swaying and muttering indecipherable insults, but there's no way I'm letting her have the last word, even if I don't know what it is.

'Get back in your lake, you old trout.'

I roll up my napkin like a snowball and throw it at her. Batting at it, she falls backwards into her chair, panting heavily. Game, set and match. The Little Donkey employee crouches by her, holding her hand and fanning her with a menu. I think she might be having a heart attack, and can't find it in my own heart to be sorry.

'I think you'd better go,' the staff member says over his shoulder, and I nod, but can't resist giving Grotbags the finger when he turns around to her again. It's only then I notice Petroc has already gone, and catch sight of him striding off down the road. Snatching up my bag, I follow him.

'Wait up!'

He faces me, his expression stony.

'Do you want to find somewhere else to have lunch? We didn't get to eat much there. Or crack that Astral1 brief.'

'Not really. I've lost my appetite.'

'I know, what a bitch. A face to turn the milk sour.'

'I didn't care about her. It was you who turned my stomach.'

I stare at him in amazement. 'Me? What did *I* do?'

He sets Lafayette on the pavement, with the usual result. 'You're not my knight in shining armour. What did you think you were doing, starting a fight on my behalf? It wasn't a fight I wanted.' He's gone red again, which clashes with his beautiful suit.

'Well, she started it. I wasn't going to sit there listening to that bigoted crap.'

He snorts. 'She was a sad old woman. She just wanted someone to notice her.'

'But if we let things like that slide . . .'

'There you go again! It's not your fight! Do you think I haven't encountered that sort of stuff before? And much worse besides? I deal with it in my own way, which is not throwing food. You know what people saw then? They didn't see you standing up for gay rights. They saw you harassing an old lady, making her ill. It doesn't further the cause, darling.'

I don't understand. For the first time in my life – all right, the fourth or fifth time today – I'm able to defend myself and my friends, and this is the thanks I get. If I wasn't feeling so sunny, I'd be quite disgruntled.

'Right, well, I'll keep my mouth shut next time.'

'Do.' He picks up his useless dog, who has been cawing like a seagull the whole time. 'Enjoy your day, Shirley Temple.' He stalks off, Lafayette looking daggers at me over his shoulder.

I bloody will. Half a burrito was not enough of a lunch, but I think it's time to dial things down a little. I'm going shopping.

# 12

Although I didn't get to wear it, I did actually find the wedding dress of my dreams – the green one with the bustle – in a vintage shop on the Essex Road. That was when we were still living in London. It cost £185 and although I tried it on, and stared at myself longingly in the mirror, I didn't buy it. The one my mother chose cost £1500 and, despite the fact that she insisted on purchasing it, she did not insist on paying for it. It was a corseted fishtail, strapless and entirely unsuited to my body shape. She also demanded a veil, which made me feel like Miss Havisham. I guess in the end, given how the ceremony panned out, the netting was helpful.

My mother wanted a September wedding so she could wear her autumn colours and everyone could say 'Rose, you look divine.' She wanted tradition, and grandeur, the kind of God-fearing pomp and ceremony that made Britain Great. Robbie would have stood up to her if I'd let him, but I was so terrified of rocking the boat that I begged him to just go along with it, let her have her way. An easy-going guy, he shrugged and said as long as the whole thing resulted in us being married, then that was fine by him. I thought the same; surely the end justified whatever means she chose?

During the rehearsal with Father Stephen, I'd ascertained the problem in the church, one which made me faint with worry, but one which I knew we could do nothing about. I did try to mention it, but my mother just rolled her eyes to the roof and said 'Don't be so silly!' My sister Maz was catatonic once she'd got over the vulgar flowers, possibly thanks to a few too many glasses of Bucks fizz in the hotel that morning. Maz is somewhat alcohol-dependent during family events with our mother, and I didn't begrudge her numbing the pain in that way. Meanwhile, keen golfer Father Stephen was already on the first hole in spirit. So as usual it was only me having an internal meltdown, wondering how I'd get through it all. I didn't want to resort to booze like my sister, so ended up begging a Valium off my maid of honour Susie, who'd recently been prescribed it by a dubious GP for her restless leg syndrome. She would only give me half, because she said she needed the other bit to stop her fidgeting in the pew. I took it at 1.30 p.m. and by the time the ceremony was due to start, I was desperate for a nap, but no less frightened.

The organ fired up at 2.10 p.m., ten minutes late, not because we were, but because my mother said that was proper. Standing in the entrance to the church, I could see Robbie near the altar conversing with one of his brothers and his best man Jonathan, and there was something about the set of his shoulders that told me he'd noticed the buzzing too. As the music began, he looked up at me, and he smiled but I could see it in his eyes. He'd seen our uninvited guests hovering, and he knew how upset they made me.

Dad wasn't walking me down the aisle because Rose wouldn't have her ex-husband in a leading role, so instead it was my uncle Harold, her brother, who tends to get overemotional at these events and already had tears streaming down his cheeks. Venetia the flower girl was in front of me, sulking in her cape, holding a basket of petals she refused to scatter. Maz was behind, wearing violet and a dazed expression. We began the procession, with diverse paces. Robbie nodded at me, as if to say 'It'll be OK' and all the way down I determinedly didn't look up, just straight ahead, trying not to fall asleep or fall apart. At least the music drowned out the angry drone, initially. I think one of the strangest things about it was that no one in the congregation seemed to have noticed – I suppose if you're not attuned to that sort of thing then it isn't a problem. But it was a problem for me, and I couldn't see how I was going to get through the next forty-five minutes.

Sobbing, Harold delivered me to Robbie, who took my hand, squeezing it firmly. I met his eyes, saw the understanding there, and it made me very glad I was about to marry him; I just wished it wasn't here, with a late-summer wasps' nest in the rafters that Father Stephen was too tight to get rid of. I suppose he trusted in God, but God was about to let him down.

I'm scared of many things – suspect packages on trains, heights (in planes, on stepladders), snakes (specifically, those lurking in toilets), to name a few. Wasps have been a major fear since I walked into a nest on a river bank during a day trip to Ross-on-Wye in 1984. We were staying with Uncle Harold and his wife Trish (who has now sadly passed) in their bungalow in Goodrich. Our parents – still together then – were drinking in the White Lion, and it took the locals a while to locate them, by which time I'd had calamine lotion applied by a nice lady who ran the pharmacy, and been given some lemonade by bar staff at the snooker club. My abiding memory of that moment is the embarrassment of running down the street screaming with wasps in my hair, and the overwhelmingly kind and solicitous reaction. Because of course, when Rose arrived, she was appalled I'd made such a fuss, and told me off in front of the crowd who'd gathered, saying I was an attention-seeker. My mother is the kind of woman who believes it's unladylike to raise her voice, so she didn't actually shout, just looked down at me sitting on a folding chair someone had brought out, sorrowfully shook her head and murmured 'What a scene. Dearie me, little Miss Panicky, aren't you? Such a palaver.' Then she apologized to the baffled chemist, describing me as a tiresome exhibitionist: 'I'm a martyr to her meltdowns, I really am!' Luckily, we were all distracted by Maz, who'd fallen into the river, and arrived dripping wet, holding a fish in a jam jar.

The trauma of that day lingered and laser-focused on the wasps, even though of course they were blameless, just doing what they do. Even now, I'm more scared of my reaction to the insects than the insects themselves. The idea that I might make a fuss, cause a palaver . . .

I really wanted to be a beautiful, radiant bride, but the bodice of the dress was slipping down my bosom, and I kept having to hoist it up, make sure as much of my skin was covered as possible in case of attack, not look up towards the roof, not fall asleep, and definitely not scream if I saw a black-and-yellow monster loitering. Just smile and look at Robbie, my rock, and occasionally Father Stephen if I absolutely had to, then smile again and repeat some words, and wait for it to end.

Susie did the reading, which was from Ephesians, chosen by my mother, and not even glanced at by my best friend before the service. She read it with a growing incredulity: '*Wives, submit yourselves to your own husbands as you do to the Lord* . . .' Robbie's lips twitched throughout, even though he was trying to be anxious for my sake. Then, halfway through, she suddenly slammed the book shut with an almighty thunderclap, causing the entire congregation to jump.

'Sorry,' said Susie. 'Wasp in the Bible.' I risked a glance at my mother, who was clearly hoping God's wrath would smite my friend. Robbie's shoulders were shaking, but he squeezed my hand again, as Venetia let out a small wail.

'Ohhhh . . . oooohhhhhh OUCH.'

'*I am talking about Christ and the church*,' continued Susie sternly.

Venetia's mother Ginny was obviously cast in the same mould as mine, because at a glare from her, the little girl subsided into hiccups, as tears poured down her face. My heart was beating erratically, but I also longed to lie down on the cold stone and sleep for a thousand years. Please let this be over without anyone else getting killed or stung.

'*However, each one of you also must love his wife as he loves himself, and the wife must . . . the wife must . . .*' Susie looked up, distraught. Everyone waited.

'*The wife must *BANG* her husband*,' Susie declared, slamming the book shut on the word she objected to.

My mother's face was impassive, but the fingers gripping her bag were white with rage. Luckily Uncle Harry's loud sobs distracted her, and she had to attend to him, passing him a handkerchief and hissing at him to shut up. Father Stephen continued with the service, but didn't notice a wasp crawling over his shoe, and into his trousers. He asked if there were any impediments, and then cried out, clapping a hand to his knee.

I was sweating by that point, my skin clammily damp, which made the bodice even more slippery. My hands were shaking as we exchanged rings – during which time two more of our guests were targeted and scurried out of the church, clutching their arms. My mother sat bolt upright, staring straight ahead, even as a wasp clambered delicately over her fascinator. It was fascinating; I watched it creep under and actually saw the moment it stung her. She flinched slightly, and flicked it away, then ground her foot firmly but quietly on the tiled floor. I suppose at least she practised what she preached.

'You may kiss the bride,' Father Stephen gabbled, and barely waited for a peck before striding towards the vestibule, his cassock flapping. We didn't see him again; the curate said he was unfortunately indisposed. Outside the church I thought I might faint with the relief of it being over. My father kissed me and said 'That was lovely. Anyway, got to get a wriggle on . . .' because he had a flight booked back to Spain, home to his second wife Valentina who shouted a lot and never bothered keeping herself trim.

Still, at least we avoided a scene, eh?

# 13

With my original wedding dress in mind, I hop in a taxi to Broadmead to buy a nice outfit. It's the Red Eye wrap party later, and although I had no intention of going, I am starting to think that maybe I should. Maybe it can't be avoided. On the way to the Shopping Quarter, I ignore two calls: one from Vince, and another from my mother. She's been phoning a lot lately, and usually I dutifully listen to her carefully modulated moaning for twenty minutes before pretending one of the kids needs me. 'You are too indulgent,' she always says. 'They're better off without you.'

One of Rose's firmly held beliefs is that the sooner you leave children to their own devices, the sooner they acquire the skills to find success in life. Thus, I was able to make an omelette by the time I was five, otherwise we would have regularly gone to bed hungry. Although she thinks that cooking is a woman's job, she doesn't think it's *her* job. She preferred to spend her evenings going out to dinner with friends, leaving me and Maz under the indifferent eye of a local girl called Annis who just wanted to watch *Dynasty* and didn't care if we went to bed or not as long as we didn't bother her.

Anyway, I didn't want to think about why my mother had been more communicative of late; I wanted to try on a dress. When I was in my early twenties in London, one of my few pleasures was pottering down Kensington High Street looking at all the shops. I approached them much like I approach art galleries – in a kind of transfixed reverie, wandering around fingering beautiful coats, circling exquisitely dressed mannequins in wonder. I loved trying on stuff I couldn't afford, telling the assistant on the way out that 'The fit wasn't quite right,' as if that and not the extortionate price prohibited me from buying it. Occasionally though, I would be so quelled by a raised plucked brow that I'd end up splashing out on something eye-wateringly expensive and then have dry bread for dinner for the rest of the month to make my rent. I've still got a pair of Jimmy Choos that I can't wear because whenever I put them on they make me feel hungry, remembering the culinary sacrifice.

Of course, when my children came along, clothes shopping became a thing of the past, unless it was for them, in which case it consisted of pushing a trolley up and down the rammed rails of Tesco, rifling for bargain, easy-care ensembles while both of them hollered at each other and tried to knock over anything remotely breakable. Now I can afford the stuff, I don't have time to try it on. Instead, once a year I go to the Bicester Village outlet to stock up on my trouser-and-blouse uniform, and buy Gap jeans and jumpers online for the weekends. That's it. So today, for once, I'm going to cavort round Cabot Circus in search of something that makes me want to do a little dance. I've got the hair; now comes the killer dress and the fuck-me shoes. An accommodating killer dress, and comfy fuck-me shoes – since lockdown I can't wear anything too restrictive.

I buy some black leather ankle-strap sandals in the shopping centre, then joyfully wander round various high street chains, marvelling at the skinniness of skinny jeans, the shortness of denim shorts, the skimpiness of the crop tops. Occasionally I puzzle over the function of the garment I'm holding, a flimsy item with various holes and no discernible top or bottom. Which body part is it supposed to cover? Whatever it is, I'm sure it's designed to flatter curves smaller, firmer and less stretchmarked than mine. After examining something that might be a skirt, I conclude that this particular establishment probably caters for younger clientele and decide to move on.

Outside on Philadelphia Street, I scan the surrounding shops for a more likely target. In doing so, I accidentally catch the eye of a man who's standing holding a sign that says 'MOBILE REPAIR SHOP – FAST FIXES →'

'Smile,' he says. 'It might never happen.'

This kind of comment is as old as the hills, and I don't need to go into why it's unwanted and unwarranted. When Roman gladiators were gearing up for combat, I'm sure they would take the time to tell passing concubines to

'Cheer up, love.' For some reason, men just enjoy telling women what to do with their faces. This ancient form of chivalry is why I welcomed masks in the era of Covid, relishing the opportunity for facial autonomy that they offered. I've lost count of the number of blokes who've assumed they're director of the movie of my mouth, and have often felt acutely uncomfortable being the object of their jovial scrutiny, almost always offering a limp lip-lift in response before scurrying away, cheeks aflame. But this guy has a sign, and I think it's a sign. A sign that the rot stops here.

I smile at him, very widely. 'Now you,' I say.

'You what?'

'I'd like you to look . . . stunned. Like you can't believe how quick your mobile fixes are. Combine astonished and impressed in a facial expression. No one will want your services if you look bored and gormless. Go on, give it a try.'

Wouldn't you know it, he doesn't like this at all. 'No need to burn your bra about it. I was just being nice.'

'I'm also being nice, giving you a bit of free marketing advice. Now, do you want me to further your career by popping into that phone shop to let them know you're harassing women on street corners?'

'Mad bitch,' he mutters, the sign flaccid in his hand.

'You're very welcome,' I say, and move on.

Putting plenty of distance between me and mobile man, I move along the row of shops, waiting to be enticed by something wonderful. Fate decrees that today I will meet The One – The Dress that calls to me, will transform me, echoing the transformation within. Come to me, Dress of My Dreams, and together we will take on the world. If you could also have pockets, then that would be ideal.

I catch sight of it in the window at the end of the row. It's deep forest-green, with a loose raised waistline and a long swishy skirt that ends in a ruffle hem. Alleluia, it's glorious. In the absence of a bustle, a ruffle will do. With a celestial chorus echoing in my head, I gambol into the shop, already doing a little dance, because I've needed a wee since I left the gallery. I meant to go in Little Donkey but my barney with Grotbags made me forget.

'Madam. Can I help you?'

Madam. Such an insidious term. The manager in Avon House used it in the same way – to convey the sense that you don't deserve to be there and should leave immediately. But whereas the Old Clover would cower and retreat, this one is as assertive as her curls. I look down my nose at the shop assistant, even though she's taller than me.

'I'd like to try on that dress, please.'

She glances at the mannequin. 'That one? I'm afraid that's the only one we've got in stock.'

I really do need a wee. 'Well, I'm sure you've got plenty of others that will look delightful on her.' Then I just stand still in silence, until it gets awkward, which is hard because I want to jiggle to stop myself leaking. Why is everyone an arsehole today?

Finally, she relents, and heads to the mannequin. I browse the other stock in order to keep moving, feeling like I'm about to burst. After gestating and giving birth to twins, my pelvic floor is not what it was, but the dress is mostly off the model now and I don't want to waste my opportunity to try it on. The assistant hands it to me and I bear it off to the changing room reverently. By the time I'm down to my underwear in there, my bladder is bulging like the vocal sac of a bullfrog. Throwing the dress over my head, I shimmy my way in, wincing at the answering twinges in my lower abdomen. It contains a suspect package, and if I don't do something about it, it's going to explode.

Briefly distracted by my appearance, I stare at myself in the mirror. With the ringlets and the high waistline, there's a Regency feel to the look – Elizabeth Bennet, if she'd been a forty-six-year-old TV producer living in twenty-first-century Bristol. Like many women, I have an ambivalent relationship with my face and body – while I accept that there's nothing horrific about either of them, we're frequently at odds. I have very little control over my features or my figure, despite my best efforts, and sometimes when I see myself in a photo or catch sight of my back view in a mirror, I'm unnerved by how . . . *weird* I look. Unfamiliar, as if I'm inhabiting a stranger's frame and we're fighting for the upper hand like cats in a sack. I guess what I'm saying is I'm not comfortable in my own skin, which isn't a huge surprise when you consider

I've had decades of my mother saying things like 'I don't understand why you didn't get my cheekbones; it's a real shame.' Over the years, she eroded my confidence until I was just a shapeless bag of nerves. But now, for the first time, it's like I'm seeing myself, what I could be, if I just embraced the weirdness; the heightened, cartoon quality. I want to look different today – it's quite important – but I didn't expect to enjoy the change, or to want to keep it that way.

Jesus Christ, I need to pee so badly I might . . . pee. I shuffle out of the changing room, keeping my legs crossed.

'Excuse me!' I call out to the frosty assistant, who's now steaming a new dress on the mannequin.

'Yes?' She looks me up and down without commenting. Does the snooty cow even want a sale?

'Do you have a toilet?'

She purses her lips. 'No.'

'You don't have a toilet?'

She hesitates. 'Not for customers.'

More facilities that can't be used. 'OK, but I'm really desperate. Like, *really*.'

She waves the steamer wand – that dummy is getting more attention than me. 'There are public toilets in the shopping centre.'

I shake out the folds of my skirt. 'But I'm wearing this. Can't I just nip into a back room or something?'

'Against company policy.'

'I won't tell.'

She shrugs, passing the wand back and forth. I stare at her for a second, weighing up my options. 'Right.' Stuffing my old clothes in my bag, I shoulder it, and march towards the exit.

'Hey! What do you think you're doing?'

I start, feigning surprise. 'You told me there were public toilets in the shopping centre. So, I'm going there.'

'But you're wearing that!' She puts down the steamer and points at my lovely dress.

'Yes, I just told you that, and you didn't seem very interested.'

'You can't go, you haven't paid for it.'

Obviously, in normal circumstances I would agree, but as I've said, today is not normal, and now I'm really pissed off, not to mention full of piss. She could have made things so much easier and friendlier, but she chose not to, from the very beginning, and now I feel like she needs to be taught a lesson in customer relations. In fact, it would be really good for her and her future sales if I outlined a few key areas of improvement. I turn around, slowly, my hand on the door.

'I'm afraid it's my company policy not to pay for items when I'm about to wet myself. You'll just have to wait.'

Putting her hands on her hips, she inhales sharply through her nose. 'If you leave the premises, I will call the police.'

'I'm only borrowing it. Think of it as a sartorial test drive. Back in a sec.' I can't wait any more, even for banter, so I exit and walk as rapidly as I can in the direction of the toilets. Unfortunately, that's not very rapid, as my pubic area is now under such intense pressure that it's hard to walk at all. It's a sort of limp/stumble towards the ladies, which feel perilously far away, even though it's only a few hundred metres. Then they turn out to be those ones where you have to pay 20p to get through the turnstiles, so I have to scrabble around in my purse, desperately trying to find the right change, as my nether regions pulse painfully. To spend a penny, I need twenty of them. Of course, I haven't got a fucking 20p, just pound coins and a euro I kept in case I accidentally end up in France. This is unbearable, I must pee immediately. Desperately, I look around for help. Another woman is about to go in, has a precious coin ready. Lucky, lucky lady, to have that coin. I wonder if she has another?

'Excuse me, you haven't got a spare 20p, have you?'

Jealously clutching her magic heptagon, she studies me suspiciously. 'What for?'

What *for*? To play heads or tails to decide who serves first?

'For the toilet.' I gesture to the turnstile, convulsing with the urge to urinate. I'm suddenly aware of water around me – a hose being deployed outside, the drip of a tap inside, an abrupt flush as some fortunate shopper concludes their evacuation.

She sighs like I asked her to mint it herself. 'I'm not sure.'

'Could you look? I've got a pound.' I brandish it for reassurance.

Her expression brightens at the prospect of an 80p profit, and she starts digging around in her purse.

'Hmm . . . I don't think . . .'

She delves, muttering to herself, while I fidget and squirm in agony, proffering my pound with a shaking hand. What if I just let rip and flood the ladies' entrance; would it be so very bad? My usually heightened sense of embarrassment and shame is noticeably absent today, but I draw the line at public micturition. Plus, I'm worried about volume – it wouldn't be a leak, more of a torrent. Please let her have a 20p.

'No, I'm sorry, I haven't got one.' She glances at my pound coin regretfully, mourning its loss.

She's dead to me. I whirl around, searching for another saviour. 'Has anyone got 20p?' I bellow, holding my reward aloft. 'I will give you this!' Then, thinking better of it, 'No, all these!' I grab the remaining pound coins in my purse. 'Four pounds for 20p!' My kingdom for a horse.

Within thirty seconds I have three potential 20ps in return for my four pounds. The dilemma then is which offer to accept. Despite the thrumming of my groin, I find myself dithering over it, before finally taking my piece of silver from a sweet old lady who has 'basic pension' vibes. That extra £3.80 should keep her in tomato soup for a bit. Gibbering my thanks, I cram the coin into the slot and barge through. Please let there not be a queue, or I'll have to start handing out fivers to jump it.

It's quiet, thank the Lord. As I approach a cubicle, the imminent purging causes a slight anticipatory spurt – I can barely get the door closed and my pants down before Niagara Falls gushes forth. Oh, the relief. The cubicle is fairly grimy, and there's no paper, but I think it's the nicest and best toilet I've ever had the privilege of urinating in. I feel like writing a note of thanks on the wall, which is already liberally scribbled on. Charmaine was here, apparently; Billy and Danika are forever; and Boris can suck my dick. What a refuge this is; I might just stay here, reposing on the now-warm cracked seat. When I left the office this morning, I wanted to find comfort in stillness and solitude, and I've found it, here in this lavatory. Or loo, as my mother would say. As the last drops dribble out, I scroll on my phone, enjoying this rare moment of uninterrupted bliss.

Thanks to my unavoidable pre-pee trickle, and the lack of toilet roll, my pants are wet for the second time today, but my joy is profound. I skip to the boutique, enjoying the feel of the full skirt swirling around my new sandals, chucking my old clothes and shoes in one of the bins on the way. I feel like Jack Reacher hitching a ride out West – free, unfettered, and about to get into a fight. I wonder if the police have arrived yet?

Breezing into the shop, I hold my bank card aloft. 'I'm back!' I announce cheerily, slapping it down on the counter.

There's a burly security guard standing next to Cruella, looking strapping and impassive. She sneers, then turns to him, gesturing towards me dismissively. 'This is the shoplifter.'

He looks me up and down, so I give him a little twirl. 'Do you like it? I think it suits me.'

If possible, he looks even more inscrutable. Maybe *he's* Jack Reacher. A British Reacher would definitely be working in security at a Bristol shopping precinct. Just as a day job while he hunted down gangsters in Knowle by night.

Cruella sniffs. 'You stole it.'

'But I'm right here. In a stealing situation, he'd be chasing me down the high street, calling for back-up.'

A tight smile creeps across her face. 'We apprehended you in the nick of time.'

'Capital!' I'm finding the Regency style of this dress quite inspiring. 'Should he get me in some sort of chokehold, to make the story stick?'

Cruella's smile fades. 'He has the authority to make a citizen's arrest. With force if necessary.'

Reacher's inscrutable expression tips towards boredom – it's clear he doesn't take his low-level crime-fighting role particularly seriously. I bet he's got bigger fish to fry. Probably a gunrunner operating out of the docks on Harbourside. A real nasty piece of work. Forget citizen's arrests; Bristol Reacher will be pulverizing a trafficker later.

I raise my eyebrows. 'Only if there are reasonable grounds. And I think you'll find my peaceful presence here indicates there aren't.' Did a bit of googling on my phone in the bog, among other things, and it's paying dividends. Emboldened by my new legal nous, I carry on. 'I'm here, ready and waiting to pay. If you want to drag this out, then we could call my lawyer?' Robbie deals in intellectual rather than sartorial property, but she doesn't need to know that.

Her brows snap together; she's both angry and nonplussed, and it's time to wrap this up, particularly since I have no other clothes to wear, having thrown my old ones in the bin. I rest my elbows on the counter.

'I'll tell you what's going to happen. I'm going to pay for the dress, and we're going to agree it was a misunderstanding. Or else . . .' I get out my phone, fount of knowledge, source of information, locator, identifier, amplifier, online warrior.

'Or else what?' She's breathing hard now; she'll need moment in the back room staff toilet when this is all over.

Keeping my back to the stony-faced security guard, I discreetly show her my Instagram page. The hipster at Avon House was some kind of influencer with two million followers and I've picked up over fifty thousand of them since 11 a.m., thanks to Petroc tagging me. Obviously, I'm only on there because Vince insisted we 'get with the memes'. Never mind that my page is just photos of our cat, Grizelda, perching on various precarious spots around

113

the house, or that the only story I ever put up was an accidental screen grab of all my weather apps. It seems everyone is keen to view a clip of a middle-aged woman kicking against the pricks in a posh swimming pool. I'm sure my newfound fame will fall off a cliff along with my fertility, but right now it can be useful.

'I can be very kind to you here,' I murmur. 'Or I can be . . . mean.'

There's a long silence as she looks at the figure on my phone. I lower my voice, conspiratorial, chummy. 'I really want to be kind. Let me pay for this gorgeous frock, and we can all get on with our day.'

She meets my eyes, and there's grudging respect there. When you're a bitch, meeting a superior bitch can be a salutary experience. Nodding a dismissal to the guard, free to go back to his day job stopping teenagers nicking the condiments in Nando's, she takes my bank card from between my fingers.

'I can give you a ten per cent discount,' she says, and I pat her on the arm in a motherly way.

'That would be splendid,' I say, and we complete the transaction.

My mother doesn't know it, but the wedding dress she chose for me had a fitting end. Last year, Hazel got invited to a Halloween party – it was fancy dress, but she didn't find out till the last minute, and had nothing to wear. After covering her face in talcum powder, together we unearthed my £1500 meringue, and slashed it to ribbons. Then

I took a lighter to the veil, making the netting furl and blacken. Hazel sailed off as the Corpse Bride and when she came back, the hemline was muddy and the bodice drenched in Red Bull. I rolled it all up, stuffed it higgledy-piggledy in an old suitcase and left it to decay in the attic, feeling electrified by the vandalism, animated by a belated rebellion which would go entirely unnoticed. I wondered what Rose would say if she knew?

Outside in the sunshine, I do another twirl and take a perky photo of the swish for my new fans. Not *Emily in Paris* but Clover in Bristol. I've got a great new dress, and my bladder is gloriously barren. What next?

# 14

I grew up in a genteel Oxford suburb, far enough from the city that we could afford a detached house, as my mother considered semis lower-middle class. One of my earliest memories is going to some sort of play group when I was tiny. It was a drop-off thing – Rose would leave me with them to get her hair done and then collect me at lunchtime. Maz wasn't there – I think she got left with a woman who lived down the road. I must have been about four, so don't remember much about it, just that there was a floaty dressing-up skirt that me and another girl used to fight over, and they gave you milk in blue plastic cups.

But one day I do remember, I was playing with a particular toy when my mother came to pick me up – it was a drill, and if you pressed a button the chuck actually moved around. I loved it, and was running round firing it at people, in the swishy skirt I'd managed to wrest off the other girl. But there was a boy who wanted the drill who was following me round, whingeing. He kept trying to take it off me, grabbing it and pulling it – sometimes pulling my hair too. I suppose we would have worked it out somehow, but Rose had arrived and decided to get involved. She marched up and held out her hand to me.

'Now, please.'

My mother didn't ask twice, so I handed it over. She immediately gave it to the boy, who ran off with it. Then she found a toy supermarket trolley, and closed my fingers around the handle, her rings pressing into my skin as she bent to whisper in my ear.

'Much better for you,' she said. Then she went and had a cup of tea with the other mums, while I pushed the trolley around aimlessly. We went home shortly after, and I didn't know what to make of it, but I suppose on some level I did. Give them what they want. Your place is behind the trolley. Every time I wanted something, wanted to stand up for myself, say no, I'd feel her rings pricking my skin, pushing me back.

The window intruder dream didn't start until years later, but I feel like she loosened the catch, left a way in. That Larkin poem about your mum and dad fucking you up. That's what they do. Or they ensure that someone else can.

The swishy skirt though. I loved that skirt.

# AFTERNOON

# 15

After all this excitement, it really is time to slow things down a little and have the restful moment I've been craving since I face-palmed Red Eye's eager lawyer. I decide to head back to Queen Square near the office, get a drink, have a sit and watch the world go by. Maybe I'll even read my book, get past page 48.

On the way along the river, I treat myself to another peek at my Instagram page. I'm now up to 70K; I wonder if I can get one of those blue ticks that mean you're a better-than-average human being? Someone has commented 'SPLASH THE PATRIARCHY!' Perhaps I should provide some more #content for my new followers, solidify my status as a swimfluencer. Scrolling through my photos, I upload a selfie I took inside the giant shell in the gallery: 'LOVE ART_ANDRA!' and add some emojis as that seems to be what the kids are doing these days. Studying the picture again, I'm struck by how relaxed I look in it. Famously unphotogenic, usually the camera picks up the underlying tension in all my facial muscles, making me appear rictus and off-centre, like a Madame Tussauds version of me.

In all our family shots, Robbie looks as urbane as he is, whereas I have the air of someone with an uncomfortable bowel complaint. So I'm pleased with this selfie, and think it will endear me to my new fans.

'Clover Hendry, as I live and breathe!'

Interrupted admiring myself, I'm further irked to see the woman waylaying me on Welsh Back is Glynis Johnson, an absolute busybody who lives down the road from us in Keynsham. When we moved in, she was always popping round to see if we needed anything, and massively outstaying her welcome. Once she lingered for an entire afternoon telling me about her niece Octavia's gap year, when I was desperately trying to prepare for a pitch meeting. Then she started inviting me to her book group – all the women in it are at least fifteen years older than me, and only talk about three things: 1) ongoing roadworks along the high street 2) what they bought this week from the local Waitrose and 3) gynaecological issues. The book doesn't get a look-in. I know this because I've endured several of these meet-ups and lost the will to live at every single one. Never having time to read entire novels, I swotted up on *Guardian* reviews and Wikipedia entries, and considered myself fully prepared to wing it, so it was therefore galling to sit through three hours of traffic light/ Essential Kale/UTI chat without ever getting round to the sodding point of the evening.

'Uh, hi.' I'm hoping she takes the muted nature of my greeting as a prompt to make herself scarce, but of course she barrels on. Glynis is the kind of woman who talks with her eyes closed, to ensure she's oblivious to any conversational cues.

'Just the person I wanted to see! We're doing kitchen sups at mine next week to talk about the new Sally Rooney – not the filthy one, the one with the letters. You in?'

Old Clover would stutter and prevaricate before the inevitable capitulation. Such a waste of time. 'No, thank you.'

Glynis's peepers pop open. 'But I haven't told you when it is yet.'

'It doesn't really matter when it is.'

'Oh, are you going away?' Holidays are one of the few topics that allow them to deviate from talking points 1, 2 and 3. They tend to favour Florida, and Chewton Glen.

'No, I just don't really want to come. Thank you for inviting me though.'

Glynis's brow puckers as she processes the information. 'You . . . why not?'

'I didn't enjoy it last time.' It seems best to tell the truth, so that she won't broach the subject again. No point making a lame excuse, because that would just prolong the agony for everyone.

Glynis fingers the wattle at her neck. 'You didn't?'

'Not really, no.'

'Well . . .' Blinking rapidly, Glynis studies the cobbles below. Although I didn't particularly want to see her, this encounter has been useful, in saving me from future book group boredom, and possibly further unwelcome visits. If it feels like a lot for her to take on board, I'm sure she'll be shored up by Shirley, Maxine and the other literary ladies. Or perhaps she can do a Waitrose run and stock up on her favourite Belgian Double Chocolate Cookies.

'Anyway, I'd best be going.' Glynis seems disinclined to move from her current position, but I'm keen to get on with my day. As luck would have it, my phone rings, providing the perfect distraction. Waving it, I move away to answer, dismissing her from my mind.

It's Petroc. After the way we left things, perhaps he's ringing to apologize and tell me I did further the cause after all.

'Hello!'

'Where the fucking fuck are you?'

It's Vince, who I've been ignoring all day. 'You're not Petroc.'

'No, I'm on his phone because you wouldn't answer my calls.'

'That's a dirty trick. Does he know?'

'Yes; he says he doesn't like you any more because you're brash and thoughtless now. Which is exactly what I need. We've got an emergency.'

*Eyeroll emoji* Vince regularly summons us for 'emergencies' which turn out to be minor production issues. He's the TV equivalent of the boy who cried wolf, and we all wish it would eat him. When there really *is* an emergency – like when one of our contributors

124

turned out to be a spy from a rival indie – he's always mysteriously unavailable, so we end up making all sorts of major decisions that he strenuously objects to on his return. He fires people more often than Alan Sugar, but generally, if you keep your head down for a bit, he forgets about it.

'Can't help, I'm busy today.'

'Listen, it's great that you've suddenly grown a pair of balls, and we can definitely use them, because right now you need to sort out this shitshow we've got developing.'

I'm only half-listening, because having arrived at the square, I find it's completely packed – there's some sort of protest going on, people shouting and waving placards.

'I'm at a recce, could be a real opportunity.'

'What is it?' He can never resist the sniff of a fresh idea.

My eyes rove over the crowd. 'Erm . . . Activists. Really radical ones. Total nutjobs. The new Swampy. Nailing themselves to trees.' This is word salad now, but I just need Vince off my back.

'Where?'

He thinks he can catch me out, the slimeball. 'Just round the corner in the square. Big crowd, it's really kicking off and I'm right in the thick of it. Here.' I hold the phone out to let him hear the chanting.

'All right, Kate Adie, hold your horses. The nutjobs can wait, because we've got a serious situation down at Chew Hill, and—'

That snags me briefly, because it's my show, but then I'm not listening any more because I've spotted a face in the crowd; a face I know, a face I saw at the breakfast table this morning, a face I gave birth to, a face that is definitely supposed to be in school right now.

It's Hazel, my sixteen-year-old daughter.

# 16

There are no twins in my family, apart from the ones I gave birth to sixteen years ago. *Nada.* So I really wasn't expecting them, and definitely didn't want them. When we went to the first scan, I was terrified, of course. Terrified they would tell me there was nothing there; that there was something there that shouldn't be there; that there *had been* something there, but there wasn't any more. I lay stiff as a board on the ultrasound table, Robbie holding my hand tightly, trying to pretend he wasn't excited, because he knew how worried I was.

'It'll be fine,' he murmured, rubbing my palm. 'You're not as old as your mother says you are.'

At thirty, in Rose's eyes I was geriatric, delaying reproduction to do silly things like further my career.

'I might have bad genes,' I replied, thinking of my respective parents.

'Then I'll make up for them,' he said, kissing my fingers. 'Mine are top-notch.'

And then the moment I'd been dreading – the taut silence, as the sonographer spotted something, and moved the stick back to investigate. My heart started beating an erratic staccato, my thighs leaden as I clutched my husband's hand and waited. I didn't even want one baby, let alone two.

Or perhaps it wasn't that I *didn't* want one, just that I wasn't sure I *did*. I felt ambivalent about the whole thing, in a way that Susie didn't. Susie knew she didn't want children, had known since university that she just had no biological urge and never would. My old schoolfriend Laura had three children by her early thirties, really loved being pregnant and having babies – I watched her rubbing her own bump, squeezing her newborn son's dimpled thighs lasciviously, and wondered if I would ever feel that all-consuming urge to procreate. I wanted to feel strongly either way, rather than sitting on the fertility fence, waiting to see which way I toppled.

Of course, my mother was only too happy to stick her finger in this pie. 'If you don't have children, you will regret it,' she warned me. 'You cannot ignore Mother Nature.' I found it ironic that my dear mama couldn't resist the siren call of motherhood, but once her two children were born found it perfectly easy to pretend they didn't exist. It troubled me though, the idea that if I put it off too long, the choice might be made for me, as my womb withered, and that broodiness would kick in just as the last of my eggs shuffled off.

Robbie always wanted children. He comes from a loving family of four brothers, enjoyed a riotous *Swallows and*

*Amazons* childhood in the countryside, wanted to recreate it, build a swing in a big garden and watch future Hendrys kick their feet and soar as he did. Robbie's parents are still together, still devoted. His mum isn't a roaring narcissist and his dad never did a runner to Spain with his voluble mistress. Unsurprisingly, I had nothing I wanted to recreate, though was tentatively tempted by the idea of erasing my own childhood through my children. But what if I was a mother like my mother? That smarting combination of disinterest and disapproval, laced with faint malice? There was no room for us in Rose's mirrored pool, and Dad was a genial but idle father, whose quest for a comfortable life outweighed all other considerations. They weren't the best examples, but would I do any better?

Having agonized over the decision, in the end I decided to just leave it to fate and see what happened, which of course meant I got knocked up on our honeymoon (lovely spa in Heraklion, near the remains of Knossos Palace). My fertility hadn't fallen off a cliff, it was nestling ripely in the crumbling columns of Crete. Meanwhile, Mother Nature was staring at her nails and smirking, as was my own mother.

'Well, well, well,' said the sonographer. 'This is a turn-up for the books.'

In my wildest nightmares, it never occurred to me, which shows that even a prize worrier like me doesn't go far enough. As someone who firmly believes that nothing ever works as it should, it seemed incredible to me that not only could Robbie and I reproduce with such brisk efficiency, but manage to produce two foetuses in the process. Twice as much to worry about. More than twice, because immediately my (already considerable) fears multiplied and ballooned, my addled brain a lightning rod for a gazillion scenarios that included but were not limited to: Siamese, oh God, that's an offensive term, call it conjoined; one baby on each boob will just look ridiculous, like having a litter of puppies, one on every teat; everyone I know will gather in glee to point and advise; that double buggy in John Lewis was £1700, Robbie and I laughed at it and now look; I will definitely die in childbirth; even if I don't die my vagina will explode; my mother will say this is all my own fault . . .

The first thing Robbie said was: 'It will be OK.' Which was both the best and worst thing he could have said. Best because he nobly resisted punching the air, which was what he wanted to do; worst because, in the end, it was OK, but not because anyone really helped make it that way. It was OK, but not before it was terrible and frightening and uncontrolled and exhausting and tedious and the most painful and distressing thing I have ever endured. Like boiling a frog backwards – I'm in tepid water now, but my flesh has peeled off and I will never look or feel the same again. My children give me such joy and enrichment, and the love is indescribable, *galactic*. But it's a thorny, tangled, flailing thing, infused with guilt and worry and a dizzying sense of inadequacy. Moreover, the eruption of their arrival lingers like an echo.

From the beginning – or at least, from the moment the sonographer waved her wand – I wanted a caesarean. I wanted drugs, and medical intervention, and as much certainty and control as a woman in my position could expect. Major abdominal surgery terrified me – but not as much as the alternative. For once my terror made me assertive, and when my mother said 'What rot, Mother Nature knows best,' I was able to retort that in this case I knew best, and Mother Nature was going to have to step aside. But my consultant had other ideas; he said – and I quote – that giving birth naturally would be 'a doddle', and that my recovery time would be much quicker, which would be helpful looking after two babies. He was so sure of himself, of his expertise, of his unassailable right to say how things would be, that I didn't feel like I had any choice but to acquiesce. When I reported back to the midwife, I saw her hesitate, just for a second, before ticking the box. Neither the mother nor the midwife questioned the man.

I tried so hard – NCT, hypnotherapy, breathing exercises, breastfeeding classes where we practised with a crocheted tit, seventeen books on planning for parenthood and forty-seven cups of raspberry leaf tea. I bought an internal massage tool that claimed to stretch your perineal muscles and prevent tearing. It was a sort of balloon that inflated inside you, gradually increasing its size, tenderizing your vaginal walls like steak. I would sit in the bathroom blowing myself up while I read the birthing guru Sheila Kitzinger describing the wondrous euphoria of delivery, how babies eased and crept their way out. We watched endless DVDs: a woman with the smooth, enraptured face of a nun explaining how she had an orgasm during a contraction; another dreadlocked free spirit next to a pool, playing the guitar with her patronising partner during the early stages of labour – I hope during the later stages she smashed it against the smug git's head. Still, I ploughed on, trying to dismiss the dark thoughts that would surely condemn me to a difficult birth. Everyone kept telling me that it was all in the mind, that if only I could approach the process positively then it would be a walk in the park. I just wanted everyone to be pleased with me, tell me I did well, give me a pat on the head.

I went into labour on a mild midsummer night, and we hastily packed up the car and headed to the hospital. The first signs that it wasn't going to be a breeze came early. On arrival, the midwife refused to let us in because she thought I was lying about having twins, even though I was so enormous I could barely walk. 'People will say anything,' she sniffed, as I groaned through a contraction on my hands and knees.

When we finally got into the labour ward, there was a brief moment of levity when Robbie tried the gas and air, and then everything rapidly went downhill. After all the consultant's assurances, it turned out no one really knew anything, no one was in charge, and certainly no one was thinking positive thoughts. My memories of those eighty-six hours are mainly brief, violent pulses – wheelchairs, gurneys, tight faces and averted eyes, hastily inserted shunts, shunted from one room to another, being left alone, being surrounded, and then a long, excruciating moment of silence as the epidural was administered: 'Stay perfectly still, or this could paralyse you.' After hunching, immobile through the spasms with a big needle in my spine, I thought the rest of it would be the doddle I'd been promised, but the drugs didn't work, they just made it all worse, giving everything a nightmarish hallucinatory hue.

It's not helpful to describe the pain, but I'm going to. It's like the tightening of a winch, but the winch is inside you, screwing all your organs and muscles to a pitch where you can't think or breathe or bear it for a second longer – no, you will absolutely die if this continues, but it's carrying on, tighter and tighter, a scaffold of agony and panic and primal fear and utter torment and – *release*. For a few seconds, there's a delirious pause, and then it starts up again, hoisting you higher and higher with each vicious turn of the spool. In hypnotherapy, they call them surges, or waves, which is supposed to be empowering, but a better word would be lacerations, each one ripping you apart a little more. And then there's a stage – the mundanely termed 'transition phase' – where it's just one giant swirling mess of racking pain that goes on forever; there's a dimension in time and space where I'm still there, writhing and gripping and lowing

133

for all eternity. And then the most tremendous pressure hammering down on you, the most savage insistence, unbearable, no, no, push, push, push, no, I can't, push, push – *wait* . . . Now, push, push, *pusssshhhh*, no, wait again . . . One more push . . . NOW. The actual moment of birth is a spiteful blooming sting, the venom of all the world's wasps erupting in your vagina, as every sinew in your body explodes, atoms of residual burns showering around you like the tail-end of a firework.

Now imagine doing that twice, in quick succession.

In the event, I didn't. After sustaining a third-degree tear giving birth to Ethan, I was whisked into emergency surgery for Hazel, who refused to breathe for the first two minutes, probably in protest at her treatment. Luckily, I'd started to haemorrhage by that point, so wasn't available to fret myself into a fit about her. Not a great time for Robbie, who ended up being given a beta blocker – for once, he was as worried as I was.

But then, when passageways had been cleared, skin sponged down, blood clotted, perineum sewn, prick tests passed . . . there was a sense that . . . why the fuss? It was all worth it, wasn't it? You're alive, you have two healthy babies, no room to complain. So, naturally, I didn't. Didn't want to rock the boat by speaking out. Besides, I suspect there would have been nothing more than a dismissive shrug from that consultant. You're just left to get on with it, lick your wounds in private.

My mother didn't come to the hospital because they

make her feel 'icky' but when we got home, she deigned to visit, looked at my pale, wan face and said 'Goodness me, anyone would think you were ill. Buck up, no one wants to see a misery-guts.' Because of course twins made her *livid*. The waters of her pool had been rippled by me doing something that everyone else thought was unusual, special. She bashed aside the balloons, shifted the baskets of muffins off the kitchen table to the floor and told me about the horrors of laying her new patio, while I sat on a ring cushion with my itching stitches and dry mouth.

But when she'd gone, and I was left, with these miraculous tiny babies who had once been foetuses caught by the sonographer's wand, I looked into their little alien faces and allowed myself a tiny, fleeting moment of positivity: yes, this was going to be tough and sometimes unrewarding and mind-numbingly tiring and baffling and, in many ways, utterly awful, but I wouldn't ever be as bad as her, and it wouldn't be as bad as what came before, and in the end . . . in the end, it *would* be OK. More than OK. Sometimes it would be wonderful – worth every last twinge.

# 17

'Well, well, well,' I say. 'This is a turn-up for the books.'

Hazel doesn't notice me, and I watch her for a while, interested to see this zealous streak of activism I'd hitherto been unaware of in my daughter. It seems to take the form of her lounging against the square's central plinth, a placard under her arm, while scrolling on her phone, frowning at something and tossing back her hair. Hazel's hair is possibly her chief concern in life, and she spends a great deal of her time and my money making sure it pulls focus. I must admit, it is nice hair – it's my hair, if mine were any good. A lush, rich brown, with all the thickness of youth. She's grown it nearly to her waist, spends hours brushing it, conditioning it, smoothing it, buffing it like a racehorse. If only Hazel was as dedicated to her school work as she is to her grooming regime, she'd be gunning for Oxbridge. As it is, she's an indifferent scholar who I suspect is on the lookout for a rich husband. As a mother, I hope I am not like my mother, but sometimes wonder if my daughter is going to be a wife in the mould of Rose Ashton. Decorative, self-obsessed, dissatisfied.

At other times though, I berate myself for such unmotherly thoughts. Hazel can be great fun, and she's funny – a dry, withering wit that makes me think there is a brain under that barnet. I can deal with a vain child but not with a humourless one. And to be fair, she does have plenty to be vain about – in addition to the fairy-tale version of my locks, she has Robbie's elegant frame and my mother's much-vaunted cheekbones. Although I enjoy attractive people very much, and (to a certain extent) relish my own daughter's beauty, I worry that good-looking folk don't bother to develop a personality because they don't need one. Having said that, Hazel is a vegetarian, which I've always thought was a good sign, and, in light of today's turn of events, a sign of things to come.

'Hazel Hendry!'

At the sound of her name, she whirls around in alarm, the placard dropping to the ground. It says 'THE WRONG AMAZON IS BURNING', which is rich given the amount of bilge from the right one that comes through our letterbox addressed to her. Only the other day she bought a silk pillow slip which is an absolute bugger to wash.

'What are you doing here?' She stumbles over her billboard, picking it up and holding it in front of herself like a shield.

'You've stolen my script,' I reply genially. 'I am a working adult who's left the office on important business. You're a schoolgirl roaming the streets.'

'I'm on study leave.'

'Then why aren't you studying? You're supposed to be getting an education.'

She grimaces. 'This *is* an education. It is my future.' Which is a good point, but it's parroted, like she heard someone else saying it.

'OK,' I said. 'Before I read you the riot act, I'll give you a chance. Imagine I'm a tetchy pensioner who objects to you snarling up his square. Change my mind.'

My daughter gapes at me, her wooden message slack in her hand. 'What?'

'You obviously feel very strongly about this, to take time out. Outline the issues. Wow me with your powers of persuasion. Turn me green.'

'Erm . . .' She swallows. 'They're . . . ripping up forests . . . and the orangutan has nowhere to go.'

'Is that a Christmas advert you saw in 2018?' She hangs her head. 'You're going to have to do better than that, love. Why don't you tell me about the Paris Agreement, or what we should do about plastic in the ocean, or where the people of Tuvalu are going to go?'

She fiddles with her sleek sheet of hair, hiding behind it and her sign.

'Hmm, I'm not feeling waves of ecological enthusiasm here. Why are you really here?'

Eyes down, she mumbles something indistinct.

'What?'

'A boy . . . invited me.'

Instantly, I'm wildly intrigued. First, that there *is* a boy, and second that she actually told me. I was vaguely aware something was going on, because the other day I heard Ethan lazily teasing her, and her hissed response, and mentally put it on my list of parental gardening. I intended to dig deeper, assuming it would be firmly buried; now here she is offering it up, brushing off the dirt so I can breathe in the heady aroma of a budding romance.

'*What* boy?' I try not to grin like a jackass.

She jerks her head and I see him straight away, in the midst of a group. Oh yes, of course. Anyone would go on a march with him, he's to die for: chiselled and unselfconscious, with adorable curls that fall across his forehead. His placard shows a picture of the earth drowning in rubbish, and says 'WE NEED TO STOP'. Ain't that the truth. Something about the way he's holding it tells me he made it, and he really means it. I adore him, and would happily welcome him into the Hendry fold.

'And he's into this stuff, is he?'

She nods, her face on fire. 'Never mind,' she mumbles. 'I'll go back to school, just don't tell Dad.'

But I'm looking at the boy, thinking that if I was thirty years younger then I'd be following him around with a placard too. And I remember when I was a teenager, a lad at school who was really bookish, and for the while I fancied him, I read a lot of John Steinbeck, and then stopped fancying him but carried on reading. Also, thanks to my various neuroses, I was a virgin until I was twenty, which is not good for a young girl, not good at all. I was so inexperienced, so callow, so trusting, so goddamned eager to please that what came after was almost inevitable. If only I'd been a bit savvier then I would never have—

'No,' I say.

'*Please* don't tell Dad. I know I shouldn't have done it, but—'

Even as I interrupt her, I'm thinking it's telling, that she doesn't want her relaxed, lenient father to know all this. She wants to please him, be a good little girl. How deeply this is wired, too deep to dig up.

'No,' I say again. 'You should stay.'

Hazel breaks off the begging, dumbfounded. 'What?'

'Sit.' I take the sign off her and put it on the ground, pushing her down with it, and kneeling behind her. As I grope in my bag, I continue: 'You should stay, but if you're going to do this, do it properly.' In a side compartment, I find what I'm looking for, and start sectioning the lovely hair on the head that sleeps on a silken pillow from Amazon. 'Show some commitment, do a bit of research, talk to people. You're quite right; the world is burning and it's your future that's at stake. You should be here, shouting, protesting, making a fuss. You should be getting to know that very nice boy who cares about the planet.'

'But . . . what about school?' she says in a small voice, as I wind and tug like Sasha did to me earlier. It's years since I've done this, and it feels good, to groom my daughter, make her ready. Robbie and I have always been very strict about school – my mother made me and Maz go even when we were at death's door, as she didn't want us under her feet all day, and I've carried on the family tradition. Hazel is in the middle of her GCSEs, and on non-exam days is supposed to be attending various revision sessions designed to cram last-minute facts into that glossy head of hers. *Supposed* to be. Well, I guess we all have places we're supposed to be today. Sometimes you just have to bunk off.

'Fuck school,' I say, and hear her shocked snort of laughter. 'Just for today, fuck school.' I get to my feet, pulling her up with me. I've woven her beautiful hair into two plaits so thick and solid they look like weapons. Holding her face in my hands – that face I gazed at all those years ago thinking *It will be* OK – I say 'Go and save the world.'

She laughs again, and steps back, her brows knitting as she looks me up and down. 'You look different,' she says. 'You *are* different. I saw something on Instagram . . .' She holds up her phone, puzzled.

I shake my head. 'Never mind me. I'm sorting my own world out.'

We all exist in our spheres, whirling round feverishly, obliviously, brushing up against each other occasionally but mostly keeping to our own orbits. When your kids hit their teenage years, they begin to build their own lives; their own messy, complicated, giddy circles, and you're so busy with your own that you barely have time to register – as long as they're still spinning in some form, you leave them to it. But in slowing down my own rotation, I realize I need to get more involved, adjust her path, stop her making the same mistakes I did. Hazel needs to be pushy, proactive, unapologetic, worldly. She needs to break the rules. She needs to do what she wants. I want that for her. I want that for me, too.

Hazel is still frowning, but her focus is pulled by the boy. She fingers a plait self-consciously as she regards him.

'Go and make a scene,' I say. 'I'll see you later for a planet pop quiz.'

'OK.' She picks up her placard, already looking more purposeful. 'Great hair, by the way.'

The ultimate accolade. 'Thanks,' I reply, and head off.

# 18

Since the square is out of bounds, I decide to make my way back to the river for a stroll, pick up a coffee, soak up this beautiful summer's day. Ignoring another call from my mother, I wander past the Old Vic, its impressive façade glazed gold in the sun. After Covid, I imagined I would rush there as soon as it reopened, told myself I'd see *anything*, just for the pleasure of being in a theatre again, feel the rustle of expectation as the lights dimmed, look forward to drinks at the interval. But of course, a combination of late work nights, ferrying the twins, slightly-too-esoteric productions and my own tendency to not-be-arsed, I never booked anything.

Amidst the various to-do lists in my head and on my phone, there's a more diverting note called 'One Day' which features fun things I'd like to do if I had the time and the energy. There are those box-ticking exercises on Facebook – 'How many of these have you done?' – and it's all 'Get a tattoo', 'Throw yourself out of a plane' and 'Dive the Mariana Trench', but I have no desire to do any of those things. Mine is the tamest of bucket lists, and varies according to my mood – 'GET A MANICURE' often features since my nails are a bitten-down mess and I think I'd feel like more of a grown-up if they were glossy and well-shaped. Similarly, my life would be vastly improved if I ever managed to 'GET EARWAX MICROSUCTION' – I've heard the process is satisfying and the results impressive. On a more ambitious note, *One Day* I'm keen to go on a 'SLEIGH RIDE', though I realize this would involve considerable logistics and expense. But a more manageable notion is 'SEE MATINÉE'. An afternoon play seems like such a glorious indulgence, shutting out one world to lose yourself in another.

So, I'm standing there outside Bristol's famous theatre, staring at a neon sign that says 'Come on in', thinking *Why not?* I could go in, see whatever's on. Never mind if it's some inscrutable Beckett or a 'bold' series of shorts – I'll wallow in the thespian atmosphere, frolic in a theatre-bath, and come out enriched by the auditorium, the glorious echoes of trodden boards. Yes! I will do this, I will—

'Fucking hell, Clover, it's like chasing a fucking fox.'

My matinée idyll dies a Shakespearean death as I turn to see my boss looming above me. Vince travels everywhere by Segway, zooming down streets like a demented kids' camp instructor in a flat cap, shouting at pedestrians and shaking his fist at cyclists. He thinks it's a quirky characteristic that will endear him to commissioners, but unfortunately, his habit of refusing to take no for an answer in pitches tends to negate any fond emotions engendered by his 'wheels'.

'Oh,' is all I can manage, because I'm mentally still in the dress circle having a sneaky ice cream.

'Is that the welcome I get? I've been halfway round the city looking for you. What happened to the tree-fuckers?'

I scratch my head, trying to gather my wits. 'They . . . were dispersed.'

'Right, so you left the office to recce an empty square. Can we get back to work now?'

I have no intention of going back to the office, even if I have to push him off his stupid scooter and do a runner.

'I'm a bit tied up at the moment, I'm afraid.'

He steps off the Segway. 'Like I said, I'm digging this Ferris Bueller schtick you've got going here, love your new finger-in-a-socket style.' He gestures to my curls. 'But I need that nose at the grindstone, not sniffing the summer breeze.'

'I haven't had a day off in months.'

'Then book one. Don't just fuck off.'

But I didn't know I needed it until today – until the headache, the forks, the email, the briefcase, everything in a pile-up until the only answer was to break out.

'I can't; got some stuff to sort.' It's true. Everything I'm doing needs to be done – a list I didn't even know existed till now. And I'm starting to see where it's headed, see the boxes that have to be ticked, and don't want to veer off course. I'm on a Segway, zooming towards the finish, shaking my fist at everyone.

'You're damn right you've got stuff to sort. Firstly, I had a call from Avon House. They've revoked your company membership.'

'Good, no more pitching on sunloungers. It buggers up my back no end.'

'It buggers up my business if you waste the perks I've worked so hard to get for you. Why have they booted you out, what did you do?'

I think back to this morning in the pool, which already feels like ages ago. 'It involved a semi-naked man, and a violation of special privileges.'

He wrinkles his nose in distaste. 'I don't want to know. Anyway, you've got bigger problems. Your wine show. David Lyon-James has got cold feet.'

That pulls me up short. 'What?'

Vince nods, fishing out his phone. 'He called me this morning, then sent this email. He's worried his vineyard won't be seen in its best light.'

Reading the email, I harrumph. 'He knew the deal. What's changed?'

'He watched Oz's show.'

I read on, with growing annoyance. David, the owner of Chew Hill vineyard, the location for my latest production, has watched a series made by Oz Phillips called *Would Like to Meat*. It's about young apprentices learning to be butchers – and shagging on the side. It's a daft show, as many of Red Eye's are, but it's buried on an obscure digital channel, so I'm surprised David stumbled across it.

He's worried about the tone, wants reassurance that his show will be a classier number. I haven't told him yet that our pitching title was *More Than They Can Chew*. But he certainly knows that a load of binge-drinking youths are going to descend on his estate to be taught a more refined way of quaffing booze. What does he expect?

Of course, he expects what we told him, which is that this will be a 'meaningful journey' for the cast and an education for the audience. It's going to do for winemaking what *Clarkson's Farm* did for agriculture. Beautiful West Country backdrops, rolling hills, the sun setting on ripening rows of vines. It will be all that, but obviously it will also be drunken twenty-somethings running amok, snogging each other's faces off and knocking back pinot noir like it's Ribena. I sort of assumed that, deep down, he knew it. Yet here he is, having a wobble. We need Chew Hill – it was by far the best place, and filming starts next month. I've already got a team down there setting up.

We can't lose him. It's a £1.2 million pound commission.

For a second, I actually care, then the shutters come down again. 'Send someone else,' I suggest, handing back the phone. 'Petroc can go.' Petroc's good at talking people round, he'll say anything to get a show made.

'Don't be ridiculous,' says Vince, pocketing his phone. 'It's your baby. Besides, Petroc got some really good intel from his Astral1 lunch, and he's working on that.'

I'm about to dig my heels in, steel myself to fight Vince on this pavement for my right to fuck off, when I remember my first visit to Chew Hill, in the autumn of last year. It was another beautiful day, and David Lyon-James took me and Flora, our assistant producer, out onto the terrace at the back of the house, looking out over the Mendip Hills. We drank a bottle of delicate sparkling rosé and, even though it was work, it was one of the few restful, pleasurable moments I'd had in months.

After various lockdowns, vainly trying to engage the twins in Google Classroom, juggling back-to-back Zoom meetings sitting cross-legged on the bed in the spare room, writing pitches while I made endless snacks for everyone, scrabbling to secure an elusive Ocado slot, pretending I was going for a run just to get out of the house, coming back to clear up all the mess and make dinner with whatever we had in the fridge, going to bed to have a million mad dreams (or sometimes nightmares) and then getting up to do the same things all over again, day in day out . . . It's fair to say life had been a bit of a grind. Instead, there we were, sampling an award-winning wine, watching clouds move across a vast blue sky as someone friendly and knowledgeable explained the process of fermenting. The novelty of it was charming, and I suddenly feel the urge to sit on that terrace again, maybe try the barrel-matured Madeleine Angevine David mentioned.

'OK,' I say. 'I'll go. But you have to send me in a nice car.'

'It's only half an hour away, I'll send you in a fucking Uber Lux,' returns Vince, which gives me a thrill, because that could easily feature in my *One Day* list. 'You're coming to this party later, right?' he asks, as he orders the cab. 'I'm saying it like it's a question, but it's more of a North Korean decree.'

My head pounds briefly, a reminder of the migraine and what really set it off. The wrap party. Imogen's list. Viewing a show called *Blind Dinner Date* with TV's great and good. I'd rather ride naked round Bristol on Vince's Segway.

'Absolutely,' I say. 'I'll be there. You can count on me.'

# 19

I never meant to work in television; it was never my ambition. After university, what I really wanted to do was go back to university, start again as a first year, maybe just keep repeating the course until I got a first, which would probably take about twenty years of repeats, or do a different degree – anything to stay in my cosy little house-share in Leeds, where our biggest challenge was seeing how many bottles we could get through in a weekend, and continuing important experiments like finding out how deep dust could get, and how long you could leave a duvet cover unwashed.

After university, real life was such a letdown. Fuelled by Blairite bonhomie, I moved to London in the summer of 1997, because that seemed to be the expected relocation, what everyone was doing. But we all scattered in different directions and the city is so massive it felt like I was on my own there, grubbing a Dickensian living by day and crawling home at night wondering how all my uni friends could afford to go out. I temped for a bit, which was the most miserable experience imaginable. In one placement,

I had to stand in a back room on my own, shredding paper. For seven hours a day. The company was based at an industrial estate in North-West London and there were no shops where you could buy food, so I would sit on the floor of my 'office' eating a packed lunch I'd made in the silverfish-riddled kitchen of the basement I was living in. Stale cheese sandwiches and a wrinkled apple, staring at the shredder. Sometimes I used to read the documents I was destroying, which they'd told me not to do, as they were apparently highly sensitive, but instead of top-secret redacted MI5 reports, it was just mind-numbing minutes from meetings about some sort of corporate takeover. Sometimes I wove the shredded paper into little mats. Once I shredded the bread from my sandwich, just for a change. One lunchtime, someone had left a newspaper on the table next to the shredder and, before I shredded it, I saw a job advert in it that began 'DO YOU BELIEVE THERE'S SOMETHING OUT THERE?' Stuck in that windowless room, I really wanted to believe it, so I applied for the role.

As part of my application, I had to write an account of my own supernatural experience. In my twenty-one years on earth, I'd never been aware of anything *un*earthly – not so much as a cold draught had troubled my sixth sense. But I was desperate to get out of the shredding room, which was opening up a portal to hell, so I wrote a story about doing a Ouija board at a hen weekend, and it spelling out the name of a boy who died in the house we

151

were staying in. This was actually my uni friend Hima's story; not only had I never used a Ouija board, but I'd never even been on a hen weekend. I called Hima for a bit of background in case they asked me more about it, but she said she could never talk about it again because a tarot reader told her not to.

The interview to join the team of *Ghostly Goings On* was at the production company HQ in West London, with one of their producers, Delia Smith. No, really, that was her name – she said it looked good on credits so she'd just gone with it, and was waiting for the real Delia to sue. Later, she married a man called Jason Partridge, and so became Delia Partridge and the real Delia never had to get involved. Anyway, Delia was a great exec – loud and gossipy, but got things done. She always wore a big feather boa as she said it got her noticed, made her memorable. I suppose it worked, as I frequently heard her referred to as 'that mad bitch in the boa', though mostly she was known as 'Other Delia', even after her marriage.

In my interview she asked me about my Ouija board story and then drilled down, which was what I was afraid of, so I told her I could never talk about it again, because a tarot reader told me not to. She hired me, even though I had no experience in TV research, no driving licence and no gumption whatsoever. Their tech guy taught me the basics of using a camera, and they sent me off in search of spooks, long before the days of health and safety, or due diligence, or any of the stuff that's factored into production nowadays. Just me and my trusty Canon XL1, going into strangers' houses, hoping they were scary.

The main lesson Other Delia taught me was: Make It Happen (one of the great tenets of TV production). Do whatever it takes to get a show off the ground. Tell people what they want to hear, don't take no for an answer, railroad, dissemble, charm, evade, get them to put it in black and white, don't *you* put anything in black and white, and don't worry too much. Just get it on camera, and it'll all come out in the edit. A TV producer needs shameless brass neck, rhinoceros hide and chutzpah.

Obviously, I had none of these things. Early on, I was constantly hung up on, doors slammed in my face, emails ignored, and every night I cried myself to sleep worrying about what I was expected to do. But the alternative was the shredder, so I had to get on with it. Fudging my way through, I clumsily climbed the career ladder, but the truth is, unlike Other Delia, I'm not a great executive producer. I find it hard to delegate, and end up doing everything myself. It feels like an imposition to say to someone 'Would you mind doing this job we pay you to do?' so I end up doing most of the jobs we're paying them to do, running myself ragged in the process. My teams have a ball because now I bring in please-like-me bagels instead of doughnuts, and they never have to go the extra mile – I always go there for them. I have my mother to thank for that – don't be a bother, be a good girl, you push the trolley.

I also find it hard to lie to people, which always seemed to be a requirement of the profession. Not because I mind about lying, I just mind about being found out. Petroc and Oswald make all sorts of wild promises they can't possibly keep, with a sublime disregard for the fall-out. Whereas I'm always thinking three – or thirty – steps ahead, worrying about the consequences. So I lie, but without the necessary conviction. People smell it on me and retreat, hanging up the phone, slamming the door.

I know I haven't done the greatest job with David and Chew Hill, because I liked him, and thus found it even harder to maintain the vague web of deceit we needed to secure his involvement. Oz would have looked him in the eye and told him that the series was guaranteed to win a BAFTA, because we had an internationally renowned director on board, when in fact it's Tristram Barnes, responsible for masterpieces such as the distinguished talent show *Grease Me Up*, the acclaimed celebrity journey *Titty-Ho to Twathats* and the esteemed documentary *My Post-Prison Party*. It's hard to talk up a filmmaker whose biggest hit featured an ex-con called Mad Dog Matty having a knees-up with his feral family in Burngreave. As such, my equivocation didn't seal the deal.

One thing I am good at, though, is post-production. I'm great in the edit, love sitting in a darkened room, taking a shoddy bit of footage and making it sing. Like gathering the shredded pieces of paper, weaving them into a smooth glossy sheet full of revelation and intrigue. A tweak here, a cut there, a sound bed there and hey presto! A story is told. I can do the lying and dissembling and charming, but only if it's locked in an edit suite. Because that's the other tenet of telly: nothing you see is real. It's someone looking at a wasteland, painting an oasis. We can turn a villain into a hero, and vice versa. David's worried he's going to be the baddie, and now I've got to persuade him otherwise, whatever it takes.

I often think about Other Delia and that show *Ghostly Goings On*; the path it set me on, what it led to, the steps ahead I didn't see coming. Because in many ways, I've been haunted ever since.

# 20

My Uber Lux is a Mercedes driven by Danny, who, on learning my profession, is keen to tell me all that's wrong with it. We're entering a shitty age of television, apparently – everything is dross and we should be ashamed of the pap we produce. I find it extraordinary how much of this pap he's managed to watch, because he seems to have an opinion on everything from *I'm a Celebrity…* to *Line of Duty*, via *News at Ten* and *Gogglebox*.

'Don't get me started on the soaps,' he says, as we edge our way out of the city. It's still early afternoon, and the traffic isn't too bad. We should make it to Chew Hill well before three o'clock.

'All right, I won't,' I reply, checking my phone. Another missed call from my mother. I text my sister Maz: **Baby Jane keeps calling, what's up?** and then devote myself to gazing out the window, trying to ignore Danny's drone. I like being driven around in cars; it makes me feel like a VIP – protected, anonymous, conferring responsibility for my life onto someone else. It's the same in hotels and restaurants – someone else is doing all the hard work, taking on the load, aiming to please. There's something about crisp white sheets and tablecloths that makes my internal winch slacken, like the opposite of a contraction. However, despite the Lux-ury of this vehicle, my driver's infernal monologue is getting on my nerves.

'The trouble with these daytime quizzes is—'

'Danny, can I stop you there?'

He pauses, raising his eyebrows at me in the mirror as he takes a swig of his Monster energy drink.

'Thanks,' I say, going back to my phone. Maz has replied: Something brewing. She wants to have dinner tonight.

No ducking way, I tap furiously. I'm busy, got a work thing.

I can see the ellipses as she crafts a reply. Maz isn't usually so prompt in her responses, which means Rose must have rattled her. My sister spent most of her twenties in therapy recovering from our mother's parenting methods, and her psychiatrist told her she had to find three things in life that would keep her on an even keel. After careful consideration, she chose alpacas, IKEA, and alcohol. Now she lives near Crediton in Devon, on a smallholding that's a short drive from a flagship branch of the Scandinavian store. She takes people for healing walks with her calming camelids Mabel, Dorcas and Tilly, and when her anxiety flares, she goes for a Nordic fix, browsing the displays and treating herself to meatballs in the café. Whenever she encounters our mother, she manages to maintain an impressively constant low level of inebriation at all times, like a Glastonbury festival-goer downing a shot before braving the rancid toilets. Sometimes I think she's the most sorted person I know.

**Wondering whether to get it over with.** Maz's reply startles me. She takes the alpaca by the reins, not the bull by the horns, and I'm confused by her willingness to interact with Rose, who will surely have something up her flowered sleeve.

**Rly?** If my sister is ready to have dinner with our mother, then I will have to as well. I'd rather stick poisoned pins in my eyes, but I can't let her face the tinkling music alone. Maz and I may not be the closest siblings, but where Rose is concerned, we stick together.

**I can drive up, she can get someone to drive her down.** Rose lives in Stroud, and occasionally deigns to come down to 'see the gorgeous grandchildren', which is shorthand for 'disapprove of everything and daintily bemoan her lot in life'. She doesn't stay with us, ostensibly because she's allergic to cats, but actually because the original oak beams in our house in Keynsham make it too dingy for her. Luckily, she has a 'dear friend' with a penthouse flat in Redcliffe who lets her stay in a vague mutually beneficial arrangement which makes me wonder if my mother is a kept woman. After our father left, her famous stiff upper lip was firmly coated in fuchsia as she battled to maintain the façade that he was simply away on business. Since Dad was already shacked up with Valentina in Torrevieja and showed no sign of returning, this was a difficult front to keep up, so the story gradually evolved, and now she tells the beau monde of Gloucestershire that she is a widow, banishing my father from most family events. At my wedding, she referred to him as a distant cousin, and even though everyone knew exactly who he was, no one dared mention the elephant in the room, least of all my dad, who likes an easy life. He's taken to pre-empting her by calling himself Cousin Jack, and sometimes I do too, because it seems to sum up our amiable but slightly insipid family connection.

OK but don't let her book anywhere too £££. Rose insisted on an extended family meal at the Dorchester for my fortieth birthday and sailed out after liqueurs without paying, leaving me to foot the bill. I have no intention of letting her get away with that this time, but also I don't like her choice of restaurant, which is always the type that serves tiny portions with 'jus' in a jug on the side – her idea of a place posh people go to, as, in her head, my mother is marginally better-born than the Queen. If I have to hear her tale of woe then I want to tuck into a hearty shepherd's pie while I do it. And not too late, need to be done by 9. That's when the Red Eye party starts, which is a good excuse to get dinner over with.

Understood.

An evening of hell reluctantly arranged, I sit back to enjoy the views, as we're now out of Bristol, heading south towards Chew Magna. On balance, I'm glad Robbie persuaded me to leave London so he could fulfil his dream of a country house with a garden, even if my mother laments the low ceilings. He wanted space in the sense of more rooms and land, whereas I wanted something more abstract. Whatever it was, I found more of it in the clear horizons of the countryside than I did in the hemmed-in capital. When I watched him building the longed-for swing in the garden, I felt settled in a way I never had before, like I'd successfully escaped. But I suppose I hadn't really, just kicked the can down the road, as this morning's email proved. Talking of roads, there's a gorgeous view of the valley from the one we're on, and I tell Danny to stop so I can get out to enjoy it. This day is about pausing to be in the moment, and I'm going to do it, over there in that meadow.

Grumbling, he pulls up on the kerb, and I set off down a dirt track to get a better look. Gazing across fields peppered with dandelions, I can see the reservoir glittering beyond – perfect for this period of reflection I intend to take. It's lush and beautiful – so far removed from the endless tarmac and crowding towers of London. Layers of vivid green with pockets of remaining yellow, shimmering silver blue and then the deeper blue of the sky above. Like a Constable painting, if he'd used nice bright colours. I start some mindful breathing, but something is nagging at me – not just the things I didn't manage to escape, but something I've just seen out of the corner of my eye. What was it? Turning, I look back up the track. There's another car parked there, one I passed on my way down – an old muddy Golf, with a Countryside Alliance sticker on the window screen. I traipse back up and peer in. Jesus Christ. A cowering ball of fur on the back seat. It must be nearly thirty degrees, and the windows are closed.

Unlike Maz, I wouldn't describe myself as an animal lover. I like Grizelda well enough, but mainly because she keeps the mice down and looks good on Instagram in front of an open fire. However, this is not on. It's likely whoever owns this car has gone on a lovely country stroll – why couldn't they bloody well take their dog with them, rather than leaving it to roast? I've read about these stories before and know what I'm supposed to do. In fact, when I read them, I fervently hoped it would never happen to me, because I couldn't imagine how I would deal with it, so it's lucky it's happened today, when it won't be a problem.

'Danny!' I holler, beckoning him. He's got the *Daily Express* propped against the steering wheel and he's eating a packet of Wotsits. I march over and tap on the glass. He looks up, annoyed, and lowers the window.

'You have to come and help me,' I say, opening the door for him. 'It's an emergency.'

'Help you do what?' He gets out, wincing as he stretches his legs.

'Break into a car,' I reply, stalking down the track.

'What's wrong with my car?'

'There's nothing wrong with your car.'

'Then why'd you want to steal another one?'

'I don't want to steal it, I just want to break into it. Look.' I point at the ball of fur. 'Poor little thing.'

Shading his eyes, he presses his face to the glass. 'It might be dead already. Leave it.'

'I will not. Help me find a brick.'

We can't find a brick, but we do find a big stone on the track. With my eyes closed, I hit the front passenger window with it. Nothing happens. Car window glass is reassuringly tough. I hit it again, harder; nothing.

'You do it.' I hold out the stone to Danny. 'You're stronger than me.'

He shakes his head. 'No way, that's criminal damage, that is.'

'It's justified if an animal is in danger.'

'Not if you haven't told the police you're going to do it.'

'How are you suddenly such an expert?'

He gives me a withering look. 'I'm an effing taxi driver, ain't I.'

I get out my phone. There's no signal, so instead I take a photo of the little cringing creature whose life I am about to save.

'Right, stand back.' From about a foot away, I throw the stone, hard, at the window. It shatters, I duck and Danny yelps, but when we come to, there's a huge jagged hole. Bingo.

'Now you've done it,' says Danny.

'I know I've done it, I meant to do it.' Exasperated, I push him aside, carefully reaching in to unlock the car.

Then I open the back door, gather up the hot dog, and pass it to Danny.

'What am I supposed to do with this?' he splutters.

For someone with such strong opinions on popular culture, he's not very proactive. 'Just take it back to your car.'

'Aren't you coming?'

'There's something I've got to do first.'

Clutching the bundle, he turns and trudges back up the track, as I contemplate the legally damaged Golf with my hands on my hips. Far from being unable to do the deed, I've discovered that, in fact, the deed wasn't enough. I'm still vexed with the heedless owner of this vehicle, who left his dog to die in it. He – for I'm sure it is a man – needs to be more comprehensively punished for his malign neglect. I assess the track, speculatively. It slopes downwards in a fairly straight line towards a field with an open gate. There's a big oak tree just beyond. It's an extremely bucolic scene.

I open the passenger door and lean in to look around. Although I didn't pass my test, I'm familiar with the basics. Checking the gearbox is in neutral, I release the handbrake, and step back hastily. This turns out to be unnecessary, as the car stays exactly where it is. Slamming the door, I go round to the boot and start to push, my sandals scrambling on the gravel. Just as I'm wondering if I'm going to have to call Danny again, the car begins to trundle down the track, gathering momentum as it goes. It's as satisfying a sight as the gently rolling valley. By the time it reaches the end of the lane, it's got up to quite a speed, and the crash as it hits the tree is gratifying, causing me to do some spontaneous mindful breathing as I appreciate the vista. It's definitely enhanced the view, like a sort of modern *Hay Wain*. There's a faint hissing sound coming from the bonnet, but I haven't got any more time to stand around admiring my own work. Dusting off my hands, I return to Danny's car, climbing back into the rear passenger seat.

'How's the dog?' I ask, putting on my seatbelt.

'I'm sorry to say . . .' begins Danny, in sombre tones.

'Oh God, don't tell me it's dead.'

'No,' he replies, holding out the ball of fur. 'It's not dead, but . . . it ain't no dog.'

I take the trembling, cashmere-soft bundle from him and arrange it on my lap for inspection. He's right. It's not a dog, it's a rabbit. A massive, floppy-eared bunny.

'Right,' I say, as its back legs scrabble painfully against my thighs. 'My mistake.'

'Seems a bit much to smash someone's car in for a rabbit.'

I was thinking along those lines myself, but I'm damned if I'll admit it. 'That's a very prejudiced view. Anyway, who the hell leaves a rabbit in a car?'

'Maybe they thought it would get shot in the field.'

Who knows why people do what they do. The fact is, I've destroyed a car to save Bigwig here, and I'll just have to own it.

'Very well,' I say. 'Drive on.'

# 21

Despite Maz's love of animals, we were never allowed a pet. My mother professed herself allergic to cats, and said she'd once been bitten by an Irish terrier, leaving her with a lifelong fear of dogs and Ireland, but the truth was that neither beast would have been conducive to her quest for an immaculate house. My sister's alpacas could be viewed as a massive metaphorical finger to Rose – free to embrace four-legged friends, Maz chose the biggest, smelliest ones she could find. Perhaps Grizelda is my subtler, more refined rebellion. And now I have abducted a rabbit.

Inspired by our encounter, Danny launches into a tirade against a show called *Good Dog, Bad Dog*, which is in fact a series I made a while ago which took two contrasting examples of the same breed and . . . contrasted them. I'm actually quite proud of that show because we made it with all sorts of Covid regulations in place, and, after shivering my arse off in bleak parks for six weeks, I managed to avoid hypothermia. It seems my driver objects to us having paired a 'good' Golden Retriever with a 'bad' yellow

Labrador – technically not the same pedigree, which made a mockery of the format and disappointed Danny hugely. I stroke Bigwig's butter-soft spine and wonder if he is a good bunny or a bad one.

David's estate is looking particularly exquisite as my Mercedes rolls along its lengthy cypress-lined driveway shortly after 3 p.m. The vines undulate across the Somerset slopes in pleasingly uniform rows, and the elegant Georgian manor house ahead is burnished amber in the afternoon sunshine. In the show *Good Vineyard, Bad Vineyard*, this would definitely be the former. It really will make a lovely setting for a series about shitfaced millennials. As we pull up outside, I can hear the crunch of gravel, as if we've arrived at Downton for a murder mystery weekend.

'Right,' I say to Danny. 'I'll only be half an hour or so – can you wait here?'

'What about Flopsy?' He jerks his thumb at my new pet, who is sprawled on the leather seat, his back legs sticking out like one of those animal-hide rugs.

'Well, unless he wants a wine tour he'll have to stay here.'

'I can't have him hopping everywhere.'

'He's not hopping, he's flopping – look at him.'

The rabbit sleepily rolls an eye.

Danny sulks. 'What if he makes a mess?'

'Charge it to Mr Chapel's account.' I get out of the car and pat the roof. 'Thank you, Branson, that will be all.'

Pushing the doorbell, I ready myself to play hardball. Old Clover would be quaking at the prospect of rescuing a million-pound show, but she was a wet blanket, and New Clover is made of sterner stuff. Like weak beer versus hard liquor. Cheap plonk versus finest Cristal.

The housekeeper answers the door, and I manage to refrain from curtsying and asking if the master be in. She shows me to the drawing room, which I've seen before, but am happy to see again, as I like ogling how the other half lives. It has parquet floors and heavy drapes, several camelback sofas and numerous oils on the eggshell-blue walls. It's very tasteful, but I couldn't live here. How would you settle down to a night of Netflix and salted caramel Lindors in a room like this? It's more the kind of room where you sit bolt upright reading Keats. I wonder if they've got a secret lounge where you can loll and fart and leave remote controls lying about.

The door flies open and my series producer, Caroline, barrels in.

'Thank God you're here,' she pants. 'It's all gone to shit.'

Caroline is thirty-two, with a blunt-cut fringe and an attitude. She was great in her interview – frank and friendly, with just the right balance of go-getting and submitting. You want someone driven but not too aggressive, who can give orders but also take them. Once she'd got the job though, it turned out Caroline didn't really like the submitting/taking orders bit. She frequently goes rogue and does it her own way, blaming underlings when anything goes wrong. Also, I've noticed she's only nice to people above her in the pecking order, and despite the fact that I clearly outrank her, somewhere along the line she decided she doesn't need to be nice to me – probably as a result of all the bagels I bought her. The further we got into pre-production, the more her manner edged towards truculent, pushing back on my decisions or ignoring them entirely. Well, Princess Caroline's about to get her comeuppance.

'David's thrown his toys out the pram,' she begins. 'You need to get him back on board, and also tell the casting team to stop giving me all these character profiles because they're doing my head in. Then you need to—'

She falters as I hold up a hand. 'Let's not talk about what I need to do, Caroline. Let's talk about what *you* need to do, which is stop addressing me like I'm your servant. The casting APs are sending you profiles because that's their job, and it's your job to stay on top of it, not come bleating to me every time you're required to lift a finger.'

For a second she gapes at me, then collects herself. 'I . . . I . . . didn't mean to . . . It's just been very stressful out here, trying to organize everything.'

I blink conspicuously. 'Caroline, correct me if I'm wrong, but aren't you an SP? It stands for series . . . *producer*. Isn't organizing everything . . . your thing? Otherwise, you're in the wrong career, and should change tack pronto. Maybe you'd be more suited as a hand model or a mattress-tester or something.'

My series producer's neck is now bright red, and she looks as if she's struggling to speak. 'I'm sorry if I . . . I'm doing my best.'

'That's the trouble: I don't think you are. I think you're leaning very heavily on the team, making them do all the hard work, while you swan around issuing orders. I heard you last week having a go at Flora because she hadn't sent the latest treatment to the channel commissioner, but that was supposed to come from you, wasn't it?'

Her eyes fill with tears. 'I'm sorry about that. I'm having a difficult time at the moment. My boyfriend—'

'I'm afraid I don't want to hear about how your boyfriend made you be rude to a colleague. We all have our personal issues, but we don't have to bring them into the office.' No, I think – when we have personal issues, we make sure we're nowhere near the office. 'Now, run along, and see if you can't be a bit nicer to everyone on less money than you. I'm going to talk to David.'

Flushed and teary, Caroline scuttles off, while I take a turn about the room to inspect the portraits. Frederick Lyon-James looks like he's half man, half pig. Arthur Lyon-James definitely had the pox. Geraldine Lyon was clearly a mad old battle-axe, and on closer inspection is wearing a locket with what looks like her own face on it. Saluting her, I move on. Charles Rupert Lyon is surrounded by his own kills, pheasant and partridge draped all around him. I wonder if I had a portrait done, what I would be surrounded by? Washing, probably. A fully loaded Lakeland air dryer.

'Clover, how good to see you.'

The latest in the Lyon-James line enters, giving me a neat little bow. He really is quite dashing, in a silver fox kind of way, though I guess his family are fox-killing types. So, more of a distinguished deerhound – gentle, polite, dignified . . . but destructive if not treated in the right manner.

'David, thank you so much for sparing the time.'

'Shall we go outside? It's so hot today.'

Oh goody-goody, I'm going to get a nice cold glass of something. Sure enough, out on the terrace, the table is already set with a bottle in a terracotta cooler and two glasses. David is an excellent host.

'This is a Domaine Servin chablis,' he says. 'Not one of ours, of course, but it's a tolerable vintage for a sweltering afternoon.'

'I adore chablis,' I reply. I do. And chardonnay, and châteauneuf, and champagne, and anything he wants to pour down my throat. He hands me a vessel as delicate as Cinderella's slipper, filled with heaven's juice. Taking that first, luscious sip, I sigh, soaking up the glorious view of the valley. This is the life. If only David wasn't already married, he might want to marry me and make me lady of this manor. But I've met his wife Isabelle, who is also charming in a fragile, ethereal way, as breakable as this glass. I can't imagine her stamping on grapes, whereas I would get stuck in. I'd make David a fine wife.

'So, I gather Vincent has spoken to you about my concerns?'

I rearrange my face in a serious expression. 'Yes, I came down as soon as I heard. What can we do to reassure you?'

David pinches the bridge of his nose. 'I'm not sure,' he says eventually. 'I was a trifle perturbed anyway, but then I watched that . . . that meat thing.'

There was no television in the portrait parlour, so he must have a secret lolling room after all. Why on earth did he choose to watch Oz's telly guff, of all things?

'*Would Like to Meat*? But Oswald's show is an entirely different genre,' I say. 'That was a reality series, whereas ours is a formatted documentary.' People always hear the word documentary and think high-brow. Sure enough, David nods encouragingly.

'Yes, of course, and you were saying your director . . .?'

Last time, I waxed less than lyrical about Tristram because I didn't want to overegg the pudding. But now it's time for lashings of egg.

'It's no exaggeration to say he's one of the true greats,' I say. 'Right up there with Jackson Bezalel, Teresa-Ann Sutcliffe, Samuel J. Allen . . .' He won't have heard of any of them, because I'd guess that, unlike Danny the driver, he watches very little television – probably just listens to *Front Row*, and only watched Oz's show for research because he had the jitters. If he were to look them up, he'd find out that they're mighty filmmakers, and way out of Tristram's league, but he won't, because in about five minutes' time, his mind will be at rest, and he won't need to.

'*Last of the Summer Vine* is a truly great opportunity to share Chew Hill with the nation, show the public the backbreaking work and expertise involved in creating world-class English wines.' I'm pleased with the bullshit title I've just come up with though there's no way we'd be allowed to call it that – it'll probably end up being called something shouty and on-the-nose like *Binge-Drinkers' Vineyard* or *Good Drunk, Bad Drunk*. 'With a renowned director on board, and a cutting-edge independent production company behind it, this show has the potential to be a breakout hit.' I take a gulp of my wine; delicious. 'The channel heads are already talking about awards. BAFTA, Rose d'Or, maybe even an Emmy . . .' That's going to be a major talking point at future Lyon-James dinner parties, I'm sure.

'It does all sound rather impressive,' says David, taking a pensive sip. 'You're very persuasive, I must admit, but . . .'

But what? Just pocket the location fee and spend it on more noble grapes or trellises or whatever. David obviously isn't short of a bob or two, but in my experience rich people always want to be richer and no vintage bouquet is as aromatic as the smell of hard cash.

'What about the, er, youngsters who'll be staying here?' His brow wrinkles. 'Izzy is worried they'll be . . . high-spirited.'

That's one way of putting it. One of the 'youngsters' we've cast likes to drink a four-pack of Diamond White prior to a night on the town. Then it's beers at the local, followed by Goldschläger shots in a club called 'Dixy's Lyrix', rounded off with kebabs and a tactical vomit before bed. Izzy's going to have the biggest migraine of her life.

I press David's arm reassuringly. 'I understand absolutely, but we have a wealth of experience in finding contributors for upmarket documentary formats like this. Our casting producers have found a wonderfully diverse group of young people who are eager to learn all they can about vinification and your successful business here. Think of it as having a team of unpaid work experience students!' The yummy wine is going down very easily, and I'm absolutely nailing this.

'And I suppose your vetting process is rigorous?'

I nod solemnly. 'We cast *very* carefully.' That much is true. We have to cast incredibly carefully to hit that sweet spot of contributors who are borderline insane enough to be entertaining, without actually being certifiable. Our psych evaluations are on a knife-edge. If only I'd known it was this easy, to say what needs to be said, what people need to hear, without a care in the world. I'm even starting to believe it myself. Maybe we *will* win an Emmy.

David sits back, cradling his glass in his palm. 'Well, I know about the director, who sounds terrific, and I know about your very talented casting team, but there's one more thing I'd like to know.'

'Of course!' I beam, ready to lay it on with a trowel. I'm prepared to say that Caroline is the industry's most dedicated series producer, Vince is a TV guru, and Red Eye is the UK's most dynamic, ground-breaking indie. I'll tell him the cameras we use are made of gold.

'I'd like to know about *you*, Clover. You're the mother of this show. Tell me about yourself.'

# 22

I got my second job in television via the first. That's often how it happens – word of mouth, recommendations, ears to the ground. So, a producer on *Ghostly Goings On* put me in touch with someone in HR at the production company, who found me another show they were making, and the producer of *that* show found me another, and before I knew it, I was a working junior researcher specializing in the paranormal. I met a lot of psychics, who were mostly useless apart from one who told me to look under the bed for the missing item – I found a pair of socks which weren't necessarily missing, but which were useful all the same. I met many, many people who believed they'd been taken by UFOs, which only led me to wonder why aliens choose to abduct such dim specimens, and don't look further afield for superior samples of the human race, like Barack Obama or Paul Rudd. I attended several séances, and found it extremely hard to stop myself giggling and disrupting the spirit communication. Everyone (living) was so earnest, and all the mediums wore scarves and big earrings.

It might seem strange that such a resolute non-believer would find herself in this murky sphere, but firstly, it was really good fun, and secondly, a deeper part of me *wanted* to be proved wrong. I wanted to believe, to be convinced that there was something else out there beyond my basement flat and fractious calls from my mother. Maybe one day a medium would help me make sense of it all, or a ghost would at least prove death wasn't the end. All the hokum gave me hope.

By early 2001, I was a researcher (no longer junior) finding contributors for a show called *Bump in the Night*, which was about people doing house renovations who were finding disturbing things behind plasterwork, or having their home makeover disrupted by unwelcome apparitions. It was a difficult job, because it loaded extra layers on the casting process – house refurbs AND supernatural claptrap. Plus, Susie wasn't there any more, having picked up a gig on *Songs of Praise* – one of the resident exorcists on *Ghostly Goings On* was also a vicar who asked for her number. She was busy finding bell ringers to take part in some competition they were running, and had developed tinnitus as a result. Whenever I called her, she just shouted down the phone about how the reverend was a real letch, but couldn't hear anything I said in reply.

So, this time round I was on my own, pretty much, touring the country by train and in taxis, trying to find fixer-uppers fed up with their phantoms. I was also writing treatments for the production company, Beatnik Media, and found I'd started talking in the same style when I pitched the show, using a lot of alliteration on doorsteps. Because I was often crippled with embarrassment, I'd write myself a little script to parrot, to stop myself stammering and petering out on the phone, and it carried on when I got over the threshold, a steady format-patter that ensured there were no awkward silences or tricky questions.

Luckily, I hit the jackpot early on, finding a couple who were renovating an old vicarage outside Chipping Norton and had encountered all sorts of freaky things. Re-laying the lawn, they'd discovered a strange air raid shelter in the garden which led to a network of dripping tunnels. When they started converting the attic, they found a crawl space which may or may not have been a priest hole, but had unnerving child-like drawings on the walls. Finally, they were pretty sure there was a partition in the cellar that led to a hidden room. I'd persuaded them to let us film them knocking it through, just in case there was anything juicy behind it. I was very pleased with myself for securing them, and it made up for the lacklustre semi in Woking whose loft renovation had unearthed a mysterious locked box labelled 'Do Not Open' which, when we filmed them opening it, turned out to be completely empty. Mysterious, but not in an interesting way. As my series producer, Sharon, said, 'That's two minutes' footage, max. Move on.'

The vicarage rapidly became the focus of the show, as more and more ghoulish stuff started happening. One of the garden's underground tunnels had a pentacle drawn on the wall, and when the builders knocked through the house's cellar partition, they found an old iron bed behind it, which really freaked everyone out, and when we researched the history of the site, it turned out that one of the previous residents was a vicar called Humphrey Ecclestone, who killed his entire family, followed by himself, in one of the bedrooms. The new owners, Jillian and Edgar, were no longer as keen on their new property after that. They were renting a cottage in the nearby town while they did the works, and decided to put the vicarage back on the market, so then the story became them trying to find a buyer for their creepy-as-fuck house. By this point, the entire staff of Beatnik Media were obsessed, all angling to come up and have a poke around. Personally, I didn't ever see anything spooky there, but there was no doubt the place had a bad feeling. The best way of describing it was there was a sort of echo. Like the silence after an unearthly scream. But I'm aware that sounds fanciful to the point of foolish.

By the time the series was finally finished that October when I'd just turned twenty-six, we'd filmed in a number of 'hair-raising half-finished haunted houses' across the country. Jill and Eddie had managed to find a (mad as a hatter) buyer and we decided to have our wrap party in the empty Ecclestone vicarage with its spooky dripping tunnels. Because, you know, telly people. They're absolutely nuts. The production co-ordinator arranged for a load of booze to be delivered and everyone turned up in Halloween fancy dress. Nowadays, wrap parties are much tamer affairs – like the viewing for *Blind Dinner Date* would be tonight, just a few drinks and nibbles laid on as you show everyone a teaser trailer or the rough cut of an ep – but in those days they went large. They were different times, a culture of excess and devil-may-care that filtered down through the ranks until everyone was frothing on MDMA. Vince, for all his foot-in-mouth tendencies, is a pretty benign figure compared to what I saw going on at Beatnik.

It got out of hand pretty quickly, that night. Production can be intense, and everyone wanted to let their hair down, even if it involved shutting each other in the dripping air raid tunnels or coming out of the Bad Bedroom sniffing and rubbing their gums. A group of creatives were trying to play spin the bottle with a supernatural twist, waiting for the bottle to spin on its own, and just snogging each other randomly. I passed a couple of interns who were looking for the iron bed so they could shag on it. All around were the sounds of yells and cackling laughter – Humphrey Ecclestone would probably have been in his element. Maybe he was in there somewhere, dropping an E and groping a researcher.

And me? I was pretty pissed, obviously, but didn't go in for any of that stuff. Too strait-laced, and worried about the consequences. When I was about fourteen, I read the *Sweet Valley High* book where Regina the former deaf girl does a line of coke and instantly dies of a heart attack, and knew that kind of scenario was my destiny. Stay out of trouble, Clover. Be a good girl, like my mother told me. I thought that if I behaved myself then everything would be OK, I wouldn't get into trouble. And yet . . .

Later, the vicarage was still lit up like a jack-o-lantern when I stumbled away into my taxi. I went back to the hotel we were all staying in, curled up with a hot water bottle to read *Atonement*, and tried to forget all about it. The twin towers had just fallen, the world was changing, everything was a mess, ruined, *ruined*. It couldn't be fixed, a fire that couldn't be put out. Before I turned the lights off, I put a chair against the locked door, checked the windows were secure and got back into bed. There I was, tucked up, safe and sound. Move along. Nothing to see here.

\* \* \*

I realize it's been a while since David asked me the question, and I haven't said anything, just gazed down the valley and on, to the clear horizon beyond.

'Well?' he says. 'Tell me your story.'

I gulp my wine. 'Not much to tell. I'm very boring, I'm afraid.'

'Surely not,' he says, gently. 'With wine, I can glean so much just by looking. I don't even have to taste it. The hue, for example. Did you know, the colour of a wine comes from contact with the grape skins after the grapes have been juiced? The longer the wine comes into contact with the skins, the more they will impart their colour on the wine. The skins have their own characteristics, just like the

180

zest of an orange has a stronger flavour, or an apple skin contains more fibre. The longer the skin of a grape is in contact with the wine, the more of its own characteristics it imparts.'

I don't think we're discussing wine any more, but I don't know what he's talking about, or how I'm supposed to respond, so I just look at him.

'Tell me about the grape skins,' he says. 'The ones that gave you your colour.'

Thinking about my job, the people I've rubbed up against . . . If they've left a mark, I don't want to know.

I finish my wine and set down the glass. 'Gosh, I must be water, then. Anyway, back to the show, I really think . . .'

Back to the hard sell, to the thing I do best. New Clover can do the spiel, even without a script. When David delivers me back to Danny's car, I'm still going, making sure all bases are covered. He can't back out now.

'Goodbye, Clover,' he says, lifting his hand. 'Thank you so much for coming. It's been extremely edifying.'

I think that means I nailed it.

'Home, James,' I say to Danny, gathering a dozy Bigwig onto my lap for a cuddle. With my face buried in his downy fur, no one can swirl me in a glass or tell how long I've been aged in oak. I'm safe here in the car; cocooned, protected, anonymous.

No one can touch me.

# 23

We've barely left Chew Hill's grounds before Vince calls, wanting an update. I answer, stroking Bigwig's head with one finger, feeling like Blofeld.

'How'd it go?'

'Had him eating out of my hand.'

'You what? That's disgusting.'

'It's a figure of speech, Vince.'

'Is it? What does it mean?'

'It means he's back on board.'

'H-excellent . . .' I can almost hear him steepling his fingers. 'I'll talk to the channel execs, they might want someone to go down and be wined and dined there. Probably just wined.'

My finger circles Bigwig's silky head. 'Meanwhile, you can wine and dine *me*.'

'You what? That's—'

'I mean,' I interrupt him. 'In a metaphorical sense. Literally, you can start remunerating me sufficiently.'

Silence from the other end. He's wondering if he can pretend he doesn't know what 'remunerate' means.

'I want more money, Vince. A lot more.'

There are a few coughs and splutters. 'I pay you a fortune! A fucking fortune!'

'No, you don't. Not comparatively. Not as much as Oz.' I don't know exactly what Oz is paid, but am sure it's more than me.

'Not even Elon Musk earns as much as Oz.'

'But we do the same job,' I say. 'And I do it better.' It's outrageous – not to mention illegal – that I'm on less than Oswald, and, I suspect, Petroc, but until now I've been too weak-kneed to do anything about it.

'How about I send you to Babington House for a massage?'

This is Vince's go-to for stressed-out employees. The female ones, that is. He sends the male ones to the Kendleshire Golf Club.

'No, I want you to salary-match me with Oz, or I'm going to work at Tin Roof.' Vince particularly loathes them because they were the ones who embedded one of their producers in our panel show for Dave, so they could steal our ideas and pitch them to BBC Two.

'You wouldn't dare.'

'Try me. Or I might just see if *Broadcast* want to run a story on the gender pay gap in the industry, starting with me.'

He can hear the conviction in my voice. Today has been so useful. 'OK.' He sighs. 'Talk to Layla in HR and she'll sort you out. But know that you've made an old man very unhappy.'

'I'll take it to my grave.'

'See you at the wrap later.'

'Hundred per cent.'

I hang up and give the rabbit a kiss.

'Jenny Big Potatoes,' says Danny.

'You'd better believe it,' I say. Having longed to ask for more money for years, watching my salary rise barely in line with inflation as my credits stacked up and my roster of shows lengthened, it's only today I've been able to pluck up the courage to broach the subject. And in fact, I didn't have to pluck up the courage at all; I just demanded it as my due. There's nothing remotely embarrassing about asking for something you deserve, about doing yourself justice. Maybe my problem was I didn't believe I deserved it; thought I was lesser somehow. But the way I just dealt with David proves I've got what it takes. I'm a ballbreaker, and if that's what Vince needs, then he's going to have to pay for it.

We're driving past the bit of road where we stopped earlier, and as we pass the dirt track, Danny slows, both of us peering out. The dented Golf is being pushed up the hill by a man and a woman, both slipping and scrambling on the gravel. Danny grinds to a halt, leaving the engine running as we stare at them. They're clearly a couple, and not a happy one – the woman is gesticulating furiously with one hand, jabbing and pointing at the man. He has sweat pouring down his face, which is set in a mutinous expression. They obviously regret their choices today, and that gives me a sense of enormous wellbeing, having engineered this pastoral scene; a Cold War Steve version of *The Hay Wain*. They're bunny boilers and they deserve all they get.

'Shouldn't you go and give them the rabbit back?' Danny is eating his Wotsits like popcorn.

'That might open a can of worms.'

'You can pretend you found it, just hopping round.'

I look down at Bigwig nestling on my lap and think no, if I hadn't rescued him from that car, then he would have been dead meat, and besides, I have a feeling he's also going to be useful in ways I can't yet comprehend. My phone pings – it's a text from Maz that says **Booked The Brycgstow, 7pm**. It looks like a typo so I google it to see what she really means and it turns out it isn't a mistake but the name of a new restaurant in Clifton, near the river. Scanning the menu, I see they serve shepherd's pie and conclude that my sister has done me proud. We may have to endure our mother's jeremiad, but at least while my ears are sad, my mouth will be happy. I wonder what they do for pudding? But while I'm scrolling to see, my phone rings again, an unknown number, and I accidentally hit the answer button trying to browse the restaurant's dessert offerings.

'Hello? Hello?'

Hearing the voice echoing out of my phone, I suppose I'd better answer it. At least it isn't Vince.

'Hi there, Clover Hendry speaking.'

'Good afternoon, Ms Hendry. This is Gardenia Cusack, from the Sion Triangle.'

'The what?'

'Sion Triangle? The art gallery? I believe you visited our exhibition earlier today? Ms Hendry?'

I don't say anything because I have an inkling she's not calling to conduct a phone survey on customer satisfaction.

Taking my silence for assent, she continues. 'I'm calling because there was an . . . incident involving a child, and we have reason to believe you were involved.'

'What reason?' I'm willing to bet no one noticed me hoik little Lucifer into the mesh pit.

'CCTV footage,' she replies crisply. Busted.

'How did you get my details?' I know exactly how, but am playing for time.

She clicks her tongue. 'You provided them when you booked the ticket.'

'Well, what's the problem? The kid was wandering around on his own, I was worried about him. I take it he wasn't harmed in that . . . that playpen thing?'

'No, *he* wasn't harmed, but, Ms Hendry, it was an artwork. A highly expensive piece.'

'Get stuck in, did he? Well, that's not my fault. He's not my child. Have you spoken to his father?'

'Yes. Yes, we have. And his father is extremely upset.'

'He should have looked after his son then, instead of lying on the floor leaving everyone else to do it. What was he thinking?'

'I might ask you the same question. Why did you put his son in *Kinder Kraal*?'

'*Kinder Kraal*?'

'That is the name of the artwork.'

'Oh. I thought it seemed . . . an appropriate enclosure. I just wanted to help. You know, with childcare.'

'Lucas caused a great deal of damage during the ten minutes he was in there. And I'm afraid Mr Andra is holding you personally responsible.'

'Mr Andra?'

'Art Andra, the artist.'

'Why isn't he holding Lucas's father responsible too?'

'Mr Andra IS Lucas's father.'

Shades of *Star Wars*. So the man on the floor was Art Andra. 'Well, he's a better artist than he is a parent. Just about.'

'I must tell you, Ms Hendry, that Mr Andra is considering prosecution for criminal damage.'

'Seems a bit harsh to consider prosecuting your son.'

The tongue-click again. 'Prosecuting *you*, not Lucas. I feel like you are not taking this seriously, Ms Hendry. For offences of criminal damage where the damage caused is over five thousand pounds, the maximum sentence is ten years' imprisonment.'

'*Kinder Kraal* is worth over five thousand pounds?!' I wouldn't have paid a fiver.

'Indeed. Considerably more.'

I suppose this could be termed a pickle. But in the

general scheme of things, I'm heading towards a whole wall of chutney, so figure I should spear this one and move on to more important matters. My firefighting TV producer's brain is buzzing, crafting and rejecting potential scenarios until I reach one that will do the job and also be enjoyable. I check the time – nearly 4.15 p.m. – and quickly assemble a mental production schedule.

'Would you tell Mr Andra that I am deeply, deeply sorry for the damage done to his miraculous artwork, and that I would very much like to apologize in person?'

'I'm not sure he would be willing to see you.'

'Then give me his contact details and let me appeal to him myself. Please let me rectify this terrible error of judgement.'

'I'll ask him to call you, but I can't promise anything.'

'Thank you from the bottom of my heart. Tell him to call me straight away – I can't rest until this is put right.'

Hanging up, I immediately call Susie. 'Where are you right now?'

There's the sound of traffic. 'I just left the house on Cheltenham Avenue that I told you about.'

'The collector? What's it like?'

'Incredible.'

'Has he got paintings and stuff?'

'Everywhere. It's practically the Louvre.'

'And where is he now?'

'Dubai, I think. Why?'

'Because I need his house.'

'What?'

'Just for a bit. Can you meet me there?'

'No. What are you talking about?'

'I just want to hang out there for a bit. You're always saying I should see these places.'

'I don't trust you. You're crazy today.'

'Half an hour, that's all.'

'I don't understand.'

There's another call coming in. 'Thank you, love you, see you there, bye.' I switch lines. 'Hello?'

'Hello, is that Clover Hendry? This is Art Andra.' He has a kind of strangled American accent, like Loyd Grossman.

I give a little gasp. 'Mr Andra! You don't know what an honour this is. Thank you for taking the time, for picking up the phone, for blessing me this way.' Since he has an interesting accent, I decide to have one too, and go for something vaguely Eastern European.

'I'm *very* upset about this.'

'Of course you are. Of course. I can't imagine . . . But please, I can explain everything. I wondered if you would do me the additional honour of coming to my house—'

'I don't think so—'

'—my house on Cheltenham Avenue, so that I can offer you a proper apology, an explanation, and perhaps some light refreshment?'

There's silence at the other end, the address doing its work. Cheltenham Avenue is the most desirable street in Bristol – the average house price is at least two million. Everyone wants to live there, or at least have a nose around.

'It's near the gallery, with lovely views of the green.' Before this I was just a random woman; now I'm a random *rich* woman.

'As you wish,' he says, as if he's doing me a huge favour.

'Thank you so much, you're too kind. Shall we say five p.m.? I'll message you the address.'

As I hang up, Danny catches my eye in the rear-view mirror. 'Playing a deep game, ain't ya.'

I clasp Bigwig against my chest. 'You have no idea.'

# 24

That's what TV producers do; we clear up the mess. Sometimes we make it too – omelettes, eggs and all that. But firefighting is a prerequisite of a good programme-maker; fearlessness in the face of chaos. Sometimes things unravel quite spectacularly – presenters throwing strops, contributors backing out, the production haemorrhaging money, commissioners shifting goalposts. The producer keeps a steady hand at the tiller, guiding everyone through. At least, that's how it's supposed to work.

The problem is, normally, I don't do fearlessness. Tidying up is OK, stemming the frenzy, keeping things together, ticking over – that's doable. But managing all that without bricking myself is something I've never quite achieved. Pretty much every production I've ever worked on has added years to my life in terms of stress and anxiety, repeating Other Delia's mantra '*It'll all come out in the edit, it'll all come out in the edit . . .*' to calm myself down. In our catch-ups with Vince, I'd listen to my fellow executive producers Petroc and Oz casually mentioning the various production issues they were battling, and find it hard not to grab a paper bag to hyperventilate into – how were they not made *dizzy* by the things they had to deal with? As execs, we were near the top of the tree, production-wise, which meant that lightning struck us first. Of course, *they* were delegating the worry down to someone else, which is something I've never been able to do. Sometimes, you clear up the mess by giving everyone a broom and telling them to get on with it.

After he helped me out with Vince and the head of development job, Petroc and I had become friends, regularly sneaking off to the pub round the corner to snark about colleagues, commissioners and the industry generally. He'd been at Red Eye for longer than I had and, although professionally we were equals, I'd come to rely on him as a sounding board – or at least someone I could let off steam with. He has a certain sagacity – laced with sarcasm of course – that I find reassuring. Most of the time, anyway. Sometimes he fucks up, just like everyone else.

One day, I was in my office watching casting tapes and eating honey-and-sesame-coated almonds that someone had brought back from Turkey. We have what Vince inappropriately calls the 'Fat Shelf' in the communal kitchen, where people leave treats out – chocolates they've been given, leftover birthday cake, holiday harvests. It's where I left my doughnuts, where I leave my bagels – ostentatiously, so everyone knows I'm being generous. Someone had left the almonds out that morning, and after telling myself I definitely wouldn't have any, I took a handful and lined them up on my desk, resolving to only eat one when I came across a contributor I liked on the tape. I'd eaten three almonds when Petroc burst in, looking grey and unhinged.

'Kill me now.'

He threw himself into my armchair, which is a prop from a celebrity interview show we made. It's orange, designed to pop on camera, which only served to heighten the zombie tones of Petroc's face. He looked distraught, so I offered him a nut.

'I can't eat, I feel sick,' he declared, passing a hand across his sweating brow.

'What's happened?'

'Call the TV police, I'm going to jail.'

Petroc was making a popular science documentary about people who like immersing themselves in ice water. It was niche stuff, for a natural history department, who wanted an excuse to feature stunning frosty backdrops, with a bit of lunacy thrown in. But Jonno, the commissioner, was becoming increasingly obsessed with getting the presenter, a survival expert, to join the ice enthusiasts in their pursuits. Petroc felt it would compromise her gravitas, and that Jonno really just wanted to get her in a swimsuit (she was a very easy-on-the-eye survival expert), so he was pushing back.

'I was so pissed off with him,' he explained. 'He kept saying "Couldn't you just get her to have a dip in Lake Windermere?" But that wasn't the point. We were going back and forth arguing, and then Vince bumped into Jonno in Avon House and Jonno tried to get him on board as well. Suggested putting Harriet in a bikini. I lost my rag.'

'What did you do?' I'd now eaten all the almonds.

Petroc put his head in his hands. 'I sent Vince an email. Said Jonno is a pervy old man who knows nothing about programme-making, and should get in the sea, which is about eight degrees this time of year. See how he likes it.'

'So?'

He splayed his fingers to look at me with haunted eyes. 'I accidentally sent it to Jonno.'

'Holy shit.'

'I know.' He buried his head again. 'What shall I do? Maybe *I'll* get in the sea. Just wade out and never come back, like Reggie Perrin.'

'He *did* come back.'

'Well, I won't. You have to help me. I don't know what to do. Apart from go into witness protection.'

But I was busy thinking, fuelled by sugary nuts. Because it wasn't me in the firing line, for once I felt fearless and driven. 'When did you send the email?'

He sighed dispiritedly. 'What?'

'When did you send it?' Something in the sharpness of my tone pierced him, and he sat up straighter, uncovering his face.

'Five minutes ago. Why? Can you save me? Save me! Do it! What are you thinking?'

'I'm not sure, but I've got an idea.'

Sweeping almond dust off my desk into the bin, I stood up and walked out into the open-plan section, trailed by a hangdog Petroc. Everyone was tapping away, staring at their screens. Ian Gittings had his feet up on the desk, headphones on, chortling at old episodes of *Seinfeld*. I carried on, past them, towards Vince's corner office. His shelves are lined with awards – not awards he's won, just random trophies he's swiped to make himself look illustrious and successful. Some of them are his son's football cups.

Vince's PA sits just outside her boss's office, in case he wants her to do a coffee run or help him out technically – he's a terrible Luddite who still tries to send people faxes. She was typing up one of his reports, squinting at his terrible handwriting, and drinking from a Red Eye branded coffee cup, which are universally known as the myxomatosis mugs.

'Imogen, can you spare a moment?'

She looked up vaguely, her eyes readjusting. 'Yes?'

'Jonno Ritchie.'

She made a face. 'Yes?'

'Do you know his assistant?'

'Lizzie. Nice girl.'

'Do you think you could give her a call?'

Under my direction, Imogen called Lizzie, but she was having a day off, so Imogen spoke to a temporary assistant, Sian, who spoke to Jonno's colleague Petra's assistant Anita. With Anita on the phone, I explained the situation and, luckily, she understood perfectly. It turned out Jonno was in a viewing and was unlikely to have seen the email yet. We all agreed that it was in everyone's interests if he never did. Anita went into Jonno's office, logged on to his computer and deleted the message from his inbox and trash, erasing all evidence of Petroc's indiscretion. Petroc cried with relief, and tearfully took himself off to the Fat Shelf to root out a slice of carrot cake, which he gorged on to restore his blood sugar levels. Then, at my behest, he contacted Bloom & Wild and arranged to send Anita a nice bunch of flowers to say thank you. Assistants are the lifeblood of the TV industry, of any industry. They know everything, everyone. They're the power behind the throne, and you need them on side.

Back in my office, I spotted a rogue almond on the floor under my desk. I crawled under, picked it up and ate it. That's what producers do; we clear up the mess. Sometimes we even enjoy it. Now Art Andra is my mess, and I'm going to wipe the floor with him.

# 25

When Danny drops me off at the house on Cheltenham Avenue, Susie's outside looking like thunder, but I've got precisely fifteen minutes to get ready for my visitor and don't really have time for explanations. As she unlocks the door and starts messing about with a devilishly complicated alarm system, she throws questions over her shoulder at me while I stand on the steps, drinking in the imposing façade. It's gigantic, with Juliet balconies and a carefully shaped magnolia tree in the elegant front garden. Thinking of my own front garden, full of withered pot plants and flourishing weeds, I wish I could achieve this level of pruned perfection. But that would require professional help; maybe a whole team of dedicated gardeners and landscapers. If only I had staff – people to pick up my dry-cleaning, power hose the patio, renew our TV licence, make my hair curly every day. I would be so much more productive if there was a team of people taking up the slack, being productive for me.

'What's going on? Why are you so weird? What on

earth have you done to your hair? Is that some sort of creature in your bag? Where did you get that dress?'

I deal with the most important thing first, putting down Bigwig and my bag to give her a twirl.

'It's got pockets!' I jam my hands in them to demonstrate their capaciousness.

She gives me a grudging nod. 'That's really nice, how much did it set you back?'

'McMany Pounds, but I got a discount thanks to some hard-nosed haggling.'

'See, that's what I mean.' Susie beckons me onwards and, carrying Bigwig, I follow her across the hallway and up the stairs, already goggling. 'The Clover I know doesn't haggle.'

'Over the next hour or so, you're going to get to know another Clover. Just go with it.' I gaze around the room she's just led me to, at the back of the house. 'Bloody hell, this is . . . unbelievable.'

'This is the old ballroom.'

We're in a vast space lined with long Georgian windows. The ceiling is covered in intricate cornicing, picked out in brilliant white against a beige background, and punctuated by three huge chandeliers that glint in the afternoon sunlight. The floor is smooth polished oak; I can imagine Regency couples bowing to each other and circling, while dowagers look on disapprovingly. But now, instead of dancers, the room is populated with sculptures – a huge marble head emerging from rough-hewn rock; a series of metal spikes set in a concrete base; a big looping resin blob with a hole in it; an enormous shiny balloon animal; and an elongated bronze figure of a man who appears to be leaning against the wind. This is the second rich person's house I've been in today and once again I can't imagine what they do with the space – what is the point of a sculpture room? Do they come and stand here of an evening, finger to chin, mulling on the curves of the blob?

Susie continues. 'On this floor, there's also a library and a drawing room. Six bedrooms on the second, third and fourth floors, including a huge suite. Downstairs is the kitchen, dining room, cinema room, and then below that is the basement where he keeps all his cars.'

'Huh. Some collector.' I run my hand over the marble face – even on this warm day, it feels cold to the touch. 'This is the real deal, right? I mean, worth a few quid?'

She grimaces. 'He loves telling people. I've been going through a lot of the stuff for our catalogue. His car collection is worth about a million, and the art is worth more. There's a Gainsborough in the drawing room, and in the library, he's got a cigar case that belonged to Isambard Kingdom Brunel. He tried to buy the Banksy that got shredded, but he got outbid.'

'Why does he live *here*?' I'm not knocking the West Country, but couldn't this guy lord it in London or LA? I'm sure everyone has a sculpture room in La La Land, along with a gym and a chakra-realigning pod.

'He's Bristol born and bred. Divides his time between here and the UAE. I'm starting to think he might be an arms dealer. Which is why I'm really not happy about you being here.'

'I'm just your assistant, here to help you with your cataloguing. You said the kitchen was downstairs?'

I take a quick peek in the drawing room – perfect for my purposes – then jog back down the sweeping staircase. The kitchen is underneath the ballroom and is almost as big, industrial-shiny, with all sorts of anterooms for storing wine and doing laundry and stuffing swans. While Susie follows me round exclaiming and complaining, I do what I need to do, and when the doorbell rings just after five, I'm ready.

'Could you get that please?'

'Who the hell is it? We've got visitors now? Jesus Christ!'

'It's an artist called Art Andra, and it's only for half an hour, and then we'll be out of your lair.'

She takes me by the shoulders and looks into my eyes. 'What are you up to? Just tell me.'

For a second I meet her gaze. 'Not yet. But I will. You've just got to trust me. I know what I'm doing.'

She stares at me searchingly, before releasing my shoulders. 'OK. But you owe me, big time.'

'OK.' I watch her walk away, my best friend, who knows everything – not quite everything – and will do this mad thing for me, on my say-so, on my day-of-days, and I think: yes, I do owe her. More than a basement of supercars or a ballroom of sculptures. And I'll pay her back, another day, just like I did for Petroc. I catch sight of myself in the gilt mirror above the fireplace and zhuzh my crazy hair. My eyes have a light in them; it's the martial light of Lucas Andra, my visitor's demonic son. I'm going to need it.

# 26

The Clover Susie knows doesn't haggle. She doesn't negotiate, doesn't push, doesn't quibble. She pays full price, tips poor service, accepts her lower-than-market-value salary meekly, is grateful. Sometimes I hate her. She's so darn spineless, she makes my blood boil.

I keep thinking back to moments when I let my natural cowardice get the better of me, allowing myself to be ignored, slighted, overlooked, rebuked. My innate fear of rocking the boat condemned me to a life spent tiptoeing around, polite smile plastered on, apologizing and throwing my cloak on the floor for everyone. Mostly my mother, admittedly, but it's a habit that bled out and infected every part of my existence, until I'd effectively erased myself.

'Don't make such a fuss!' Rose always said, when, as a little girl, I scraped my knee, or was scared of the dark, or got lost in Woolworths and the staff had to do an announcement. Her vision of the perfect child was one who was neither seen nor heard, blending into the soft furnishings until we were as accommodating and forgiving as one of her many plump velvet cushions. It became ingrained, that urge to please, to acquiesce, to make everyone else comfortable, even if I was being sat on. Maz dealt with it in a different way, tuning her, and then most of the world, out, but I slogged away, keeping the plates spinning, doing my best to stay serene, a good girl. A husband, two kids, a career, nice house, an (almost) size ten body that functions, shiny hair.

And I'm so fucking tired of it.

I get that I'm lucky to have it all, and know that others have it so much worse. And it's not that I don't want those things any more. It's just that to get them, keep them, maintain them, was and is so much effort. Sometimes I feel like I could give up work and just spend every second of every day dealing with the humdrum minutiae of life – pruning plants and sorting Tupperware cupboards and recycling pens and filling in forms and ordering compost bags on Amazon and buying birthday presents and changing duvet covers and de-ticking the cat and fixing the loose tile in the bathroom and touching up my roots and queueing at the pharmacy and making sure Ethan does his homework and going for a run and prepping dinner and throwing away the rotting vegetables in the fridge and remembering to put wine in for later and dammit I forgot to charge my toothbrush.

And that's just the 'fun' stuff. Then there's smear tests, and checking your boobs for tumours, and pulling hair from the plughole of the shower, and rinsing the fat-clogged filter in the dishwasher and hosing shit off a child's welly, and listening to a friend tell you about her mum who has Alzheimer's and worrying about when that might be your turn, and smiling when the man tells you to smile and hating yourself, and reading about how your children will perish on a fiery earth, and knowing that when you sit down to dinner there are wars raging and people who can't afford food, parents who can't feed their kids, and you're so *lucky*, you should just sit for a while to think about how goddamned lucky you are, but you just don't have time, because the washing cycle finished and there's another load to do.

There's just too much going on. Keeping everything ticking over without breaking down is a full-time job. And I have a full-time job. 'A woman's work is never done!' my mother twinkles inanely, but that doesn't begin to cover it. Makes it sound like you're ticking off a list, one by one, and things keep getting added to the list. But the reality is more than that. It's more like the vault in *Harry Potter* where he's looking for the goblet, but everything he touches multiplies, until they're all suffocated. More like that. I'm suffocating in cursed goblets, trying to rise above it with a smile. I guess I need to stop touching stuff, stop smiling.

And I will. But first I want to burn the whole thing down.

# 27

Susie leads Art Andra into the drawing room, where I'm sitting on a chaise longue with my knees together like the Duchess of Cambridge. As he approaches, rolling his shoulders, I can tell he's already slightly intimidated, working hard to hide it. Shock and awe, that's what I was going for. I get to my feet more gracefully than is natural to me, and shake his hand.

'Mr Andra, so good of you to come. This is Suzanne, my assistant. Please, take a seat.'

While I was setting everything up, I practised my accent under my breath, and really think I've got it down now. Hearing it, though, causes Susie's eyes to widen, only to narrow again as she's introduced.

'Champagne?' I gesture towards the bottle set on the table between us, along with two glasses. I'm doing a David Lyon-James. Susie was apoplectic when she saw me nick it from the owner's wine fridge, but there were loads in there, and he'll never notice, particularly as it's only Moët, the arms dealer's equivalent of tap water. Pouring us both a glass, I check out Art Andra. I couldn't see him properly on the floor of the gallery, but it turns out he's a fairly unprepossessing figure anyway – quite short in stature, with close-cropped dark hair revealing his pierced ears. He's wearing rolled-up black trousers, a neck chain like Connell in *Normal People*, and one of those ampersand T-shirts. His says 'Claude & Camille & Alfred & Auguste & Edgar'. What a wag.

As we lean forwards to clink, we're briefly interrupted by Bigwig lazily hopping across the Persian rug between us. I had to let him out my bag as I wanted him to have a run-around, but Suzanne my assistant is on hand with wipes.

I gently caress his back as he lollops past. 'My emotional support animal,' I explain. 'Essential to my wellbeing in these times of turmoil.'

Art dips his head sagely. I feel we're already bonding. 'Can I start by saying I'm a huge admirer of yours.' I raise my glass to him. '*Six Weeks* is a miraculous piece.' That's the title of the big posseting baby figure, which was the only thing I really liked in the exhibition.

He looks disgruntled. 'That's one of my earliest works,' he says. 'I've been experimenting with form since then.'

'Ah, well, I'm glad to learn that I have been a fan since the very beginning. Your latest exhibition is a tour de force.' Picking up my phone, I show him the Instagram selfie in the shell, my shelfie, making sure that he notes my following, which is now up to 90K. Then I put the mobile face down on the table in front of us and continue sorrowfully: 'Of course, you are here to witness my profound and heartfelt apology for the damage I caused, and I can offer that to you now, wholeheartedly, along with a confession.'

He takes a sip of champagne, looking intrigued, as is Susie, whose eyes are on stalks.

'Alas, I suffer from a very unusual and strange complaint which causes me to behave in an inappropriate way around artworks that I find particularly moving. I realize this sounds bizarre, and admit I am at a loss—'

'Stendhal syndrome,' he butts in, his face transfigured. He's delighted. It's like taking candy from a giant posseting baby.

'I beg your pardon?'

He leans forward eagerly. 'It's a recognized psychosomatic condition. Also called Florence syndrome, after the city.' Obviously, you puffed-up twat. 'It causes the sufferer to react hysterically when in the presence of great beauty or antiquity.'

I raise my hands to my cheeks and take a shuddering breath. 'I am also this way in the Roman Baths . . . Is it possible that you have diagnosed my affliction?'

Art Andra sits back, taking a triumphant gulp of his champagne.

'Suzanne, this makes sense of so much. Remember when we were at the Rijksmuseum?' Susie nods, very slowly, saying nothing. I point at the Gainsborough. 'It took me six months to look at this without feeling nauseous. Mr Andra,

I cannot thank you enough. Please, come with me.'

He puts down his glass and follows me out, towards the ballroom, Susie trailing behind us like a harassed PR girl.

'I would love for you to see a few of my little pieces. There are more, of course, in my house in Berlin, but this is what I call my cosy collection.' Throwing open the doors with a flourish, I beckon him inside. He stops short in the entrance.

'This is . . . This is quite something.' He's fiddling with the neck of his T-shirt like he's overwhelmed.

I put my hand on my heart. 'You do me too great an honour. An art lover's trinkets, merely.'

'But this is a Jeff Koons!' He hurries to the balloon animal. 'C-can I?' He runs his hand wonderingly over its shiny surface, then heads towards the bronze man. 'And is this a *Gormley*?'

I figure it's safe to nod. He then proceeds to take me through all my own artworks, telling me about them. Apparently, it's quite a collection. When he's finally finished, I think his throat might be sore, so suggest another glass of champagne, which he's very happy to accept.

'The blob is *not* an Anish Kapoor!' hisses Susie in my ear as we repair to the drawing room. 'It's an up-and-coming Portishead artist called Elba Delaney.'

But it doesn't matter that Art Andra doesn't know his Anish from his Elba. He's right where I want him, standing by the balcony overlooking the green. As we enjoy our second glass, I ask for his business card.

'There must be nominative determinism in play here,' I say, fingering the corners.

He looks at me, puzzled. 'You're called Art,' I explain, showing him his own name.

He shrugs, like he doesn't get it. 'Short for Arturo,' he says. 'My family is Italian American. Where are you from?'

Slightly dangerous territory. 'Serbia,' I hazard, thinking that's obscure enough to be safe. 'Clover is short for Clovjana.' Behind me, Susie snorts.

He knocks back the last of his drink and raises the glass. *'Ktoh ni riskuyet, tot ni pyot shampanskava!'*

Fuck. I can hear Susie's intake of breath, but hold my nerve, shaking my head and pursing my lips.

'Russian,' he says. What's Russia got to do with Serbia? They don't even share a border. This man's a total crayon.

'Your accent is very strange to me,' I reply. 'As they say in my country, *Ususivač je pun I potrebno ga je isprazniti!'* Which roughly means 'The vacuum is full and needs emptying.' We had a Serbian cleaner for a while, and I used to have to say it to her every week without fail, feeling that the request might seem less passive aggressive if it came in her native language.

'May I ask why you brought your delightful son to the gallery this morning?' I'm still intrigued as to why none of the staff seemed to recognize the boy.

'I like to visit my work incognito, to get the authentic experience. Lucas was with me as a cover,' says Art Andra, like a true visionary.

I slap my forehead in wonder. 'Inspiring. I was right about you, Mr Andra. Aside from my intense and fervent apologies, which I offer again, I also wanted to say that one of my many companies dabbles in a little television here and there.' I press my own business card on him. Thanks to Vince's odd whims, it says 'Clover Hendry, Creative Director, Red Eye Productions'. Vince hands out nonsensical titles willy-nilly, and Red Eye has about five creative directors, all doing completely different things, but Arturo Andra doesn't need to know that.

'You would make a wonderful presenter in the mould of Grayson Perry, but more heavyweight. Perhaps a thoughtful, recherché series on BBC Four, meeting your own heroes of the art world, visiting a few iconic pieces?' Like anyone would watch that.

Art Andra is transfixed. His day has gone from disastrous destroyed artwork to a dazzling, daring world of showbiz opportunity and adventure. He's probably picturing a major international travelogue where he gets to hang out at the Uffizi, which is in Florence, the city, and look meaningfully at the camera occasionally before swanning off to his hotel on the piazza. I won't bring him back down to earth by telling him a BBC Four budget wouldn't get him into the Filton Premier Inn. Oz is always meeting people and promising them presenting careers in order to make himself look like a mover and shaker. I've lost count of the number of beautiful blonde physicists/gardeners/archaeologists/ballerinas who've left parties clutching his card, which reads 'Oswald Phillips, Vice-President, International Development, Red Eye Productions'. Is it our fault if they fall for this baloney? These people delude themselves, believing they're worth it, that this is their destiny, that they deserve it. We might show them the sun, but they made their own wings and it's up to them where they fly. Anyway, Art Andra can't prosecute me now – I'm practically his patron.

Rather than leave it to my assistant Suzanne, I show Art Andra out myself, waving him off as he heads into the summer heat with a spring in his step, all thoughts of lawsuits forgotten. Best of all, I had some champagne in a gorgeous house, and my support animal got to have a little hop about. Job done, mess cleared. On a console in the hallway, there's a golden statue of a hand giving the finger that I'm very much drawn to. It's heavy in my own hand, and conveys a powerful artistic message. I put it in my bag, which I left by the front door. It's stealing, but it feels justified, because I really want it.

Back in the drawing room, Susie is collecting glasses, wearing her previous thunderous expression.

'What's wrong? I thought that went rather well.'

She huffs, tucking the mostly empty bottle under her arm.

'Well, apart from the fact that I still have no idea what the hell that was about, it was really mean, what you did.'

'What do you mean? He was so happy.' I start searching the room for Bigwig, last seen nibbling on the cord of a floor lamp.

'He was bamboozled. You promised him the moon on a stick. The poor man thinks he's going to be on TV.'

'It's not my fault if he believes it's actually a possibility.' I check behind the chaise for a tell-tale tail.

'Well, it is, since you *told* him it was a possibility.'

'You're taking it all very literally. I was just throwing creative ideas around.'

'Didn't sound like that to me. Sounded like you were conning him.'

'Don't be dramatic.'

'You're a grifter. What was that ridiculous accent?'

I look under an antique table with clawed feet for more clawed feet, but can't see him. 'I thought it was pretty good. It lent me an air of sophistication.'

'Lent you an air of insanity, more like. When are you going to tell me what's going on?'

On my hands and knees, I look up at her, wondering if now is the time, here in the drawing room of an arms dealer's house, which I've appropriated and pillaged. But we've got to wash up, and I've lost my rabbit. So I duck again to check behind the curtains, and she goes downstairs to rinse the glasses and hide the bottle in the recycling. After ten increasingly frantic minutes, we find Bigwig up in the palatial top-floor bedroom suite, nibbling on a valance. For such a lazy lapin, he doesn't half move fast.

That goes for me too. It may look like lolloping, but I know exactly where I'm headed, and I'm picking up speed, ready for the crash.

# 28

Everything happens for a reason, one of Maz's therapists used to say. I don't think that's entirely true – some things happen for no reason at all, like spontaneous human combustion, which always terrified me as a child. But in general, I guess that's the way it is – things happen because other things happened to make them happen, like dominoes. And in the same way I've always looked fearfully forward – 'What if . . .?' – anticipating the repercussions, I've always glanced behind me too, unpicking the series of events that led to my current situation, going right back to the tiny horseshoe nail. There's that short story where the guy travels back in time, kills a butterfly, and when he returns to his present, everything's changed, and not for the better. It was just a butterfly, and yet . . .

The problem with worrying about this stuff, is you have to tread so carefully, as there are butterflies everywhere. You're treading on your dreams, your anxieties, your hopes, your mistakes, every step a potential disaster. Sometimes I think it would be better not to go out at all, just to impose a voluntary isolation and keep yourself in stasis to ensure you don't do any damage, to yourself or anyone else. When we were all confined during the pandemic, there was a certain comfort in it, the custody – a consoling hush as everything died down, everyone kept their distance, out of danger. I would go out into the garden and stare up at the flight-free sky, thinking of all the planes that definitely wouldn't fall from it now. But obviously that was a fallacy, butterflies getting trodden on until you couldn't see the ground.

I remember that time in my twenties, burned out and broken by my time at Beatnik, *Bump in the Night*, the wrap party. For months after that night at the vicarage, I was in lockdown, long before it was a thing. Although I was getting up and going to work, just about, I wasn't really there at all, just going through the motions, waiting to be let out again. After declining so many invitations they fell away, I would just go home to my basement flat and shiver in bed, afraid to go to sleep because of the nightmares, afraid to be awake because my mind would dwell on the what ifs, backwards and forwards, over and over again until I wasn't sure if anything was real and maybe the whole thing was a dream.

Banishing bad things as a figment of my imagination was the solution, it turned out, the same way I would if I caught sight of a ghostly figure in an empty room. Shake your head, snap out of it, it doesn't exist, wasn't there. Some people choose to believe; I chose not to. So I dragged myself out of bed, put one foot in front of the other, and let myself out again. And it was OK. Having dealt with her letchy vicar, Susie found a job for me on *Songs of Praise*, and I found God. Well, I didn't, really, but it felt like I'd gone from Hades to somewhere lighter and purer. I was going up in the world, professionally, spiritually and also physically. Thanks to Susie and my credits, I was now an assistant producer, finally leaving the paranormal behind, and thanks to my pregnant friend Laura, I was able to move into the ground-floor flat she'd just vacated in Herne Hill, which had a very sweet and absent-minded landlord who hadn't got round to putting up the rent.

It wasn't happily ever after, by any means. The flat was still punishingly expensive, my promotion meant harder work and more responsibility, and I remained an emotional wreck. But working on *Songs of Praise*, I was asked to write a treatment for a show about Richard Madeley embracing his own spirituality and becoming a monk, and then the BBC gave us development money, and I booked a train to Northallerton to recce a ruined priory and there met a lovely young lawyer with an interest in relics, and an even bigger interest in me. I may not have found God, but I did find a husband, my perfect match, the one who could restore the balance. One thing leads to another, and everything happens for a reason.

# 29

I'm starting to wonder if I should take Vince up on his offer of a massage at Babington House. My bag is so full that it's really dragging and I might end up with a rotator cuff injury. In addition to my unread *Blind Assassin*, it's now Bigwig's carry-case, and also the repository for my latest acquisition, the golden finger. My bag is huge, one of those Mary Poppins holdalls for all the bumf that, as a woman, you're obliged to carry. Not just your own stuff, like tampons and lip balm, but items for others – tissues for snotty children, plasters, snacks, water bottles, sun cream, chargers and sunglasses for Robbie, because he always forgets them. I got rid of most of the crap to fit the rabbit in, but despite the bag's commodiousness, it's straining at the seams, and so is my shoulder.

I'm also feeling quite light-headed, since I've had a skinful this afternoon on very little food, so I decide to pick up something tasty and take it to the green. In a café nearby, I find a dainty selection of gateaux and buy a maple pecan slice, and a coffee to sober me up. I even get an apple for the rabbit. The park is fairly busy with the post-work crowd, but I find a tranquil corner under a tree to have my picnic, settling on the grass and spreading out my spread. Bigwig presents a problem initially – it feels unfair to leave him in my bag, but I don't want him hopping off to find a new warren and fight General Woundwort. I decide to let him out, and keep a close eye on him – in the event, there's no need, because as soon as I put him down next to me, he ignores the apple, stretches out and falls asleep. He really is the world's most bone-idle bunny. I'm starting to get quite fond of him.

At nearly six o'clock, the punishing heat of the day has subsided, and it's pleasantly warm sitting there, scoffing my treat, sipping my drink and contemplating world domination. Having spent the day flexing my new superpowers, I figure I'm ready for what lies ahead. A plan is coming together, the pieces steadily slotting into place to form a revelatory scene. It will require nerves of steel and lashings of audacity to pull it off, but I don't think I have a choice. When I first saw the name on Imogen's list, I thought I could ignore it, run away, like I have done for years, but gradually it's become clear that the ghosts are gathering, pointing, showing me the way. Yet I have the sense – maybe a sixth sense – that when it's over, I'll have the moment of peace I've been craving.

I suppose I should tell Robbie I won't be coming home till late tonight, even though he'll be working late anyway, as he always does. There'll be no one to make the twins' supper; unlike five-year-old Clover, they don't know one end of a wooden spoon from the other and will undoubtedly resort to Deliveroo for their dinner, but that doesn't matter. Some things matter, but not that. I have always sweated the small stuff, and now I see I used it as a distraction to stop me seeing the bigger picture. Like being in a field with a raging bull, and worrying about nettle stings.

Munching my pecan slice, I call my husband. 'Hi, it's me.'

'Hello, what are you eating?'

'Carrot sticks.'

'Is that why you're calling? To boast?'

I snigger. 'No, just to tell you I'm going to that wrap party tonight after all.'

He sighs. 'You didn't want to go. Did Vince reel you in?'

No, I saw an email that changed everything, turned the world upside down, sparked a revolution. 'Something like that. You know how it is.'

'You can say no, you know.'

That was always the trouble. I never could. 'What will you do for dinner?'

'I'll rustle something up.'

'Takeaway?'

'How dare you? Yes. Enjoy your carrot sticks.'

I lie back on the grass with shortbread crumbs on my lips, staring at the sky; an abiding, deepening sapphire, fringed with horse chestnut branches that stretch out across my vision in their network of ever-narrowing boughs. There are the sounds of summer – children shouting; aeroplanes overhead, filling the skies again; a mower in the distance, rumbling away, seagulls crying as they soar over the gorge. I close my eyes and just listen, my senses tapering like the tree, until it's just the music of city life, weaving together in a gentle counterpoint to carry me through this moment of repose.

'Excuse me. I said, excuse me.'

Opening one eye, I realize there's a woman leaning over me. Since I'm looking up into the sun, her features are indistinct, but when I raise myself onto my elbows, I see she's tall and lean, sporting leisurewear and carrying a rolled-up foam mat. Her thick blonde hair is piled into a careless topknot and everything about her screams 'natural beauty'.

I squint, with one hand shading my face. 'Yes?'

'Would you mind moving? This is our area.' Smiling, she gestures to the patch of grass I'm lying on.

'Whose area?'

'Christchurch Yoga Group. We're here every week.' She points to a group of women standing behind her, also with mats, all staring at me like I've just defecated on one of the park benches. A couple nearby who were lounging on a blanket hastily get to their feet, bundling it up and hurrying away, ushered by another woman who's wearing a tank top that says 'BELIEVE, ACHIEVE'.

'Oh, do you book the space?'

Blondie laughs as if I've just said something hilarious.

'Bless you! There's no booking system, as such, but we're always here and it's become our special place. You're welcome to join us, if you'd like. If you think you could keep up?' She tilts her head, eyeing my thighs sympathetically.

'No, thank you, I'll just sit here with my rabbit.'

'Well, you can't really sit here while we do the class?' She says it like she's coochy-cooing a child.

I lie back, arranging Bigwig in the crook of my arm. 'Don't mind me, I won't get in your way.' Closing my eyes again, I try to tune back into the buzz – the laughter, the planes, the seagulls, the mower melody.

'Ahem.' Blondie is clearing her throat and, when I sit up, she's put down her mat and folded her arms. I take it that's not a yoga pose, more a declaration of intent. Bless her, she has no idea. 'I'm afraid you *are* in our way. You can't stay there while we're doing the class.'

'Why not?'

'Because it's our space.' The other women – five of them – have now flanked her, all of them adopting combative stances in their leggings.

'It's a public amenity, open to everyone. I was here first, but I'm willing to share. You go ahead.'

Blondie is now wearing the fixed, stunned expression of a medieval queen who's been spat at by a serf. 'You don't understand,' she says. 'We're here every week.'

I shrug. 'And I'm here today.' Today is my day, and no Nimby Namaste is going to shift me.

There are scandalized mutterings from the henchwomen

as Blondie bends towards me, smiling broadly. Up close, it's obvious that her lustrous lashes are false.

'Let me make myself clear,' she murmurs. 'You are going to pick up that monstrous sack of yours, and that *creature*, and you are going to take yourself off somewhere else, far away, and leave us to our important business.'

I laugh, loudly, provoking a collective gasp from the coven.

'Important business?' I chortle. 'Would you classify your downward dogs as crucial to a functioning society? If you miss a sun salutation, will Surya smite you? Give me a break. Why don't you and your harem take yourselves off somewhere else, far away, preferably in the road, to do your posing, and leave the rest of us to enjoy this egalitarian municipal space?'

Blondie rears up, staring down, pert breasts inflating. I think they're false too. 'You're making a very big mistake. I'm warning you.'

'Oh, bore off, Bendy.'

'How dare you!' Blondie now has two burning spots on her cheeks, the hands gripping her hips white with rage. 'I am *well-known* to the park wardens here. One word from me and they will issue you with a public order offence. And that . . . that *beast* should be on a lead.'

I cackle. 'If this beast should be on a lead, then your hellcats should be tethered as well.'

'Aeeeergh!' A scream of fury and frustration spews forth. Poor Blondie, I don't think she's ever been crossed, or crosser. But it seems I've tipped her over the edge, because she suddenly leans down, plucks Bigwig from my arms and . . . *throws* him into a nearby bin. Her acolytes gasp, either in shock or admiration, and she pants, torn between triumph and consternation. Unused to being challenged, she knows she has Gone Too Far.

'What the fuck?' I am *livid*. Snatching up my bag, I rush to the bin and peer in anxiously. Bigwig is sitting on his haunches looking up at me with an injured expression, but thankfully no injury. I reach down and gather him up in my arms. During my brief absence, the she-devils have thrown down their mats and are now smugly standing on them with their hands pressed together – I will wipe those smirks off their St Tropezed faces. They will rue the day. Marching off, murmuring words of comfort into Bigwig's lop ears, I think of the sounds I was listening to earlier. The shouting children. The aeroplanes. The seagulls. The mower.

After settling the rabbit back in his bag, I find Blondie's good friend the park warden riding his vehicle a few metres away, his face set in concentration. Raising my arm, I wave him over and he stops the mower, pulling off his headphones.

'Ere?'

'I'm so sorry to trouble you.' I sharpen my diction, a precise RP to denote a respectable, upstanding member of the community. 'But there's a gentleman in the bushes over there' – I point in the opposite direction – 'who is filming young female joggers. I thought you should know.'

'Bleedin' 'ell, that wrong 'un again!' He leaps off. 'Wherezit to?'

I point again, far away, and he lumbers off, leaving me with the machine. After circling it, I climb on, slightly gingerly, because I've never ridden one of these things before. But how hard can it be? He's left the key in the ignition, so I turn it, and grind my teeth in frustration when precisely nothing happens. He was just using it a second ago, why won't it work for me?

I'm not giving up though. Fishing out my phone, I find a ninety-second YouTube video titled 'How to Ride Your Lawnmower' and watch it. Apparently, you have to press the clutch down – there it is – and make sure the mower is in neutral – done. I turn the key again and the vehicle roars to life. Whoopee. With my skirt rucked up to my knees, it feels quite powerful between my thighs – if it were a motorbike, I'd rev the engine, but that's not an option, so I simply gun for my previous position, taking great pleasure in the immaculate trail of freshly mown lawn streaming out behind me. I could use this machine for my own overgrown front garden, not to mention our field out back. Maybe Robbie would buy me one, a little weekend runabout. Cars might be beyond me, but mowers are more manageable.

My picnic spot is now occupied by a handy line of zoned-out yogis. Deep in their lotus positions, they don't see me coming, but they do hear me. One by one, heads turn, mouths open, and then it's a mad scramble of legginged legs as they fight to get out of my way.

'SHIFT YOUR SKINNY ARSES, MOTHERFUCKERS!'
Cruising through the yoga mats on my reaper, there's instantly a rubber snowstorm, causing more screams and shrieks as the finest Lululemon runners are ripped to shreds. The grinding sound as blade meets elastomer, and the subsequent flurries, are deeply gratifying, as are the yelps of distress from the Christchurch Yoga Group as they struggle to save themselves. Don't fuck with the buck, ladies, if you want your posing rugs intact. Sadly, the mower only makes it to the last one before spluttering and dying, after a surfeit of foam. The owner of the untouched mat is cowering in a forward bend, and I feel a pinch of pity because it's not her fault she was dominated by the Blondie Lilith, who is currently on all fours, crawling through the detritus, howling like a jackal.

Sitting there, surveying my destruction, there's a split second where I think *'What am I doing?'* Riding roughshod like this, making women flinch and scream, lying to nice people who don't know any better, stealing, taking advantage, wreaking havoc, pleasing myself in the most high-handed, heedless way. But I feel like everyone has a quota of this kind of behaviour, and I never used mine up, never even went to the vault where the vial was stored. So I'm going to give myself this moment to crow like a seagull over Blondie's lithe, writhing body, and imagine her later, teeth chattering over a wheatgrass shot as she recounts the story, casting me as the mat-ricidal villain. And I'm going to allow myself to not give a rat's ass. Everything happens for a reason; there's a good one for this.

I climb off the mower, and check that Bigwig is safe in his sack. Noticing my new artwork burrowed alongside him, I pull it out and brandish it at Blondie, giving her the golden finger she deserves.

'Screw you, Bikram bitch!'

And then I march off, towards the pub, because I'm meeting Maz for a pre-dinner drink and now I'm late.

# 30

How did I get that all-important promotion, propelled to the lofty position of assistant producer on *Songs of Praise*? Jobs in telly are like the horse chestnut tree. You start on the tiniest twigs on the outermost branches, and gradually work your way inwards and up, leaping from bough to bough. Ideally you want to find bigger, firmer branches that will bear your weight safely, with the ideal destination the solid trunk. In this particular metaphor, that would represent the dizzy heights of a permanent staff position, rather than the shaky, perilous life of a freelancer. Obviously, you want to be fairly high up the tree so you can have a good view, and throw conkers at people nearer the ground. I'm one of the core team at Red Eye now, meaning I get definite indefinite employment, plus numerous other company benefits like private health cover and childcare vouchers. In addition to my Avon House membership (now sadly revoked), Vince also offers key employees more unorthodox perks like cosmetic dentistry, hypnotherapy and, for reasons I've never understood, guitar lessons. I'm yet to take him up on those things, but it's nice to know they're there. However, it's been quite a climb to reach my current branch.

I started out as a junior researcher, but within a few leaps was elevated to a researcher position. I then remained stuck on that branch for ages, even though several of my contemporaries were easing their way up. There was one guy – a mouthy public-school type – who leapfrogged straight from intern to assistant producer through a mix of hustling, entitlement and bare-faced lies. When I joined Beatnik Media, I timidly asked when I might expect to move up to AP level and was told I didn't have enough credits, but I knew the only credits that really counted were in my head. If I'd been prepared to bulldoze, then I might have got somewhere, but as it was, I was just clinging to my twig while others scampered over me.

Of course, there were other ways to get on. You could get taken under the wing of a great senior producer, who would show you the ropes, and drag you up with them. A mentor. Given that I seemed unable to help myself, it wasn't unreasonable to hope that someone else might help me. Some ambitious player might spot my potential and groom me to be their second-in-command, their apprentice, their protégée. When I worked for Other Delia, she had a producer called Yufei who she always hired – they had an easy familiarity that I envied, born of numerous productions where they'd relied on each other, propped each other up, drowned their sorrows together when it went wrong, toasted each other when it all came together. When Delia eventually became a commissioner at the BBC, she got Yufei on her team and they continued the working partnership. You might call it nepotism, I suppose, but isn't that how the world works? I thought that was how the world worked. I thought I knew, at the grand old age of twenty-six. So I got my head down and slogged away, dreaming of getting a leg up like that.

And in the end, I suppose that's exactly what happened.

*　*　*

Maz is already in the pub when I arrive, sitting at a table in the corner with a bottle of wine that she's already halfway down. Rosé for the upcoming encounter with Rose. I've never seen my sister drunk, or even tipsy, because that's not how she reacts to alcohol. It's more like a dimmer switch that slides her into a faerie dimension. That's how she copes with our mother, who very much exists in the Real World, where you Get On With Things, and Show Some Backbone. Maz is thinner than me, because she's not so interested in food, and she's dealt with the crap hair issue by cutting it all off in an elfin Mia Farrow style that works quite well with her face, which has a permanently faraway expression, like Holly Golightly singing 'Moon River'.

She raises her glass when she sees me. 'Don't think . . .'

'Just drink,' I reply, pouring myself a generous quarter-litre. If I'm going to have dinner with Rose, then I want to be safe with Maz in Cloudland.

'Is that a rabbit?' Maz reaches out to stroke Bigwig's head, which is poking out of my bag. 'How nice.'

'Hmm. How are the girls?'

'Dorcas just had mites, poor love, but some Frontline did the trick. People keep trying to feed them things, even though I've put signs everywhere. Tilly bit a child, but it was the child's fault, as I explained to the mother, and I think she understood. Alpacas don't really like people.' She sips serenely. 'How are the Hendrys?'

'Robbie's working too hard, as usual. Ethan's not, as usual. Hazel is now an eco-warrior.'

'Isn't it a bit late for that?' Maz is affably but irrevocably convinced we're all doomed, and there's no point in bothering to do anything about it. She says humanity doesn't matter, and that without us the planet will be fine.

'Maybe, but she might get a boyfriend out of it.'

'How nice.'

'So why does Rose want to see us?' May as well cut to the chase before Maz zones out entirely.

'I think she's having some sort of crisis.'

'Why?'

'Why is she having a crisis or why do I think that?'

'Both.'

'She came on an alpaca walk.'

'Jesus.'

Maz nods, a faint smile on her face, which counts as animated. 'She booked herself in online, like a regular customer.'

229

'When?'

'Last week. And when she turned up, she pretended not to know me, just took Mabel's reins and went off.'

'So what did you do?'

She shrugs. 'Pretended not to know her too. I think we'll get on much better that way.'

I take a slug of my wine, ruminating. 'So, what's the crisis?'

'Mabel wouldn't say.'

I ponder. Last time I saw Rose was when she summoned me to Stroud to help her move some garden furniture, and she spent the afternoon complaining bitterly that her next-door neighbours were getting a hot tub installed. It was the beginning of the end, apparently – next it would be pampas grass and keys in a bowl. Then she told me I was thickening around the waist and I'd best start 'reducing' or Robbie would get a wandering eye. When I look back now, I really don't understand why I didn't just piss on her pristine patio, but of course that was Old Clover, who dutifully shifted her mother's new Laurel outdoor dining set, arranged the bunch of flowers she'd bought without getting a word of thanks, and caught the train back via Swindon in time to make the kids' tea.

'Maybe she's met someone.' I'm thinking about the hot tub, how there seemed to be a degree of pique in Rose's voice when she talked about swingers. Our mother has a number of what she calls 'gentlemen friends', but they seem to exist only to give her lifts into town and squire her to

local events. Then there's the owner of the Redcliffe flat . . .
The idea of my mother as a sexual being makes me want to
heave but I force myself to consider it. Her merry widow
act might have palled; oh God, what if she's getting married
and intends to have an actual wedding? Rose would *love*
that . . . She'd have me and Maz trussed up as middle-aged
bridesmaids, with herself in virginal white . . . I reach for
the bottle of wine and drink straight from it. New Clover
will be able to sort this out, even if she personally has to
firebomb all the bridal shops in the Cotswolds. I will not
walk down the aisle behind my mother.

'What did you conclude?' Maz points at the now empty
bottle.

'She's getting married.'

'How nice.' Maz drinks steadily, draining her glass. 'She
can put right all the wrongs from your wedding.'

'At least she won't have to invite Cousin Jack.'

'She'll do it at Christmas, so she can spray everything
with fake snow.'

'She'll book King's College Choir to sing.'

'At Westminster Abbey.'

'Princess Anne will be her maid of honour.'

'Jacob Rees-Mogg will give her away.'

'For a substantial fee.'

'How nice.'

By this point we're laughing, wheezing, gripping the
stems of our glasses, our noses near the table. I briefly
begin to cry, because I've got a big evening ahead, but soon

pull myself together. Maz doesn't say anything about it, but squeezes my hand and stands, picking up her bag.

'Shall we go on an alpaca walk?'

I blink back tears, confused. 'I don't think we've got time to nip to Crediton.'

She smiles her slow, sea-cow smile. 'Sometimes you don't need a real one. The imaginary ones are actually better behaved.'

So, outside the pub, we each take a rein, and walk towards the restaurant with our animals. Maz says she always names her pretend-alpaca Geraldine, 'after the goat in *The Good Life*,' so I name mine Barbara. We agree Barbara has good energy, unlike Geraldine who has pugnacious tendencies and seems inclined to veer left. But both of them give us comfort, as we stroll through the quaint streets of Clifton admiring the Brighton-coloured cottages, festooned with fluttering Jubilee bunting. It all has a seaside holiday feel, as if everyone – not just me – is taking the day off. Looking towards the Mendip Hills, we spot a hot air balloon that punctuates the deep blue sky like a full stop. It's in the shape of a giant koala head, with two round ears poking out and a piece of eucalyptus emerging from its mouth. I feel glad to be surrounded by these gentle beasts – Barbara Good, Bigwig, and the floating marsupial – as we prepare to confront a more dangerous one. When the kids were younger, Robbie and I used to take them to Bristol's annual balloon fiesta, watch the great gasbags inflate and lift off, holding hands and staring open-mouthed at the multi-coloured vista above. I feel sad that they don't want to do it any more, don't want to hang out with us. Maybe Hazel will let me go on marches with her, and Ethan will let me . . . sit in his room. I rub Barbara's head affectionately and she butts me for treats.

I now have not one but two support animals to sustain me through the difficult night ahead. Part of me is dreading it, but another part is rubbing her hands. It's time to get on, lay the ghost. It's time to shake that tree, and see what falls.

# 31

'Do you believe in God?'

The producer of *Songs of Praise* asked the question like any other in an interview, in the same way she asked how I got into television, and where did I see myself in five years' time. In any other job, it would be irrelevant and maybe even inappropriate, but I guess for this one it was OK.

'Um, I'm sort of ambiguous. Agnostic? But I do believe in fate.'

Oh, I believed in fate. In karma, kismet, destiny. But not in a serendipitous way. I believed in a universe that required a strict balance of goodness versus evil, of happiness versus misery. If you had too much of one, you were due a dose of the other. In my case, it was best to be as good as possible, and avoid too much joy, lest it provoked a corresponding hit of hardship. However, at that point in my life, I felt I was in line for a windfall, which was why I was there. I was daring to take a step, even if it meant treading on a butterfly.

'Well, of course it doesn't matter either way. An openness to the possibility is helpful though.' The producer pointed upwards, presumably to indicate God's potential presence.

I embraced that openness, simply because I would never presume to deny His existence, as it would have felt like far too much of an affront, a taunt or provocation that invited a thunderbolt from above. I didn't want to get into any fights, even with a potentially non-existent supreme being. As far as God was concerned, I was Switzerland.

'And why do you want to work on *Songs of Praise*?'

Because I wanted to get drunk with Susie on location – not the kind of drunk where I tearfully confessed what happened in my last job and sobbed harder when I saw her look of horror, but the kind of drunk where we hiccupped hysterically and tottered back to our hotel, our arms around each other to keep ourselves upright. I wanted to hear choirs sing and revel in the righteous boom of their voices, and wander round churches, letting their sacred majesty seep into me and purify me, and I wanted to make a new start working in a different kind of television where I could leave the ghosts and ghouls behind. Because I wanted to be an assistant producer, without needing anyone to elevate me to that level. Because I really, really wanted to leave Beatnik. I wasn't sure I believed in God, but I was sure that all those things could make me better, tip the balance back towards happiness.

'I've always admired the show, and think that you're doing really interesting things with the format.'

With key points written on my palm to prompt me, I proceeded to outline all the excellent ways they were bringing religion to the masses. I sang the praises of *Songs of Praise* and, like with David Lyon-James twenty years later, had its producer eating out of my hand – literally, in this case.

'Now, to the issue of references . . . You've given Martin Haggard as a contact at Beatnik Media, but is there anyone else there you would like us to speak to?'

There was no need for my notes at this point. I looked her in the eye and said 'No, thank you, Martin is fine.' My links at Beatnik had to be reduced to one slender, brittle branch which could be broken off once I'd scampered across it. No one else there would speak for me.

Outside the producer's office, I walked past Susie's desk and she winked at me and made a call sign. Later, I got two calls – one from her and one from the producer, telling me I'd got the job. The sigh of relief I gave went straight up to the heavens.

\* \* \*

I've always had nightmares, ever since I was little. After the Ross-on-Wye wasps' nest incident, I used to dream there were insects in my bed, crawling all over me, tangled in my hair, a spider dangling just above my face. The visions were so vivid, so real, that I would get out of bed in my sleep, brushing off the bugs, slapping my pillow, pulling off the duvet to check. Even after I woke up properly, I couldn't convince myself that they weren't there, that it was all just a figment of my imagination. Sometimes I would sleep on the floor, because the bed felt contaminated – whenever

Rose found me there in the morning, she would exclaim 'Goodness me, *again*? We'll have to get this baby a bed guard.' And then she'd yank the comb viciously through my birds' nest hair until I was made neat to match the house.

During my teens, there was a recurring dream about forgetting my lines in a play. Or rather, not having any lines to begin with. I'm standing in the wings, and no one has shown me the script but everyone's waiting and I just have to get out there. Once I've stumbled on stage, I realize pages of the script are lying around, behind a sofa, under a table, taped to a grandfather clock, and I have to make my way there, find my line, learn it, say it at the right time before anyone realizes what a mess I'm in. Can I rescue the production? Or will the audience see through me? I always used to wake, panting and drenched in sweat at the precise moment the pages ran out, when I was left high and dry, my panic at a pitch. When in real life I was asked to audition for the school production of *Blithe Spirit*, I couldn't face it, because I was sure the dream would come true. When I told Rose, she laughed and said 'Oh, I don't think so! No one would be able to hear your mousy little voice!' So that was that.

And then the window dream, which started when I was twenty-six. Someone trying to get in, and I haven't closed them all, haven't left things secure as they ought to be. I'm running round, starting at the top of the house, working my way down, slamming everything shut, worrying that

I'm too late, he's already in – but rather than look for him, I want to know which window was open, which one was it? Which was the nail that led to my lost kingdom? I must close it, must finish the job, get it done, make everything right and tight. So rather than escape from him, get away, I just go round with my checklist . . .

I don't have the dream so often nowadays. My brain is probably gearing up to give me a fresh and juicy nightmare scenario. But I did have it a few times during lockdown. You'd think that being away from the office might calm me down, give me the space I craved, but it didn't. In fact, it blurred the boundaries between work and home, made me feel like I couldn't escape. My home was always my refuge, a switch-off, but now it was my office too – a window had been opened, and all these jobs and worries and obligations had filtered in, overwhelming me. So I started having the dream again, thrashing around in bed until Robbie's arms around me woke and soothed me.

'Shhh,' he said. 'It's going to be OK.'

'It's my fault,' I panted. 'It's my fault.'

He stroked my hair. 'Not everything is your fault, Clover. Sometimes it's just theirs.'

'No.' I found that hard to believe.

'It's going to be OK,' he said again, his hands warm and secure.

But I knew it wouldn't be, until I closed the window.

# EVENING

# 32

The Brycgstow turns out to be a pub with ideas above its station. Maz says she was perching at an island in one of the IKEA showroom kitchens, and heard a couple talking about 'Bristol's hottest new riverside inn', saying the cocktails were deadly and it had an 'ambience'. When we arrive, we stand by a lectern for five minutes being ignored by numerous bustling staff who all look like busy fools. It's a big, airy space, with heavy oak tables, a flagstone floor and pictures of ye olde Bristol on the walls, so I go over to have a gander while we're waiting. One of them is a sepia photo of a Victorian woman alongside a cutting from an 1885 newspaper. She was a barmaid called Sarah Ann Henley, famous for throwing herself off Clifton suspension bridge:

## SKIRTING CERTAIN DEATH…

Her daring leap was the result of a lovers' quarrel. The lady's young man, a porter on the Great Western Railway, determined to break off their engagement, writing a letter to the young woman announcing his intention. She, the jilted lover, filled with despair, rushed to end her life by a fearful drop from the Suspension Bridge.

Thankfully for Sarah Ann, she was saved by her crinoline skirt – a billowing effect caused by an updraught of air turned it into a sort of parachute, slowing her fall, so rather than plunging to her death, she landed in the muddy banks of the river and was rescued by passers-by. Despite her injuries, a taxi driver refused to take her to hospital in case she dirtied his cab, so they got a stretcher from the police station instead. As she recovered in hospital, news of her misfortune spread, and she received several proposals of marriage. It's one way to find a man, but not one I'd recommend.

The next photo is from 1896, of two children surrounded by policemen. The girls are Ruby and Elsie Brown, who were thrown from the suspension bridge by their father, and rescued by a passing boatman. Their murderous papa, Charles Albert Brown, had money problems, and was deemed insane at trial, but by 1901, he'd been released from prison and was back at home with his wife and daughters. I suppose whatever else she's done, at least Rose hasn't tried to throw us off a bridge.

These tales of attempted suicide and murder are interesting design choices for this establishment, which clearly sees itself as a cut above your average boozer. I wonder what Sarah, Ruby and Elsie would make of their photos on display in a gastropub near what was supposed to be their final resting place. Still, they're not around to object, and it certainly lends an 'ambience'.

None of the staff have approached us yet, and eventually I have to get their attention.

'WHAT FALSE NAME DID YOU GIVE, MARINA?' I address Maz, who is reading the bookings list on the lectern. She looks up, puzzled, but the passing maître d' hears me and is with us in an instant.

'Can I help you ladies?' he purrs, eyeing my sister like she's a mouth-watering freshly cooked lobster.

'We have a booking in the name of . . . um, what did you go for in the end?' I ask Maz, who reluctantly rejoins Planet Earth.

'Ashton,' she says, in her habitually vague way, as if she's just made it up.

The maître d' scours the list. 'Ah yes, Ashton, party of three!' He beams. 'Come this way.'

'Who does he think we are?' Maz murmurs, as he leads us to a prominent table in the centre of the room.

'He thinks *you* are a famous restaurant critic,' I mutter. 'It would be helpful if you could pretend to be Scottish.'

'Och, aye.'

He settles us at our table, whipping off napkins and arranging them tenderly in our laps. As he does mine, he catches sight of Bigwig's whiskers emerging from my bag, and his face falls.

'Er . . . is that an animal, madam?'

I touch my rabbit lightly on the nose. 'Yes, it is. Sorry, should we have booked a table for four?'

He laughs like a drain, anxiously. 'Um, it's just that . . . we don't usually allow pets in the restaurant. For reasons of hygiene.'

'He's a very clean rabbit.'

'Nevertheless . . .' The maître d' is in a quandary. He doesn't want to upset the renowned food journalist who's gracing his premises, but on the other hand . . .

Maz rescues us. 'Have you got a place he could stay while we're eating? Maybe a back room somewhere?'

Her accent is all off – Edinburgh rather than Glasgow – but the management is visibly relieved at her suggestion.

'Why, of course, please follow me.' He bows, gesturing, and picking up my bag, I follow him to the back of the restaurant, through double doors, where he shows me down a corridor to what looks like a staffroom.

'Is tonight a special occasion?' he asks, as I nestle Bigwig in an empty cardboard box in the corner. His fishing is so obvious he may as well have a rod and bait.

'Oh, no, just work,' I reply cheerfully, and then catch myself ostentatiously. 'I mean . . . *not* work. My . . . er, *sister* and I are just catching up. With our . . . elderly grandmother. Who sadly has dementia.'

'My sympathies. We at The Brycgstow will endeavour to ensure you have a relaxing and enjoyable evening.' He bows again, and leads me out.

'Just nipping to the ladies' room,' I say, seeing a sign ahead.

'Please . . .' He escorts me there, holding open the door. His deference is starting to get on my nerves – hopefully he's not going to offer to take me into the toilet and help me powder my nose. I may be the sister of an undercover restaurant critic, but I just want to be left alone to do a wee in peace.

'I'll be fine,' I say, dismissing him. With another kowtow he allows the door to close, while I retreat to a cubicle to empty my bladder and rest my forehead against the cool of the crackle glazed wall tiles. Once again, one of the rare moments of quietude I get is in a water closet. At least this one is a little more well-appointed than the Cabot Circus thunderbox. According to the walls, no one's been here at all.

I think of Sarah Ann, pulling pints in an 1880s equivalent of this gastropub before rushing off to parachute into a mudbank because of a lovers' tiff. Such a ridiculous, tragic tale. Tragedies can be reduced like that, summed up by a pithy *Sun* pun when the true story is much darker and thornier and longer. In telly we're taught not to take anything seriously – you can't, or else you'd go mad – and eventually I trained myself to make everything punchy and funny, to keep a commissioner's interest – their attention spans make goldfish look focused. But I think of the lovelorn pint-puller, flailing round in her caked crinoline, and suddenly I want to cry again, like I did in the bar with

Maz earlier. Only I think if I started now, I'd never stop, just go on and on until I drowned in my own tears. Sarah's story deserves to be told properly, with all the details of the wrongs done to her. But I've only got my own, and it isn't finished yet. So I blow my nose on toilet paper, and go out to stare at myself as I wash my hands.

My hair is still pleasingly curly and dishevelled – the ringlets haven't really dropped, bouncing around my head as I shake tap water off my fingers. The dress is excellent – swishy and flowing – and my expression in the mirror is surprisingly tranquil, considering the turmoil behind it. All in all, I look great, and while looks aren't everything, they're certainly a start. Blowing my reflection a kiss, I pick up Barbara Good's reins and lead her back into the restaurant, to await the arrival of Rose, my elderly grandmother with dementia.

# 33

We moved out west a decade ago, for many reasons, but the main one was Susie. Robbie was keen to find his Englishman's castle – some dilapidated old hovel he could turn into an elegant country home. We were both sick of the big smoke – the commutes, the cramped housing, the endless grey backdrop and squeezed skyline. We'd moved to a house in Wood Green by that point, because when the twins came along the flat in Essex Road became too small. Robbie had been enthusiastic about having a new project, and intended to do the work himself, but when he ripped up the swirly eighties carpets there was just concrete underneath; no Victorian tiles, no original floorboards. For all its a hundred and fifty years, the terraced house we'd bought was just a bland, blank slate with nothing behind it – if I'd taken an EMF meter there, it wouldn't have flickered. The garden was more of a yard, with none of the charm described in the estate agent's brochure, and the windows were cheap PVC. Basically, we'd been sold a dud, and had only ourselves to blame. So we pointed the finger at London instead.

# Lucky Day

Robbie started looking for legal firms outside the capital and was offered two jobs: one in Bristol and another in Manchester. I preferred Manchester as it was further from my mother and I had tentative plans to apply for a position at the BBC's new base in Salford. But then Susie stepped in. She'd moved to a village near Swindon when she joined SOjourn, handy for travelling between London, Somerset and the Cotswolds, where a lot of their homes are based. It was Susie who found Robbie's hovel of dreams. Driving through the rural market town of Keynsham, just outside Bristol, she spotted a 'For Sale' sign and stopped for a look. Susie had spent enough evenings at ours, listening to my husband enthuse about getting his hands dirty, about a garden that was more of a field, about a higgledy-piggledy place with timber beams and a proper history, to know it when she saw it.

Stepping out of the car to view the wonky red-bricked farmhouse fringed with lapped flint, she noted that the lintel above the door had the year 1680 carved into it. The owner was an old lady in her eighties called Dorothy Fletcher who'd lived there for fifty years without doing a thing to it apart from planting a now-huge cedar in the garden, ready for Robbie's swing. She was moving to a new luxury retirement village, wanted a quick sale and was pleased to accept our asking-price offer. Our featureless box sold like a hot cake because it was near an Outstanding secondary school and our buyers could overlook the home's lack of character in favour of a local super-head who got results. Everyone was a winner.

Robbie got stuck in straight away, started stripping wallpaper the day we moved in. Unlike the houses featured in *Bump in the Night*, our new-old home kept offering up delights – a drawing of a cat scratched into the glass of a lattice window, with the words 'a catte'; beams with apotropaic markings to ward off evil; an original brick floor in the kitchen underneath the threadbare rug that Dorothy left. I went to visit her once, in her beautifully converted apartment, taking some flowers and a tin of homemade biscuits. I worried she might be sentimental about us moving into her family home, but it wasn't the case. 'Terrible old place!' she chortled, scoffing my shortbread. 'Draughty and uneven. I've got central heating here and the doors all close properly.'

But my husband was in his element in our draughty and uneven house, paring back, restoring, finding new wonders every day. He became obsessed with the provenance of the property and would spend hours searching online, or going off to visit libraries. He discovered that it was used as a meeting house, which pleased him greatly, because he has Quakerish tendencies himself. Apart from buying Orla Kiely curtains to keep out icy blasts, I didn't contribute much to the renovation, being otherwise occupied by five-year-old twins, who considered our Restoration wreck to be a great opportunity to do themselves harm. They were keen to break their necks falling down the winding wooden staircase, desperate to trip over on the irregular stone flooring, eager to impale themselves on seventeenth-century nails. When Robbie found a well in the garden, I resigned myself to them perishing in it, but thankfully he agreed to close it off. It's still out there somewhere, lurking underground like the dripping tunnels at the Ecclestone bloodbath vicarage.

For three months after we moved in, I fulfilled my long-held dream of taking a sabbatical from work – a prospect as delightful as the window cat-etching. For years, ever since I left university, I had been dying not to work. To step off the relentless nine-to-five treadmill and simply drift around, *being*. I imagined that was what I would do on maternity leave, but I didn't realize I would have twin babies and therefore be a twenty-four-hour slave. Having quit my job at the BBC in West London, I was now ready to stagnate like the ancient well.

Of course, my lovely leave didn't turn out the way I planned. We couldn't get the twins into the nearest primary school, which was a five-minute walk away, and instead they got into a school which required a forty-minute bus trip. Because I was off work, it became my job to ferry them back and forth. By the time I got home after dropping them off, had a cup of tea and tidied up, it was nearly time to set off again. The school day is *short* – frustratingly, agonizingly short, like a commissioner's attention span. And because I mentioned to one of the mums at the new school that I was on a career break, she immediately suckered me into all sorts of Parents' Association roles and charitable activities. I found myself bursar for the fundraising committee, the

*Friends of Rainbow Wood* magazine editor, and a regular caterer for the endless bake sales. It was a nightmare, but since I was unable to say no, they just kept loading me with more and more responsibilities. After six weeks of this, I'd drop the kids off and immediately phone the school down the road to see if two places had opened up, before starting all my extra-curricular chores. Eventually the twins got in, and I was able to regretfully resign from all my Rainbow Wood roles. There was a moment when the chairwoman of the FoRW looked like she was about to insist that I stayed on, with my kids in another school, and I knew that if she did, I would end up saying yes, because I can't say no. I can never say no, that's my problem. So I told her I'd just had an unfortunate diagnosis and would have a lot of appointments to get to over the next few months. For weeks afterwards, I always went into town with a scarf around my head, just in case. I considered shaving my hair off, just to avoid having to make another fucking no-nuts cake.

Anyway, the twins got into the school which was five minutes away and then the end of my gardening leave was looming and it was time to get another job before we ran out of money. It turned out there were lots of telly jobs in Bristol, and I took one that would allow me to be home in time for tea. There I was, back at the grindstone.

But in another way, I thought maybe things had changed. Although it was Robbie who wanted the space and the past, I benefitted from it, breathing easier in our field of a garden, while the house's rich history seemed to erase my own. Out here, I was a new person, turning over a new leaf. From now on, I would be more assertive, learn to say no, start standing up for myself.

I didn't, of course.

When Rose finally blessed our new home with her presence, she took one look round the dimly lit rooms with their low ceilings and small windows and said 'Goodness, what a dingy old place! I can't imagine why anyone would want to live here.' I said the kitchen was a little brighter, and suggested we go there for a cup of tea, served in our best china, reserved for visiting dignitaries.

When my new boss told me they didn't have the budget for a casting producer, and asked if I could share those duties with my assistant producer, just for a few weeks of pre-production, I didn't complain, just knuckled down and did the work. After the show was delivered, they didn't renew my contract, because the channel said the casting was patchy. I got a short-term contract with a different production company, accepting a pay cut because they were dubious about my last post being so brief. When I finally landed the job at Red Eye, a role I was fully qualified for, I felt absurdly grateful, and never negotiated as hard as I should have.

When the twins' new primary school asked me to film and edit their nativity play, then moaned because I only used two camera angles, I apologized and promised that the following year I would bring a proper camera operator in to help. The school graciously accepted, and since then I've filmed every one of their Christmas shows, even though my kids left five years ago.

It's not easy making a fuss. Standing up for yourself can be awkward and embarrassing. Causing a scene is mortifying. Saying no is hard.

But I think, finally, I might be getting the hang of it.

# 34

Rose is late, of course, because she likes making an entrance. It wouldn't do for her to sit at a table on her own looking like a Billy No-Mates – someone might see her and imagine she was dining solo, which in her book is akin to declaring herself a high-class hooker, *inviting* an approach. While we wait, Maz and I try the deadly cocktails, which are all named after sexual positions. I order a Butter Churner, and my sister goes for a Three-Legged Dog. When they turn up, both are served in big jam jars, which makes me think of the trip to Ross-on-Wye when Maz fell in the river. I shiver, and we each take a massive slug.

'Bluergh.' Maz winces. 'Tastes like alcoholic pond water.'

'At least it's alcoholic.' Mine tastes of liquorice and liquor. I can't detect any butter, but it does make my stomach churn.

The maître d', who by now has introduced himself as Alan, sidles over and presents us with some nibbles. Spiced cashews, arranged on half a broken bowl. I run my finger along the jagged edge, wondering what possessed them to serve nuts like that. My sister the restaurant critic is going to have something to say about it.

'How nice,' says Maz, staring in fascination at the shard of china.

I shovel in a handful, suddenly starving after all the booze and bizarreness. Their saltiness clashes with the sweetness of the cocktail, not unpleasantly, and for a while I just sit, watching the other diners, digging nutty nuggets out of the grooves of my teeth with my tongue. I'm starting to feel enjoyably buzzy, tuning in to the low hum of genial chat, 'Numb' by Portishead playing in the background, my sister murmuring to Geraldine as she offers her a lick of her dusty fingers.

I remember Christmases before Dad left, walnuts left out on the sideboard with a nutcracker, and he would sit pulverizing the shells, popping the kernels into his mouth as we watched *Jim'll Fix It*. Fragments from the husks coated his fingers and the floor, and Rose would make him lift his feet so she could hoover under them. After he went, she didn't need to hoover as much, but she did it anyway. Cousin Jack hasn't been back in a while, because of travel restrictions, he says, but we all know he's happier where he is, with his Spanish wife and soiled floors. Ours are filthy too – we have a cleaner, Lottie, who comes once a week and makes valiant efforts, but for some reason they keep returning to their natural state: seventeenth-century brick layered in cat hairs and cereal crumbs. Does that mean I've broken the cycle?

'What on earth *is* this place?'

Rose stands before us, resplendent in her Phase Eight finery, highlighted hair in a chignon, ladylike heels, French manicure because coloured nails are common. She won't sit because she's a) waiting to be tenderly helped into her chair and b) before that, she must be complimented on her appearance. She does look good for seventy-three, in a kind of Stephanie Beacham way – perhaps with a dash of Sybil Fawlty. I take a deep breath, because I'm about to throw us all off a bridge. I don't feel good about it, but it has to be done.

'Ravishing as ever, Rose. A face that could start a Trojan War.'

Obviously, it's not how I would normally address my mother, but then, nothing about today is normal. My opening parry produces a raised eyebrow from her, designed to cow me into submission, but this time there will be no capitulation, no appeasement. Rose is about to meet New Clover, and it's safe to say she's not going to like her. But she didn't particularly care for Old Clover either. If Rose is Helen, then I'm about to lay siege.

She can at least sit down first, and Alan obliges, hurrying over with a level of obsequiousness that meets even my mother's requirements.

'Madam, please allow me to help you.' Behind her back, I catch his eye and grimace as if she's having a bad day. Alan rises to the occasion.

'There, there, Mrs Ashton, you get nice and comfy.

Don't worry about a thing. You're at The Brycgstow now.'
He speaks slowly, patting her on the shoulder, and Rose
frowns at his forwardness.

'Let me know if there's anything you need – anything
at all.' He backs away, bowing, and my mother waves
graciously, as if she's riding through Windsor in an open
carriage.

'What an odd chap,' she says, flicking her napkin onto
her lap. 'Who booked this table? You, Marigold? Is it a
*public house*? You do make strange choices. Still, I suppose
we'll have to make do.'

'You're looking sprightly,' I say, taking a sip of my
cocktail. 'Did you come by train?'

I know she didn't. Rose doesn't deign to travel by public
transport. Sure enough, her nose wrinkles in distaste.

'Darling Ginny drove me. Her daughter Venetia is
working down here. You remember her? Your bridesmaid?
Sweet girl, though a little unstable.'

Venetia in the cape, crying at the wasp sting. I'm briefly
distracted. 'Venetia works in Bristol?'

Another nose-pucker. 'Well, she's . . . at the Old Vic.
*Acting.*' She whispers it, as if it's a dirty word. 'Hopefully
it's just a passing phase. Ginny likes to come down, check
she's applying for proper jobs.'

In my mother's world, the only proper jobs are lawyer
and doctor. Architect at a push. Until you get married, of
course – after that it should be more of a domestic role.
Needless to say, married TV producer and unmarried

alpaca farmer are both severe disappointments, to be swept under the carpet – or ruthlessly vacuumed.

'Now, Clover, what in heaven's name have you done to your hair? Please tell me it's not permanent. I know you're paranoid about it being grey and lank, but that is *not* the answer.' She glances at Maz. 'Nor is chopping it off like a you-know-what.'

My sister takes a long drink of her Three-Legged Dog. I smile, raking a hand through my curls. 'Just spicing things up. You should try it. Your 'do is getting a little . . . out-of-date, if you don't mind my saying. How long have you had that style? Since Diana died?'

For a second, Rose's mouth is a little 'o' of surprise. Then she blinks and straightens in her seat. 'Let's get on. Is there a menu, or is it just a *blackboard*?'

I hand it to her. 'Here. Shall I read it out to you? Otherwise, you'll be squinting, won't you, and you know that makes you look tipsy.'

The 'o' is now a firm line. Rose won't rise, because that would be unladylike – what she doesn't realize is I'm only firing warning shots, just limbering up for full gun warfare.

'Can't have the management turfing us out because Mother's squiffy!' I honk merrily. 'Think of the palaver.'

'*Do* pipe down, Clover,' returns my mother. 'People will stare.'

Oh, they're going to. 'If they're staring,' I say, 'it's only because they're admiring your divine outfit. You put us all in the shade.'

Unsure, Rose decides to take this as one of the compliments she was waiting for. 'Thank you.' She preens, smoothing her delicate floral print.

'Perfect for a summer wedding,' I continue, taking a gulp. 'And very brave to go sleeveless, at your age. Not everyone could pull it off.'

'Well, *I* have always kept myself in good shape.' Rose eyes my own bingo wings. 'Still the same size I was as a girl.'

'Back in 1885,' I say, swigging. 'Did you know Sarah Ann Henley?'

'What *has* got into you? Are you . . . *drunk?*' Rose leans forward, entranced. Although she's far from teetotal, one of the things she loves to lament is when people have a few too many and cause a ruckus. There was a family Christmas party when we were small where Uncle Harold got weepy and maudlin after half a bottle of scotch, and had to be escorted out by his hissing sister, while Maz and I hid under a table sharing a bowl of Viennetta. I remember the goosebumps on her skin, from the ice cream or the scene. She started pinching herself shortly after.

I lean forwards too. 'I drank a whole bottle of tequila. I even ate the worm. And now it's turned.' Finishing my cocktail, I hold the jar aloft. Alan's arrival is reliably prompt.

'Same again, please. And Mrs Ashton would like to try the Reverse Cowgirl.'

Rose now has the air of an Arctic explorer contemplating his own gangrenous foot. When the cocktail arrives, in its jam jar, she takes it gingerly, sniffing and pulling a face.

'I do find cocktails rather vulgar.'

'The Queen Mother didn't think so. She had one every night.'

'I'm sure she had more refined receptacles.'

I can't argue with that one. We've finished the nuts, leaving the broken bowl sitting dejectedly on the table like the aftermath of a fight.

'Are you ready to order?' Alan has appeared again, nodding encouragingly at Rose, who still looks pained at her ordeal.

'I suppose . . . I'll have the fish.' It's actually cod and chips, but she can't bring herself to say it. Maz has chosen this place very well.

'Shepherd's pie, please. And a bottle of the sauvignon blanc.' I need Rose to let her guard down.

'I'll have the lasagne, thank you.' Maz hands Alan the menu and he takes it reverently, as if the paper has been blessed by her touch.

'What was that?' enquires Rose, as he retreats.

'What was what?' Maz already looks exhausted – she can only take small doses of our mother.

'That *accent*. You sound like . . . like Nicola Sturgeon.' Rose loathes her. The only Scottish person she's ever approved of was Sean Connery because he was a Sir and he made her feel coquettish.

'Do I?' Maz is pleased. 'I worried I was veering east.'

'You are,' I tell her. 'You need to rough it up a bit.'

'What? Why is she speaking that way? Like an oaf?'

'Maz identifies as Glaswegian now,' I explain.

'There is no one Scottish in our family,' declares Rose firmly.

'Dad's sister Julie married a man from Inverness.'

'No one in our family,' repeats Rose.

The wine arrives, and Alan makes a big deal out of asking Maz to taste it. He clearly finds her faint 'How nice' a bit of a letdown, but she is supposed to be undercover, so he lets it pass.

'Will, er, Mrs Ashton be partaking?' Alan asks, as he pours.

'Do you want a glass, Nanna Rose?' I ask loudly. 'Or would you prefer a lovely lemonade?'

My mother is both bewildered and irritated, but she is also a lady, and this is a public place. 'Wine will be fine, thank you.'

Our glasses full, we are a trio once more, and I raise mine. 'To the Ashtons. As we slide down the banister of life, may the splinters never point in the wrong direction.'

'Ahem.' My mother coughs delicately. 'We are not Ashtons. You are a Hendry, since the occasion of your marriage. And as your father is no longer with us, I recently decided to revert to my maiden name.'

'*Parker*?' It's hardly the Cholmondeley-Fitzwilliam of surnames; I would have thought my mother would be glad to bury it. In fact, I'm sure she once said it made her sound like a valet.

'A very old English name,' says Rose. 'It dates back to the eleventh century.'

'Just like you,' I say. 'Lady Rosie Parker of Stroud. Sounds like the first line of a limerick.'

'You're very odd today, Clover. I hope you're not coming down with something. Your immune system always was weak.'

'Just a touch of gonorrhoea,' I reply.

Rose refuses to lower herself to my level, instead focusing on her youngest daughter, who is staring at the photo of Ruby and Elsie Brown with a dazed look on her face.

'So, it's just you, Marigold. Poor Marigold, the only Ashton left.' She raises her glass. 'To Marigold! My little spinster.'

We're used to this, but I can feel my blood boiling just the same. Rose constantly harps on about Maz being single, asking what's wrong, why can't you find a man, is it because you give off vibes, you mustn't seem desperate, but don't be too standoffish, you're away with the fairies, that's why no one wants you, or is it because you smell of the farm and always wear those jodhpurs, which do nothing for your figure, Marigold, you should consider wearing a dress once in a while or people will think you're a whatsit, particularly with that hair, and why don't you wear some lipstick for goodness' sake, because if you did you could be almost attractive, in a certain light . . . Oh,

I'm *joking*, Marigold, can't you take a joke? You always were such a solemn child . . .

For a second I don't register Maz's reply, lost in the chat and music and my own internal monologue. But I feel my mother stiffen beside me, hear her intake of breath and gradually process the words, wallowing in them like a spurned barmaid on a mudbank.

'I'm not an Ashton either,' she said softly, staring at the not-dead sisters, ranged by their uniformed entourage. 'My married name is Fraser.'

# 35

It's always been Maz and me against the world. No, not against the world, just against our mother, whose presence in our lives has been a constant, malign drip-drip of platitudes and can't-put-your-finger-on-it putdowns. Never openly hostile, or overtly derogatory, just gently disparaging, dismissive, distracted by far greater concerns. Rose wasn't the sort of mother who, if you fell over and grazed yourself, would comfort you and find a plaster. No; she would let you bleed until you stopped crying and controlled yourself, because that was a lesson worth learning. Then she would ask you how it happened, and tell you what you should have done instead. And then she would say 'The first-aid tin is that way, don't make a mess.'

So, from an early age, I was mother to Maz, who was such a fragile child – the kind who would cry over a cold bee slowly dying in the autumn chill. I was the one who soothed and bathed and found a cold compress. The one who made dinner when Dad was at work, Rose had gone off to her tennis club, and Annis the babysitter was watching *Dynasty*. The one who helped Maz with her homework, packed her lunchbox, plaited her hair. The one who worried when she went out. And you might think we're closer because of it, but we're not. We're further apart, because we're both embarrassed by it.

We were supposed to be sisters, teasing each other, fighting for the upper hand, enemies and best friends, but neither of us had the chance. That dynamic disintegrated long ago, leaving us floundering in our roles. When Maz got her A levels, there was a prize-giving ceremony at our school, and I came down from university on the train to be there, because although our mother was going too, I knew how it would play out. Dad was in Spain, and Maz needed someone there who would be proud of her. Rose had no interest in her daughter's academic achievements, just wanted to wear her Sunday best and swan around. I didn't want to be there, had my own stuff to do, and Maz didn't want me there either, but someone had to say well done.

We watched her get the Sociology Prize and then met her afterwards for a drinks reception they'd laid on. My little sister stood there, in her uniform, clutching the certificate they'd given her.

'Nice one,' I said, pointing. 'Not just a pretty face.'

'Pretty?' said Rose. 'Would you say so?' And then she went to chat up the headmaster, who regularly wrote for the *Telegraph*.

Later, I took Maz to the pub for one of her first legal drinks, then left her with her friends. When I went to pick her up later, she was retching over the wall of the beer garden and had to be helped home. It was classic teenage drunkenness, except I knew what – or who – had set it off. Rose was already in bed when we got back, so it was me who held Maz's hair back as she vomited, fetched her a glass of water and waited until she went to sleep, the tears drying on her cheeks. As she drifted off, she murmured 'You should go back to Leeds.' She didn't want me to bear witness any more. First thing the next morning, I left, and we never mentioned it again.

As a grown-up, Maz didn't need as much mothering, and I'd forgotten how to be a sister by then, so we have an amiable but on-the-surface connection, confined to the odd text and visit. She's a vaguely affectionate aunt who brings the twins too-hot alpaca-wool jumpers and Daim bars, and I occasionally hang out at her rewilded smallholding and work my way through her eclectic selection of spirits. Sometimes we meet at her IKEA store and wander around the showrooms before topping up my cheap crockery collection. But we never talk about anything remotely deep or meaningful – we just got into a groove of making snarky comments about Rose, without ever properly discussing how our upbringing affected us.

A few times, mostly after I'd hit her not-so-minibar, I found myself on the point of properly asking Maz about her therapy – more than just ribbing her about BILLY storage solutions – or telling her about what happened to me, and why I think it happened. But it felt like opening

Pandora's box, or maybe a window for an intruder to come in. Once he was in, that was it. It would become real, and scary, and sad and not a joking matter.

So instead, we talked about Scandi furniture, and Mabel's dislike of foot trimming, made quips about Baby Jane, and because of that I had no idea, no idea that my sister got married and didn't tell us, didn't invite us, didn't involve us in any way. No idea she was even seeing anyone, no idea who he or she might be, my sibling-in-law, our new family member.

Whoever it is, with a name like Fraser, I really hope they're Scottish.

# 36

'*Married?*' exclaims Rose, with Lady Bracknell energy.

Maz appears to be gazing into space, but I know she's looking at Geraldine, taking comfort from her calming alpaca breath. I picture the koala balloon floating away in the sky, unleashed, looking down on all of us, lowly ants scurrying round, and practise my mindful breathing, to slow myself down. None of this matters. Some things matter, but not this. Not this. Not this.

Actually, I think this does matter. My sister got married without telling anyone, it probably should go on a list of significant issues. Why didn't she at least introduce him/ her to us? Is he unpalatable in some way? Is he a *convict?* Oh God, my sister married an inmate, it sounds like one of those one-off ITV docs; maybe Vince will want me to cast her and her heavily tattooed gangster husband, and find other relationships hindered by one half of the couple being behind bars. I'll have to recce a prison, get heckled by child killers as I walk through the visitors' room; maybe one of them will develop a fixation on me and break out to hunt me down and I'll end up in witness protection wearing a wig with a new name. Or something.

Breathe, breathe. Old Clover had my head for a second there, but the new one rapidly reasserts herself. Of course, I know why Maz kept schtum. I wish I'd done the same, it would have made things a lot easier. It *is* an issue, but I have bigger things in play today, and will not be sidetracked.

'Congratulations!' I say, catching my sister's eye and raising my glass. 'To Mrs Fraser!'

Maz clinks her glass with mine and we both open our gullets for considerably more than a sip. Rose remains stock-still in her seat, staring at her youngest daughter like she's just grown a second head. Which, I suppose, in a way, she has.

'Who is . . . it?' she manages. 'This . . . this *person* you've married?'

'He's called Calum, and he's a vet.'

'How did you two lovebirds meet?' I'm starting to enjoy myself again, and see how this new situation can be used to my advantage.

'He came to treat Dorcas's meningeal worm.'

'How romantic. Was it orgling at first sight?' I was once unlucky enough to be around the barns when Maz had a guest alpaca called Barney, who attempted to mate with one of her girls – I don't know which one, and don't want to. The sound he made was extraordinary and could not be unheard.

'Do you *live* together? At the *farm*?' Rose is repeatedly smoothing her napkin along her lap and seems to have developed a tic, her right eyelid flickering. If I play this right, I won't need to do much at all.

'Cal has a flat above his practice in Crediton, but yes, he mostly lives with me.' Now she's unburdened herself, something seems to relax in Maz, and she looks rather beatific. She seems . . . content. At peace. I envy her. But I'm also pleased for her. Maz deserves this. God, she deserves it.

'Nice one,' I say softly, and she smiles at me.

'But . . . but . . .' Rose is struggling to reconcile all the unhappy news. '*Married*?'

'We didn't want a fuss,' says Maz, which makes me chortle, because it's so perfect. 'It was just a registry office thing.' Also perfect, because to Rose's mind registry offices are only for one kind of marriage: a sham one.

'But that's just so . . . downmarket,' she complains. 'So cloak and dagger. Was it a shotgun wedding? Are you in the family way?'

'No one says that any more,' I say. 'We're not in a Jane Austen novel. Though you do bring Mrs Bennet vibes to the table.'

Maz shakes her head. 'I don't want children. I've got my girls.'

It's going from bad to worse for Rose – better and better for me. To think I'd worried the only wedding we were going to talk about was my mother's impending nuptials –

which, to be fair, could still be on the cards. But now she's been upstaged by her daughter's covert union, the impact of any announcement will be drastically dampened. Maz has taken the wind out of my mother's floral sails.

'Think of *this* as Maz's wedding,' I say, raising my glass again. 'After all, you've dressed for it.'

'Clover, stop being facetious. I don't know what's got into you, but it's not *remotely* funny that your sister has eloped with a stranger.'

'He's not a stranger,' says Maz. 'Not to me.'

'But we haven't been introduced! What kind of *unnatural* daughter marries a man none of her family have even met?'

It's time to get out the big guns.

'Perhaps one with an unnatural mother?'

The silence that follows my statement is extremely awkward, or would be if I hadn't meant to create it. But Maz, insulated by her new status, looks untroubled, and I'm cushioned by the bouncy Zorb of the New Me, who's immune to embarrassment or shame. It's like Cinderella's carriage – it might not last, but it's magnificent.

'Why, you—'

'Dinner is served.'

Alan saves the day, for now, appearing loaded with dishes. Immediately, we all paste on appreciative smiles, as he presents our dinner with a courtly flourish. The smiles fade to puzzlement as each of us contemplates our . . . plates. Something is very off.

My shepherd's pie sits on an upturned metal bin lid that lists to one side on the table. The pie itself looks fairly normal, but nothing else about the meal is. Glancing across, I see that Maz's lasagne is presented in an open toolbox, with garlic bread tucked into the top tier. And Rose's cod and chips are carefully laid out on a . . . toilet seat lid. Smothering a laugh, I eye our host quizzically. He's beaming.

'Intriguing plating, Alan,' I say. 'Novel.'

'We at The Brycgstow are proud of our sustainable credentials,' he replies. 'All our presentation platters and cocktail jars are sourced from the bed of the Avon.'

'You mean . . . plucked out of the river?'

'Indeed.'

Rose gives a little moan.

'Dredgewood.' I snigger as, with another of his bows, he leaves us to enjoy our meal.

'I can't eat this,' says Rose, pushing her toilet seat away from her, which isn't far, because there's very little room. 'It's disgusting.'

'I'm sure they cleaned it when they pulled it out,' I say, through my first mouthful. It's bloody good pie, rich and filling, although I do have to chase it as the lid rolls around on the table.

'The very idea,' sniffs Rose. 'Of eating off a lavatory seat.'

'We could ask them to put it on an ordinary plate.'

'I would still know where it's been.'

Surely no trace of the riverbed remains on these unorthodox vessels? I remember what David Lyon-James said about grape skins leaving their mark. What has my bin lid rubbed up against? I suddenly feel a bit sick, but the pie is very good, I'm hungry and need to soak up the booze. Maz is attempting to close her toolbox as an experiment, and we all watch in fascination as it slowly glides shut.

'Useful for keeping it warm,' she says, opening it and breaking off a piece of garlic bread.

'That couple in IKEA were right,' I reply. 'It certainly does have an ambience here. Eau de estuary.'

'The space really flows,' she agrees.

'It's very current.'

'I bet they're laughing all the way to the bank.'

We're in danger of becoming hysterical again, but I need my wits about me if I'm going to complete this mission, so pour myself a glass of water from a metal jug that was probably covered in algae six months ago.

'Tell us about Calum,' I say, partly to annoy my mother, and partly because I'm genuinely interested in my sister's man of mystery. When this is all over, I would like to get to know my new brother-in-law, maybe get him to check out Bigwig, who I hope is safe and happy in the staffroom.

'He's from Cornwall, he likes surfing, and he has a dog called Gawain.'

Wonderful stuff; I can feel Rose bristling beside me. 'So Gawain lives with you on the farm now?'

'Yes. The girls didn't like him at first but now they get on.'

'What breed is he?' I'm prolonging this avenue of conversation purely for the pleasure of the pain it's causing the old dear. My sister in a three-way with a vet and his dog.

'Collie, but Calum thinks there's something else in there – maybe a bit of Labrador?'

'Mixed breeds are healthier, aren't they?'

'Oh yes, hybrid vigour.'

Rose, who considers herself entirely pure-bred and all the better for it, changes the subject. 'Were there *any* guests at your . . . *ceremony*?'

Maz's gaze slides away. 'No.'

'*No one?*'

'Well . . . we had lunch with his parents after.'

Rose's gasp is audible. 'And did they not think it *unconventional* that *you* had no family members present? That your own *mother* wasn't there?'

There's another silence as Maz cuts and chews her lasagne. 'No, they knew why you weren't there.'

'*Why* wasn't I there? Pray enlighten me?'

Maz swallows. 'Because I didn't want you there. If I'd had you, it would have had to be everyone. All . . . the family. You would have turned it into a fanfare.'

It's truth bombs all round today. As my mother subsides into enraged silence, I say 'Did you not want me there either?' I don't ask it with rancour – I thoroughly approve of Maz's decision and just wish I'd had the balls to do it myself, rather than enduring the wasps' nest. All through my wedding, I was mentally under the table, spooning Viennetta.

Maz's smile is sympathetic, infinitely understanding. 'You would have ended up telling her, you wouldn't have been able to help yourself. Or at least, the usual you wouldn't.'

It's a low blow, but a fair one. I would have tried to lie, failed miserably, and ruined it all. I take her hand across the table.

'Well done,' I say, and she squeezes it, her eyes full.

'You may be having a sisterly moment,' says Rose. 'But I remain appalled by this. To be treated so *shoddily*. It's made one thing very clear to me.'

Still holding hands, we both turn to her.

'Made what clear?'

Rose straightens in her seat, clearing her throat. 'We are gathered here today because I have my *own* announcement to make . . .'

Oh God, here we go. Cue Wagner's Bridal Chorus. Maz clasps my fingers and I can feel another laugh begin to build in my throat.

'I'm not getting any younger . . .'

'You're a spring chicken.'

'. . . and in my advancing years . . .'

'Twenty-one if you're a day.'

'. . . I want to make some life changes, so . . .'

'Dignitas?'

Rose taps the table, irritably, to quell me. 'My neighbours' recent *deplorable* activities have caused me to reassess my situation . . .'

'Orgies in the hot tub?'

'. . . With the result that I have . . .'

'. . . arranged a rival sex party?'

Rose glares at me. 'I have put my house on the market.'

Taking a sip of river water, I choke on it. 'You what?'

My mother raises her head, grandly. 'My house is for sale. In fact, I've already accepted an offer.'

'But, where will you live?'

Maz's grip on my fingers convulses as both of us anticipate the answer a split-second before she says it.

'With one of my dear daughters, of course. And in the light of Marigold's hasty and unwise marriage, I think it should be *you*, Clover.'

# 37

All the intruders I have fought off in my dreams all these years, and I never imagined the one that would horrify me the most would be my own mother, clawing away at an obscure window that I was sure was closed. She's sitting there, head inclined regally, fondly imagining that this is good news; that I will welcome her with open arms and say yes: see out your dotage in our dingy, draughty old house that you've never once deigned to stay in. In fact, Rose is so unacquainted with my home that I doubt she knows how many bedrooms we've got. No matter – if there aren't enough then Robbie and I can camp in the garden from now on. Anything to accommodate my dear mama.

My pensive silence is broken by Alan coming back to retrieve the river detritus. I've cleared my bin lid, and Maz has made great inroads into her toolbox, but my mother's toilet seat remains untouched. He gestures to it, anxiously.

'Was it not to madam's satisfaction?'

'Mrs Ashton's gastric bypass doesn't allow her to eat solid food,' I explain. 'She likes to order it though, so she can feel like she's joining in.' I hold up a hand to stem my mother's outraged rejoinder. 'Not now, Nanna Rose. Could we see the dessert menu? Maybe she can manage a mousse.'

'I know you must be *unsettled* by your sister's betrayal,' rattles my mother, as Alan bears the flotsam away. 'But there is no excuse for these flippant, ungodly comments. What in the world is wrong with you, Clover? You were always such a sweet, meek girl. And now you're acting like a hoyden.'

'I'm just so excited,' I reply, 'to hear about your ambitious plans!'

Rose looks mollified. 'I'll have to see the rooms, to check they're suitable, but all being well I could be in by the autumn.'

'You've certainly thought it all through.' I rest my elbows on the table. 'Which room in our house would you prefer? There's a little boxroom in the attic – if we sort out the plasterwork and slap a bit of paint over the damp bits then it should be right and tight for colder weather. You'd have to go downstairs for the bathroom, but that would help you stay in shape, I suppose.'

'Oh, I don't think that would do at all,' says Rose. 'Haven't you got anything on the first floor?'

'Well, apart from our room . . .' I begin doubtfully.

'That will do nicely,' says Rose.

'Of course, it's next to Ethan's, and he does tend to play his music quite loudly, but I think his taste is very eclectic and entertaining! He likes rap, and house, and hip-hop, and all sorts of electronic experimental stuff. And personally, I find the smell of cannabis fragrant and relaxing. Thank you so much, Alan.' Our host has brought the menu.

'Ethan will just have to keep it down. Children should be seen and not heard.'

'I'm afraid Ethan is just the opposite – we rarely see him but we always hear him and definitely smell him too! I think children should be allowed to express themselves, don't you?'

'What nonsense,' says Rose, perusing the list of puddings.

'Oh yes, you never believed in freedom of expression, did you? You preferred to keep a lid on things. Which is why Maz spent years in therapy and I'm a nervous wreck!'

'It's not my fault you both turned out so lily-livered. Your father's genes, I suppose.'

'Can I interest you ladies in something sweet?' says Alan, entirely inappropriately. There's only sourness here, but we all order with bright smiles on our faces.

'Of course, it *would* be lovely to have you around for the kids, to help them with their school work, get to know them better. Because you haven't really hung out with them much, have you?' Try ever. 'The other day, I mentioned Granny, and Hazel said "Who?" and I had to remind her who you are! "The old lady who Granddad went to Spain to get away from!"'

'*What* did you say?' Rose's eyes are flashing dangerously – her dander's up, but I'll have to do better than this.

'I'm *joking* – can't you take a joke?'

'I don't find it at all funny.'

'Isn't that strange? I don't find your jokes funny either. We must both be missing something.'

Our dessert arrives, on bricks. Rose's moue becomes even more pronounced. I've ordered a custard tart, which squats on the masonry like a little yellow toad, while Maz has a cherry cheesecake and Rose's quadrille of truffles dot the amber ingot like tiny turds. We all stare at our respective slabs, wondering where the conversation will go next. I'm still biding my time – a few light parries, jabbing here and there, waiting to put the knife in. We're nearly there – I might let her have her chocolate first though.

My tart is delicious, and I eat it loudly and messily, letting shards of pastry fall from my mouth onto the table. But Rose seems to sense I'm looking for a reaction, and refuses to rise, daintily picking up her droppings and nibbling them, ignoring me. It's time for a major feint. I push away my littered brick, and turn to face her.

'Anyway, I'm thrilled you're finally taking your life in a new direction, but I'm afraid we can't help you, accommodation-wise. Because we already have plans of our own.'

'What?' Rose finishes her final truffle and pushes the brick away in distaste. 'What are you saying?'

'You can't move in.'

My mother blinks, unable to process the idea that her

eldest child – the obedient one – could possibly be denying her. 'I'm *sorry?*'

'You can't move in.'

'I . . . can't move in?'

'No.' It's such a good word. Strong, final, definitive. A useful word. I should really use it more often.

'But . . . why ever not?' Her expression is thunderstruck. The world's dearest, most devoted mother, denied by her daughter.

Here we go. 'Because, like I said, we have other plans.' I pull out my phone. 'I had a chat with Dad the other day . . .' My mother immediately looks aggrieved, as she prefers us to maintain the illusion that Cousin Jack is dead. 'And he and Valentina are moving back to England. They want to start a business here importing Spanish rugs, Dad thinks they can get around the Brexit red tape and make a killing. So anyway, to cut a long story short, *they're* moving in with us!'

I barely pause for breath, although I can see Rose gripping the table in shock, her knuckles white.

'Just until they can get themselves sorted – six months or so, a year maybe.' A glancing blow. 'While they get themselves up and running. It'll be a bit cramped with them both, of course, but wonderful to have everyone back together, under one roof. Plus, Val's a great cook!' The blade at her throat.

'What are you talking about?' says Rose, her voice strained and faint. 'He . . . Jack wouldn't come back.'

'I know, I was as surprised as you, but they've gone for it. See.' I scroll on my phone and hold it out.

Taking it with shaking fingers, Rose reads the last text I had from Dad: Can't wait to move in. Thanks, love. The knife goes in.

'No,' she whispers. 'No.' Her face is ashen and I feel almost sorry for her, then remember she's an almighty cow. Maz takes the phone from her and stares at it, her brow puckering, then clearing.

She smiles. 'How nice.'

'Your father would never dare to come back,' says Rose, her voice trembling with rage. 'Not after what he did.'

'What did he do?' She glares at me. 'Oh, you mean, *leaving* you?'

'He left all of us,' she grates.

'Hmm, he did, but he mainly left *you*, I think. Why are you taking it so personally, after all this time? It's been years, and he's been happy with Valentina in Spain, and you've been . . . well, I'm sure *one* day you'll find a man. I don't know, maybe you're just giving off the wrong vibes, or need to update your look or something. It'll happen, don't worry.' I pat her quivering hand, as she seethes. 'Anyway, even bigger news – Dad and Valentina are talking about renewing their vows when they get back, so we'll have a proper family wedding this Christmas after all, and we can all finally meet Calum! Wouldn't that be lovely? Maybe *you'll* meet someone there.' The mortal wound. 'Would that be so very . . .'

But I don't get to the end of my speech, because it's at that point that Rose takes her brick, and hurls it through the window opposite.

'Special,' I conclude, to the accompaniment of shattering glass, and then shattering silence. I must admit I didn't expect to succeed quite so spectacularly, but having crossed the Rubicon, Rose obviously feels she has nothing left to lose and proceeds to go all out.

'How dare he!' she shrieks, her chignon loosening around her snarling face, as our fellow diners look on in astonishment and horror. 'That fucking bastard! That fucking, fucking bastard.'

It's really quite impressive, watching someone who's maintained a strictly genteel and carefully manicured façade for decades let it splinter in a split-second. Like a gently flowing stream suddenly becoming a mass of churning rapids, bringing all sorts of unwelcome debris to the surface. In a way, I think this might be good for her, get it all out, off her chest. As Maz watches, open-mouthed, Rose leans forward and sweeps her arm across our table with a guttural roar, sending glasses flying and guests ducking for cover. What a palaver! People are definitely staring.

Alan dashes over, with several staff members close behind.

'Now, now, Nanna Rose, don't go upsetting yourself,' I say loudly, moving round the table to rub her shoulder. She shakes me off, irritably, stumbling backwards into

Alan's arms. He catches her and she bats him away like a madwoman.

'Get off me!'

'I'm so sorry,' I say. 'She's very confused.'

'Do you need me to call an ambulance?'

'No, no, I'll just put her in a cab.' Alan raises his eyebrows, obviously thinking that me bundling my batty old gran into a taxi is not the most caring act, but I want to wrap this up as quickly as possible.

'Time to go home, Nanna Rose.' I pick up my mother's handbag – a lime-green Mulberry number – and escort her to the door, as everyone watches and whispers. She seems to shrink into herself as we exit, her shoulders hunched, highlighted hair falling over her face. How the high-and-mighty have fallen. I notice a few grey roots at her parting, and magnanimously resist pointing them out.

There's a handy taxi rank round the corner and I wave to the first in line, checking her purse, which has several notes in it that should see her as far as Redcliffe.

'Off you go then. Go and have a lie-down.'

She gazes out at me from deep within the cab. 'Why did you do it?'

I hesitate. Now it's done, I don't really have anything left to add. 'It's been a long time coming,' I say. 'Today was the day.'

She nods, pulls the door closed, and the cab moves away.

# 38

There was a moment, when I was twelve, when my mother put a brick through my heart. It was the day Dad left, packing his bags and heading to the airport, leaving Rose covering her ravages with extra make-up and hairspray, before sailing off to her tennis club to pretend all was well. Annis slumped round to watch whatever was on, and after I made dinner for me and Maz, and did my homework, I sneaked out to the club to find Rose. It was out of character for me – a daring, rebellious act – but I wanted to see what she got up to, what she was like when we weren't around. And it wasn't like the babysitter would notice.

It was only a fifteen-minute walk there, and the summer evening was light and warm. When I arrived, I slipped through reception without anyone spotting me and headed for the bar. There she was, in the middle of a group, talking and laughing as if she didn't have a care in the world, as if her husband hadn't just quit the family home, as if she hadn't just left her two daughters to fend for themselves, again. The bar area was partitioned, so I sat in the next section unobserved, and listened to the conversation. Rose's friend Ginny and her husband were there, along with another couple I didn't recognize, and a man they all called Dingo, which I assume was a nickname. They talked approvingly about Margaret Thatcher, disapprovingly about Nelson Mandela, and neutrally about Ronald Reagan. They had a long chat about house prices in Norwich, which nearly made me fall asleep. It was mostly predictable and boring, but the interesting part of the conversation went like this:

'Where's Jack tonight, Rose?'

A short pause. 'Working again. He never stops. I'm a Vertex widow!'

Dad worked for an engineering firm, but not hard, and while he often stayed late, I suspected it was to socialize rather than slog. He didn't apply himself to anything particularly, apart from putting his feet up.

'You're a tower of strength, Rose. A wonderful mother to those girls.'

That was definitely Ginny laying it on.

'I won't deny it's tough when he's away. But they're what get me through it. My little girlies. They're not the prettiest, or the cleverest . . .' She couldn't resist a swipe. 'But they're my babies. They're what keep me going.'

I didn't stay after that. Couldn't listen to her playing the devoted mama, gushing to her friends when she never directed any of that warmth towards us. Running home in the dusk, I felt angry and betrayed, but when I got back and saw Annis still slouching on the sofa, watching

*Tomorrow's World*, the emotions segued into a kind of flat despair. I huddled next to her, staring into the future.

'You missed *EastEnders*,' she said, her eyes on the screen. 'Angie Watts went to Spain as well. Just like your dad.' Of course, Annis knew what was going on, even if no one at the club did.

'Great,' I said. 'Maybe they'll meet up.' And she laughed, in a wheezy way, and asked me to fetch her a Coke from the fridge.

When Rose came home, paying Annis her £10 and dismissing her, I was still there, in front of *Question Time*. It wasn't until she started turning lights off that she noticed me.

'What are you doing up?' she said. 'Get to bed.'

I pointed to the TV. 'They're in Norwich this week. House prices are going through the roof.' It was an open reference to the conversation I'd heard earlier, though of course there was no way Rose would ever understand that, or suspect I was there. But I wanted to tell her, tell her I heard her say we were her babies, and were we? Because she never said it to us.

Instead, I said 'Will Dad come back?'

She tutted and snapped 'It's late, off you go.'

Some bit of backbone made me say 'But will he?'

And she stared at me, chewing her lip, then said 'Only if you're a good girl.'

I was, and he didn't. Once again, she made it my fault when it was hers.

\* \* \*

Back in the restaurant, the atmosphere is buzzing. Sheer ambience. The Brycgstow is truly Bristol's hottest riverside inn right now – practically everyone is on Twitter recounting the events of the evening and speculating the cause. I march straight up to Alan, who is directing his staff to sweep up the broken glass.

'I am *so* sorry about this,' I say. 'I just don't know what came over her. She's very . . . unpredictable at the moment. It's her condition.'

'Don't mention it,' says Alan nobly. He's cut his hand on a shard and is bleeding profusely.

'Oh, but I must.' I brandish a credit card – not mine; my mother's, filched from her purse when I put her in the cab. 'Please let me pay for the damage, along with the meal, of course.'

Rose can certainly afford it – Cousin Jack may have long since scarpered but he gave her the family home and still pays spousal maintenance, which she's always resisted sharing with her daughters, preferring us to make our own way in life as she says it's character-building. I whack £750 on her Visa and kiss Alan on the cheek.

'It'll be a superb write-up,' I promise. It's no lie – I don't know about Marina, but I'll do him a lovely review on Tripadvisor.

Alan flushes with pleasure, eyeing Maz, who has returned from the back room, bearing Bigwig, who seems gratifyingly pleased to see me.

'It has been an honour,' Alan says, bowing.

'How are you getting back?' I ask my sister, thinking that I don't want her driving home after the amount of wine and alcoholic pond water she's put away.

'Cal is picking me up,' Maz replies, settling the rabbit in my bag. 'What *was* that text from Dad about?' she murmurs, as we make our way out, followed by curious stares and muttered comments.

I chuckle. 'He and Val decamped to an Airbnb for a couple of weeks while they got their kitchen redone. It's nearly finished. Plus, he was thanking me for the photo I sent him of Hazel and Ethan.'

I showed my mother an edited version of our exchange and she saw what I wanted her to see. It's all in the edit, as Other Delia would say.

'Thought as much. Was that wise though?'

'Was what wise?'

'Riling her like that.'

'Do you think it was wrong?'

She pauses, by the photo of Ruby and Elsie. 'I've often wanted to see her pushed to the brink, and brought down. But when it finally happened, it didn't feel as good as I thought it would.'

'Oh, I don't know.' I grin. 'I thought it felt pretty good.'

My sister raises her eyebrows. 'Really? But how will you feel tomorrow?'

The truth is, I don't know. But today; today I feel OK. And I've got to push on, while I still feel this way.

# 39

I was so worried I'd be a mother like my own, and in many ways, I think I am. Constantly distracted, endlessly busy with other things, uttering the phrase 'Just a second!' continually, dashing around facilitating their lives without actually being very involved in either of them. I don't think I'm much *fun*, or as constantly loving and patient as I ought to be. Early on when they were babies, I remember being at a clinic to see the health visitor, trying to get the twins undressed, bustling between them as they kicked and bellowed. There was a mother nearby, tickling and laughing at her naked baby, and I realized I was so focused on my task, so caught up in the logistics of dealing with these wriggling, keening creatures, that my expression was completely set in concentration. Had I *ever* smiled at them? The realization froze me, my hands on their tight-as-a-drum tummies as my frown deepened. What kind of mother didn't smile at her babies? One like mine? Then I couldn't remember if *they* had ever smiled – they were over six weeks old, surely it should have happened by now, but I'd never noticed, and if it hadn't, it was because they'd never learned how, thanks to their scowling mother who was too busy fiddling with their nappies to lift the corners of her mouth.

So I smiled at them. With them on their mats, half undressed and grizzling, a slow, rictus grin spread across my face – an approximation of what they needed, wholly inadequate. It didn't reach my eyes, which were full of tears. But, miraculously, it did the job. Both of them stilled, staring at my face, and then – *then* – they responded. Two gorgeous, gummy grins that warmed me to my core and infused me with the sense that yes, in some ways, I was like my mother, but in others – ones that counted – I was my own woman, breaking the cycle. My babies. The smile became a real one, full and true; the three of us beamed and gushed at each other until the health visitor told us to hurry up and get on the scales. Ethan was underweight and Hazel had nappy rash, and so I felt inadequate again, and scurried home with both of them screaming for a feed.

Over the years I've felt less and less, and more and more, like I'm turning into my mother but I've never felt anything other than tied to her, tangled up in her thorny creepers, obsessively fixated on her failings, cataloguing her crimes, unable to extricate myself. Until I watched the taxi drive away, further and further from me. Apron strings, severed. Or am I kidding myself? As Rose's taxi disappears from view, I get the uncomfortable feeling that it isn't the last I'll see of her tonight.

Barbara Good nudges me, and I realize we'd better get on. The intense light of the summer day is fading, it's nearly 9 p.m., and the Red Eye party will be starting soon. Taking her rein, I start the short walk to the venue, mulling. Because Vincent's PA Imogen coerced me, I've been involved in every step of this party's organization, right down to checking out the venue we've booked, a sort of brasserie-cum-nightclub on The Mall. She insisted I meet her there to make sure it was suitable, so I dutifully took time out of my busy day to traipse around and approve it. Picturing the layout, it's clear where everything will be taking place – we've booked out the whole of the first and second floors, which include a large bar area, a smaller, cosier drinking den next door, along with the screening room, plus a cloakroom, and private dining room for the pre-party dinner where Vince started the wooing process with a few select guests. There's also a dressing room for when they do comedy and music gigs.

This is all mapped out in my head, and the pieces have gradually been slotting into place throughout the day, but now I have to acknowledge I can't do it on my own. It may be against my nature as an overanxious executive producer, but I'm going to have to step up a gear and – finally – delegate some responsibilities, trust someone to help me. There's only one person who can do it. I get out my phone, hoping he answers the call.

'Hi, Carrie Bradshaw.'

'Why Carrie?'

'Because you're a bitch with mad hair.'

'I'm sorry about that. I'm ringing to apologize.'

'No, you're not.'

'You're right, I'm not. I'll apologize properly another day, but right now, I need your help.'

'Can't help you, I'm at the party. Why aren't you here? You'll miss the free prosecco.'

'I'm on my way, save me a glass. And bring it to the dressing room. I'll meet you there.'

'I'm not your Stanford.'

'You're right, you're not. You're my Petroc.'

And Petroc is the only one who can handle this.

\* \* \*

Why don't I like relying on people? It makes me nervous, like stepping out onto a thin fraying rope above a canyon. A rope that isn't interested in staying taut or bearing my weight. A rope that *wants* to snap. I just assume it will let me fall. Like Rose and Cousin Jack did, always too busy to pick us up, not inclined to change their schedule to accommodate us, leaving us to get by on our own. I got used to the idea that what I wanted didn't matter, that it was better to make sure I accommodated everyone else rather than run the risk of hoping someone might indulge me. It changed, a little, when Robbie came along, because he taught me that there would always be someone at, and on, my side. But it was a hard lesson to learn, and early on in our relationship, I found myself staggered when, on a late work night, he suggested he come out to meet me and escort me home. Astounded, then anxious, because I assumed he wouldn't turn up, and then there would be an added awkwardness to my solo journey as I worked out how to never mention it again; avoid any friction by referencing his unreliability. But when I emerged from the church hall in Deptford where we'd been recording a choir rehearsal, there he was, clicking his heels together, reporting for duty. My breath caught as if I'd just heard the sweetest, most exquisite a cappella chord progression. Here was my rock, a sturdy foundation stone unmoved by the elements, that I could lean on, build my life around.

'I didn't think you'd come,' I stuttered, feeling my cheeks flush with the delight of it.

He cupped my face in his hands. 'I'm your knight in shining armour,' he murmured, grinning. With him, the kingdom was safe. He's never stacked the dishwasher in an acceptable way, but he does turn up when it counts. When it matters.

Gradually I learned to rely on Robbie, but found it difficult to widen my circle beyond him and Susie, wary of trusting anyone in case it went wrong again. The habit is hard to break. I am the rope, holding taut so that other people can cross. But it's time to cut myself some slack.

* * *

Petroc meets me in the dressing room as arranged, holding two glasses of fizz and glowering like he's changed a

294

thousand nappies. Lafayette, on the floor beside him, is yapping madly – he's caught sight of Bigwig, whose head is emerging from my bag, whiskers twitching.

Handing me my glass, Petroc is briefly distracted from his sulk. 'What on earth is that?'

'It's a rabbit.'

'What's it doing in your bag?'

'Writing its memoir. Listen, I—'

'And another thing, I'm not the only one you need to apologize to. I've just been talking to Caroline, who's in floods because you told her she's a shitty producer—'

'She *is* a shitty producer.'

He wags a finger. 'Well, it's your job as her exec to make her a better one, not bawl her out like that.'

I sigh. 'She's been winding me up for a while.'

'That's your problem, you put things off and then have to go from doughnuts straight to dressing-downs. If you'd dealt with it sooner then you wouldn't be in this mess.'

'That's the story of my life.'

'Why *have* you got a rabbit in your bag? Is it some sort of magic trick?'

I shake my head. 'I'm afraid I don't have time to explain it. I have to explain something else, and I need you to listen carefully, and do as I say.'

'Oh, go on then.'

This bit is one of the hardest things I've done so far today. Like the delegation, it's against my nature to go here, to say these words out loud. The only person I've ever told is Susie, and I was *really* drunk then, as opposed to the mild intoxication I'm currently feeling, which may or may not be booze-related. And Robbie, whose reaction was so potent that it frightened me, made me want to put the lid back on all of it. It's been fastened down tight for so long, it's not easy to prise the box open again.

As I tell him what I need, and why, Petroc's expression changes, conveying a series of emotions as his dog grumbles and prances. When I finish, he hugs me briskly, sending Lafayette into a demented frenzy.

'Are you sure?'

I nod.

'It might not work.'

I nod again. 'But I have to try.'

'You're very brave. Or crazy.'

'Or I have a head injury and am perimenopausal. Do you think you can do it?'

'Of course. Quick turnaround though.'

'Give it your best shot.'

'Will do. Oh, and Clover?'

Preparing to leave, I turn to him enquiringly.

'It's my turn to apologize. I'm sorry I was so cross with you. I know you were only trying to stick up for me. I've just been really stressed lately and didn't know how to react.'

'Your house?' Petroc's church conversion has been a millstone.

He sticks out his lower lip. 'We've found bodies.'

'You *what?*'

'Not like that. Graves, you know. In the garden. Graveyard. Whatever.'

I put a hand on his arm. 'Is it going to be difficult?'

'We're going to need God to step in and sort it all out.'

'I'm sorry. For everything.'

'I know you are.'

'I've got to go. You'll do your bit?'

'With panache, as ever. Go on, do your thing.'

And off I go, to save the day.

# 40

'Who wrote this?'

He was waving a print-out in Beatnik Media's open-plan office, drinking coffee from a mug that said 'rock and roll through and through'. He had very thick blond hair that stuck up in all directions in a way that could have been accidental or by design, it was hard to tell, and he wore his incredibly well-cut suits casually mussed, like James Bond after chasing down a villain. I'd seen him around Beatnik at various points, always doing something while he was doing something else – talking on the phone as he got in the lift, making notes as he ate a sandwich, tying his tie (carelessly) as he asked a PA to book him a table. He was all over the place.

In meetings, he would bring in work and sit unashamedly getting on with it while the managing director, a mild-mannered, harassed bloke called Martin, ploughed through projections and commissioning opportunities, boring us all rigid. I liked that about him, that he didn't care, and wished I dared do the same. There was a restless air of glamour about him, a flippancy and a sense that everything was a joke, and I liked that too, at the time.

'Who wrote this?' he asked again.

I caught sight of the show's title on the paper. 'Me. I wrote it.'

A lowly researcher, busy casting *Bump in the Night*, writing treatments on the side for their head of development, because I wanted to please everyone and couldn't say no.

He looked down at me, sitting at my desk, studiously going over my locations. 'Finally,' he said. 'We have someone around here who can string a sentence.'

The treatment I'd written was for a show he was trying to sell, a kind of climbing competition for amateur mountaineers, in various exotic locations around the world. It was a cool, if expensive, idea and I'd written it up in a tongue-in-cheek tone that I hoped would tickle him. I felt my cheeks grow warm, and focused on a Norfolk barn conversion whose owners had discovered that a farm girl hanged herself there two hundred years ago. It was an interesting story but, as my producer Sharon had asked, 'What are we actually going to see, unless there's a skeleton still dangling there?' It was a problem I had yet to solve.

'*Climb Every Mountain* is a fun title,' he said. 'But I'm not sure about the connotations. Makes me picture wimples and warbling. Can you rethink? Apart from that it's great. Do you want to come to the pitch with me?'

And there it was; a foot in the door. I'd never been invited to a pitch before – they were not for the likes of humble casting researchers. That was another winning thing about him, he wasn't remotely interested in hierarchies or who earned what – it just didn't concern him. He was a well-respected executive producer, but I'd seen him talk to interns, admin staff, canteen staff, in exactly the same way he talked to Martin. Off-hand, charming, like we were all in on the joke.

We got a cab to ITV, and talked the whole way there, about his show and mine. He chuckled until he pinched tears out of his eyes when I told him about a poltergeist in Cardiff that turned out to be a squirrel trapped in a chimney, and he had several useful suggestions for upping the ante in the Norfolk barn. In return, we discussed the mountaineering competition, the problem of litter on Mount Everest, his own plan to climb it one day. By the time we arrived at the channel we were both breathless with laughter and ideas. I felt charged, energized, and it carried me through the meeting with the forbidding commissioner who eyed me as though I was a frozen corpse on the south face. Such was the force of his personality that we left with development money to research the project further, and when he suggested a celebratory drink after I didn't think anything of it. There *wasn't* anything in it – we had a glass of champagne in a nearby hotel bar and, when we'd finished, he saluted me, said 'Nice work, Ms Ashton,' and I left, heady from the fizz and the thought that I'd done well. After that he called me 'Four-Leaf', said I brought him luck, took me under his wing, just like I'd imagined someone might. And he was the perfect gentleman, until he wasn't. Until the joke wore thin, and I realized it was on me.

As a woman, you always worry about someone coming up on you in dark alleyways, surprising you from behind, a hand over your mouth to stop you screaming. And you're taught how to avoid it – hold your keys or an alarm in your hand, don't tie your hair back, tell a friend where you'll be, don't wear that, watch your drinks. It's all on you to prevent it, to see it coming, stop it. But sometimes it's not an alleyway and it's not a sudden surprise. It's right out in the open, gradually, insidiously, worming its way in until you're stuck with your back against the wall. And, like everything else, you feel it's all your fault.

*Everything* was a joke to him, even the worst, most terrible things. Nothing mattered, and no one. Not the mightiest CEO nor the lowliest intern. Certainly not little Four-Leaf Clover, always so obliging, so ready to please.

I saw him on the guest list almost immediately this morning, eyes snagging on that horribly familiar, skin-prickling name that sent my headache off the charts, pounding away, making me groan with the pain of it. Back from America, invited to our screening, in case he wants to buy the format, take it across the pond, make Vince millions. I'd always known it was a possibility that I'd run into him again, that the box would be opened and the curses would spill forth. But I'd managed to put it off for so long and persuaded myself it was better this way – just try to forget it happened, move on with your life, keep your head down, the plates spinning. Sometimes I thought I'd managed it, but the email proved otherwise.

*But for a nail the shoe was lost,*
*But for a shoe the horse was lost,*
*But for a horse the knight was lost,*
*But for a knight the battle was lost,*
*But for a battle the kingdom was lost.*
*All for the want of a horseshoe nail.*

But for my mother my nerve was lost. But for my nerve, my career was lost. But for my career my 'no' was lost. But for my 'no' my world was lost . . . All for the want of a loving mother, all for the want of trying to please, pandering, putting everyone else's needs first. Rose got her thorns into me, ensured I was compliant, and that other people could continue the process. Over and over again, until I reached my limit.

And the headache intensified, increasing to a pitch where I couldn't bear it any more, had to do something, anything to take away the pain, make it go away. So I took the drugs, and got knocked out, and since then something has been unhinged, flapping madly, directing me, telling me what to do, what camera angles are needed, writing the script for this day, this day when I take back the kingdom.

\* \* \*

After leaving Bigwig in the cloakroom with an accommodating attendant, I barrel back into the main bar area and run slap-bang into Vince.

He folds his arms. 'Do you want the good news or the bad news?'

I don't have time for either. There's a call sheet in my head and we're on a tight schedule.

'The good news?'

'The good news is I'm saving money because you're not getting any kind of a raise. And the reason you're not getting your raise is because of the bad news. David pulled out.'

'What? I swear I nailed it. He was putty in my hands.'

'You keep using these disgusting phrases that aren't even true. He phoned me to say he doubts your authenticity as a producer.'

I can't understand it, and don't have time to try. 'I've got to go . . . got some other stuff to deal with.'

'You can deal with David, when he arrives. I've invited him here, for one last-ditch effort. So don't fuck this up.'

'Right. Right.' I'm moving away from him, pushed and pulled by the crowds who are eager to let their hair down, to celebrate the wrap. Like the Beatnik night in the vicarage, spirits high, morals low. After these past years of lockdown, cancellations, scaling back, this lot are ready to party. The music is thumping, reminding me of my headache, giving me another one. But I've got to keep going, get this done.

I scour the place, seeking him out, heart pounding at the potential proximity. He must be here, he's on Imogen's list. Where is he? I don't want to see him, but I must. I must. Just as I'm starting to panic that I've missed him, he's there, across the crowded room, and then it's a different kind of panic. He's talking to Flora, my assistant producer, and my hands tighten into fists just looking at the way his head is bent towards hers. Although he's nearly twenty years older, he doesn't look so different – still handsome, in a weather-beaten way. White teeth shining under the disco lights, no trace of middle-aged paunch. I guess that's what two decades in LA will do for you. Despite – and because of – my best efforts, I look very different. The lines and sags of a woman who bore and raised twins. More expensive clothes. Crazy hair. And also, I *am* different. A different woman from the one who couldn't say no to him. I suspect he hasn't changed. I start my mindful breathing, to steel myself.

'Thought I might run into you again.'

Turning, I let out an exclamation. It's the woman from the train this morning. Seeing her here, in this setting, I immediately know who she is, and can't believe I didn't recognize her before.

'Marcia!' She was a floor manager at the BBC, and we worked on a show together shortly after I met Robbie. I never saw her without a headset on. 'You still at the Beeb?'

'Still there.' Her gaze follows mine, watching him chatting up Flora. 'On the Entertainment commissioning team now, came over today from London to see this new dating show. We might be interested. Were you involved?'

'Nope, not me. You going back tonight?' I'm keeping my eye on him, to check he doesn't head off, or worse, take Flora with him.

'No, I've got a hotel – that's what I'm looking forward to the most, actually. Air conditioning and no kids.'

'Enjoy.'

'I see old Fingersmith over there is up to his usual tricks.'

My heart jumps in my chest. 'Do you . . . know him?'

She grimaces. 'Know him of old. Thought he had to do a runner after his antics caught up with him.'

'Hmm.' I'm finding it hard to speak, can't decide if what I'm feeling is horror or relief. He's done it before. Or after. It wasn't just me.

'Anyway, lovely to catch up.'

She moves away, and I spend a couple of seconds getting my breathing back to normal before I'm ready to go. Spotting Oz hogging the bar, I head his way.

'Oh, it's you.' He shifts along to make room, casting me a sour look, obviously annoyed by the short shrift I gave him this morning.

'Hi, Oz. I need some cocaine.' There's no time for beating about the bush. He's got it, and I need it.

In the process of taking the first sip of his pint, Oz splutters and spits it all over the bar. I possibly should have beaten around the bush a bit, just to ease him into this unexpected request.

'Sorry. Er, hi, Oz, how are you? Love the show, do you happen to have any coke on you?'

'I don't know what you're talking about. What are you talking about? As if I would ever, ever—'

He trails off as I reach into his pocket to pull out the bag. I really don't have time for this – like Petroc said, it's a quick turnaround, getting quicker with every second.

'For God's sake, don't wave it about!' he hisses, slapping at my hand, which slips the bag into my own pocket – this dress is excellent.

'Sorry about this, but think of it as a confiscation. This stuff is illegal and besides, you're really too old to be doing it.'

To my surprise he nods, wiping his mouth on a napkin. 'I know, you're right. You're probably doing me a favour. I just felt like I needed it to take the edge off.'

'The edge off what?'

He shrugs, then gestures to the gabbling crowds. 'All this. It's my show. What if it's shit?'

I'm genuinely amazed that Oz gives a toss. 'I'm sure it's not shit.' I'm not at all sure, but it feels like the thing to say right now, since I've stolen his only other solace.

'Might not come to the screening. Can't face it.'

'Whatever you feel is best.' I've scored my hit, and need to move on, not get stuck here counselling Oz in his hour of need. Leaving him nursing his pint, I make my way across the room, weaving through crew, commissioners, producers, lawyers and secretaries, heart hammering, vision blurring, as I head towards a man I never wanted to see again, a man I wish I'd never met.

'Hey there. Vince has sent me to look after you.'

He appraises me, as Flora drifts away. I'm too old for him, but he's intrigued all the same, by the novelty of the approach. He's the one who does the approaching, usually. My heart is thumping painfully, but I keep my expression open and friendly, smiling like it never happened. I don't want him to remember yet, until I've got him where I need him to be.

'Vince is an excellent host, so kind and thoughtful.'

I know for a fact that Vince will have already wooed him and other favoured buyers in the private dining room, greasing the wheels. 'He's very kind, when there's a potential deal on the table.'

'Well, I haven't seen the show yet.' He flashes his teeth, American-white, enjoying his power.

'Maybe we can help you enjoy it even more. A little birdie told me you might be in the market for a pick-me-up before the screening.' Opening my pocket slightly, I reveal my stash. In the Beatnik era, his predilection was well-known; he was always nipping off to the toilets during meetings, coming back buzzing with ideas. He once offered it to me, and pinched my chin affectionately when I stammered no. Like Oz, he's really too old for it, should have moved on to milder recreationals, but of course his eyes widen when he sees it.

'This format just got a lot more interesting,' he murmurs.

307

'Follow me.'

I lead him back to the dressing room, quickening my step as the throngs dwindle.

'You seem familiar. Have we met before?'

He can't see my expression, because I'm in front of him. My throat constricts, but I shake my head, my ringlets bouncing. 'Maybe we ran into each other at ITV?' That was where he went after Beatnik, before LA.

'That'll be it.'

We reach the dressing room. Locking the door, I chuck the packet on the long shelf by the mirror and give him a little curtsy.

'All yours.'

He sits himself down and starts tipping out the powder. 'So, do you work at Red Eye?' he asks, getting out his bank card. It's all very casual, like I've invited him to sample a canapé.

'Yep, nose at the grindstone.'

He grins, holding up a twenty-pound note. 'Bet it would rather be somewhere else.'

I laugh, remembering how he made me giggle. I liked him, he was charming and funny; still is. He hasn't changed, not one bit. My mentor, my protector, my knight in shining armour. But for the knight the battle was lost. He bends his head and I watch him snort up the line, whoosh, into that straight, clean-as-a-whistle nose. Rearing up, he sniffs and offers me the note, tightly rolled into a tube. I shake my head, backing away.

308

'Come on!' he beckons me with his roll-up.

'I've got my own!' Reaching into my bag, I pull out my purse and grab the twenty-pound note the traders gave me in the cab this morning. When I took it, did I ever imagine I'd be using it for this? This note has probably seen its fair share of coke already, so it's come full circle. I hadn't decided what I'd do if he offered it to me, figured probably not because of *Sweet Valley High* and the girl who died. Always been wary of risk. But look where that got me. Like Oz, I want to take the edge off the fear, keep me fizzing with adrenaline, help me take this next, precarious step. Rolling up my note as he hacks out another line, I fully intend to inhale, and bend to the shelf, ready to do the deed. But as he turns away, holding his nostrils, I'm suddenly revolted by the idea of sharing anything with him. Sharing this artificial euphoria, the chemicals cleaving us together. Unthinkable.

So as he enjoys his hit, I fake it, simultaneously sweeping the powder away as I snort thin air. Rearing up, I squeeze my nose and wonder how I'm going to feign a coke rush. I'm about to do something incredibly, intensely difficult and unlikely to succeed, which will be fairly traumatic and might not even have the desired result, AND I have to pretend to be high. It's a tall order, but maybe my sham snort has had some sort of placebo effect, because I FEEL AMAZING AND CAN ABSOLUTELY DO THIS.

I bend down to grasp the ruffled hem of my beautiful swishy dress, and pull the whole thing over my head.

'Whoa!' he says, laughing and rubbing his gums. 'What's up?'

'Just a bit of fun,' I say, struggling as my curls are stuck in a button. 'Help me,' I mumble, and, still chuckling, he untangles me and pulls the dress away. I pull it back, flirtatiously, and he lets go, smiling.

'What's this? Are you propositioning me? How novel.'

How intoxicating it must be, with or without drugs, to be locked in a room with someone and not worry about the consequences. To know it's fine, that you won't be hurt or violated in any way. That you can walk across any canyon, on any rope, and it will hold. Being here with him terrifies me, even though I know if I screamed, Petroc would come running. But what if I don't get to scream? What if I *could* scream, but can't make myself . . .? No, that's Old Clover's thinking. New Clover is different. New Clover can do this. I wave the skirt round in a circle, like a burlesque dancer, my grin rictus.

'For old times' sake?'

'Must be very old times,' he replies. 'Because I have to be honest, I don't remember you.'

I pout, in my bra and knickers. 'That's not very flattering. I thought I was the one person who understood you.'

'Did I say that? I say a lot of things.'

'You certainly do,' I reply. And then my voice hardens. 'You said that if I slept with you, I'd get a promotion.'

'Did I? That sounds awfully direct.' He sounds posher than he used to, affecting a kind of Hugh Grant drawl which I'm sure goes down very well in Hollywood.

'You implied it. Very strongly.'

'And did you? It sounds like a win–win.'

'Except I didn't want to do it.'

'Well, I'm sure I didn't force you.'

'I'm sure you think you didn't.'

It's strange, how I can stand here in my underwear, splitting hairs with this toad of a man, and it's OK. Without my clothes on, I guess the difference between twenty-six-year-old me and forty-six-year-old me is even more marked. I'm nothing like I was back then – I'm flabbier, and slacker, but firmer and tighter than ever. He might think it's the cocaine talking, but it's not; it's just me. I can do this. I can take him down.

He's been leaning against the shelf, long legs outstretched, but he gets up, putting his card and his note back in his pocket before strolling over to me, taking my chin in his hand, turning my head this way and that to jog his memory. His touch makes me flinch, my skin crawling as his grape skins leave their mark.

'Listen, I'm sorry if you think something went on between us, but I promise you I don't remember anything about it.'

'Get away from me.' I push him. 'So, it didn't happen? Because you don't remember? Because it meant nothing to you?'

'I think you might be taking it all a bit seriously. Just a roll in the hay, that's all. Chill out.'

'Not a roll in the hay. The Ecclestone vicarage.'

I see him remember, see the clouds lift, the smile as he recalls. 'Oh, *that* night. Clover, isn't it? Little Four-Leaf. *Bump in the Night . . .*'

The confusion and chaos of that night. I thought I'd said no. Maybe I didn't. Maybe I said yes. Maybe I implied yes. He said he was going to help me, I wanted him to help me, ergo I wanted . . . I will never forget that night, or afterwards, huddled in a taxi and then back at the hotel. It was one of those family B&Bs, not at all appropriate for a motley TV crew, and I found a hot water bottle in my bed when I got to my room. The motherliness of it made me cry, tears spilling onto the pages of my book, but I couldn't get warm, no matter where I put it against my body. I shoved a chair against the door, even though it was locked, and checked the windows, even though I knew it was ridiculous, would make no difference. He'd already got in, back at the vicarage. I didn't know how to stop him.

The muscle memory makes me shiver, leaving my naked skin clammy and cold, and suddenly I'm confused, can't remember my plan, my script, what was I saying? What do I want him to say? A confession? Remorse? What would make it better? I don't know, and don't know why I'm here, what I'm doing. It's all going wrong – he's supposed to look like a cornered rat and yet he's reclining, relaxed and assured, while I stand there gibbering in my smalls. Maybe I should have taken the drugs.

'You ruined me. You . . . you . . . I couldn't . . .' And I still can't. My mouth feels dry, my tongue thick and useless. What are my cues? I've forgotten, can't get it together. I feel woozy and disoriented, like I've just been knocked out by a businessman's briefcase.

'Anyway, like I said, it was a long time ago . . .' He studies his nails and I can see him starting to get bored, but I can't let him leave without – what? What do I need from this? What did I expect?

'I'll tell them.'

He raises his eyebrows, looking amused. 'You'll tell who?'

I gesture towards the door. 'All of them. I'll tell them what you did, what you are.'

He laughs. 'Tell them what? That we had a fling years ago? That you're put out I don't remember you?'

'I'll tell them you . . . that you . . .' But I can't articulate it. Can't sum it up in a pithy, punny, alliterative pitching line. There are no words for this. It's just a messy, unladylike, chaotic fuss, the kind my mother would deplore.

He's still smiling, but there's a glint in his eye, that demonic flash. 'How about this? *I'll* tell them what I did, what I am. I'll tell them I helped your career, years ago, and that now I'm CEO of an American conglomerate, I'm maybe going to buy their format and take it back to the US with me. Who do you think they'll want to listen to? You? Or me?'

He makes his way towards the door.

'Please, don't.' I block him, my hands full of my swishy skirt. For a second, we tussle as he tries to turn the handle, and I try to get in the way. But of course, he's too strong. I fall to one side, sliding down the wall.

'Put your clothes on before you go out, you might cause a scene. Thanks for the fun times.'

And then he leaves, while I sit in the dressing room with my dress in my hands, ruined, because once again I couldn't stop him.

# 41

By 9.30 p.m., I'm back at the party. He's mingling, chatting, pressing the flesh, and I'm standing by the bar trying to work out what just happened, trying to make sense of it all, trying not to fall apart because everything is a fucking mess and my world is crashing round my ears. Caroline's in a corner crying, and anyone who goes over to pat her shoulder shoots me a dirty look after. Vince keeps catching my eye and making throat-slitting gestures, I've ignored three phone calls from Rose, who no doubt wants to tell me I've won an award for worst daughter, and Barbara Good the imaginary alpaca has pissed off back to her imaginary barn, so is thus unavailable for imaginary emotional support. To make matters worse, David Lyon-James has just arrived in an impeccable navy suit, and Vince expects me to re-establish my authenticity as a producer and win back the £1.2 million commission. It is, as they say in the biz, a shitshow.

I stand in a corridor for a bit to do some mindful breathing but keep getting hailed by various Red Eye staff in various states of inebriation.

'Hey, Clover! Come and have a drink!'

'Heard you trashed Monty to his face this morning, you hero.'

'Hendry! Fab hair, you're looking hot.'

'Clover, are you watching the show? I'll save you a seat.'

Shaking my head, I stumble away, trying to reconcile the cock-up I've made of everything. '*It'll all come out in the edit, it'll all come out in the edit . . .*' I repeat my producer's mantra to myself and can't resist a little hysterical giggle. It does matter, it really matters, but you've got to laugh, haven't you? Otherwise, you'd cry. Or throw all the bricks through all the windows.

My phone rings again, and I'm about to cancel the call when I see that it's Robbie. I really want to hear his voice; that kind, gentle voice that told me about sixteenth-century monks' effluence all those years ago – I'll come clean with him later, but right now I just want to find out if he got a takeaway, how the twins are, whether the cat brought in any mice today. I go downstairs and outside, where it's quieter, to answer.

'Hi, are you home?' I'm imagining them carousing in the kitchen, Grizelda delicately weaving her way through the foil cartons littering the table.

'No, I'm at the police station. Hazel's been arrested.'

That really isn't what I wanted to hear. I wish I hadn't answered.

'My God! How did that happen?' I'm feigning ignorance but can probably have a stab at guessing.

'She bunked off school to go on a climate protest, and

ended up plaiting her hair to the railings outside City Hall. She called me because I'm her lawyer, apparently, though I have no idea how an in-depth knowledge of copyright infringement is going to help us here.'

'I am so shocked and surprised by this news, I had no idea.'

'She told me you saw her in Queen Square and said fuck school.'

'Shit.'

'She also said you've had a perm and you're insane, and although I'm intrigued, I can't go into that right now, because I've got to get her out of jail.'

'Oh my God, will she have a record or something?' I'm picturing Hazel behind bars, unable to style her hair. Her life will be over.

'Don't worry, it's not that bad. They're saying it's just a breach of the peace, so she won't be charged.'

'Shall I come and help?' I'm keen to get away, even though I still have work to do.

'No, you're at that wrap party, aren't you? I'll take care of it and we'll see you later. Maybe in court.'

Of course, Robbie is joking, taking this in his stride. He always turns up when it counts. And this is another task I'm very happy to delegate.

'OK, will you keep me posted? Tell her I've come to my senses and she's grounded.'

'Don't worry, I may not be the lawyer she needs, but I am absolutely the irate father.'

317

I kill the call and stand in the street, pondering. So now my mother, my boss, my producer – and everyone who's talked to her – hates me, my best friend thinks I'm a grifter, my sister got married without telling me, I've lost a million-pound commission, and my daughter has been arrested. Then there's the dressing room business, which I'm trying not to think about, and at the end of all this I have to confess my sins to my husband. It's just too much, it can't be fixed; the production's in smithereens and the fire's out of control. I sink to the ground, hugging my knees, as the tears start.

Why did I think today would make a difference? That I could change, hone the skills I needed, prepare myself for this moment and turn it into a triumph? My luck ran out, and I have only myself to blame. Glumly viewing the pavement opposite, I see a woman walking briskly, her bag tight against her body, eyes darting to survey the territory. She's clutching her keys in her hand, doing everything right, alert to danger. It might work, it might not. The danger might be waiting at home, for all I know.

'Are you OK?'

I peer up through my bedraggled curls. It's my assistant producer, Flora, bending over me, her hand stretched out, concerned. Lovely Flora, who also never moans, just gets on with it, keeps the plates spinning, doesn't complain. There are so many of us out there, struggling on, pinning the smiles on our faces even if inwardly we're raging or falling apart.

A woman's work is never done. I blink back the tears, take her outstretched hand and let her help me to my feet.

'Yes. Sorry. Just a hot flush. It's boiling in there.'

She smiles. 'I'm just making a call, I'll see you back inside.'

It's a hell of a to-do list, but I have to get through it somehow, spray a hose on the conflagration. Time to roll up my sleeves and get stuck in. Brushing myself down, I turn around and head back to face the music. It's thumping in there, everyone partying hard. No sign of Petroc. Back in the party room, I start with Caroline, who is still sniffling, being comforted by Oz, of all people. He's awful to all his producers, treats them like dirt. I shoo him away.

'Caroline, I've come to say sorry.'

She squints at me, her fringe all askew. 'No, I'm sorry – you're right, I'm lazy and horrible and no one likes me.'

She's clearly been at the free prosecco. 'No, you're not, you're a bit bossy, but that's a good thing – you just need to channel it in the right way.'

She wipes her nose with the back of her hand, watching me with doleful red eyes.

'I messed up at Chew Hill this afternoon. I should have been more constructive in my criticism. Should have been kinder. You have the makings of an excellent producer, and it's my job to turn you into one. Before, I was too feeble to do it, and today I was just a bitch. You deserve better, and I'm sorry.'

319

Caroline starts to cry again. 'It's not true! You brought us bagels! That's not feeble, that's just . . . nice.'

'Well, from now on I'll stop bringing bagels and be a bit more direct.'

She laughs through her tears. 'Can't you bring in *some* bagels?'

'No more bagels! But I can give you something better . . .' I dig around in my bag, looking for my purse. There's my twenty-pound note, still unfurling, and my mother's Visa, which also took a battering, but I don't need either of those. 'Here.' I hand Caroline a business card.

'Art Andra.' She looks up at me enquiringly.

'An incredible artist. I think he could be really good talent. You should get him in, film a taster tape. Maybe work on a format together. It can be your own project, and if you get a commission, it's your credit.'

I'm spinning her a line here, but it's not entirely untrue. Arturo Andra may be a bit of a wally, but he's renowned in the art world and has a cartoonish quality that might work on telly. He could be good on camera if only he had someone to boss him around.

Caroline flicks the card around her fingers like a majorette. 'You really think he's got potential?'

'I think he could have, with the right producer. Maybe the right *executive* producer?' I tease her, and she steps forward to hug me, which I think is a bit much, but the gesture is probably fuelled by fizz. We're never going to be friends, but I reckon we can work together.

'Thanks,' she says. 'You rock. I'll give him a call.'

'You do that,' I say. 'Tell him I said hello.'

Tick. One down, several more to go.

\* \* \*

I find David Lyon-James in the little drinking den upstairs, talking to Finn, the intern. He's holding two glasses of wine, one red, one white, swilling them, telling Finn something about the colour. That's the thing about David; he's a natural teacher who loves his subject. He'd be the perfect talent for our show, would provide a kind of benign, fatherly presence, bestowing his wisdom on our binge-drinking bunch. I realize that I really want to make the series – that I could do it well, make it funny and entertaining with a dash of something extra, something illuminating and unexpected that will take it beyond the usual Fact Ent fare. Not award-winning or august or worthy; just good, enjoyable telly.

'Hi.' I stand in front of him with my hands clasped behind my back because I don't know what to do with them.

'Hello, Clover.' He puts down the wine and regards me steadily. 'Did Vincent tell you about our conversation?'

'Hmm.' Now I'm here I'm not sure what to say. My script has dried up. 'He's sent me to change your mind.'

'Are you going to give me another speech about BAFTAs and Rose d'Ors?'

'No.' I sigh, sinking into the seat beside him. 'I think the chances of me winning a BAFTA are roughly the same as Vince deciding to donate his profit margin to charity.'

He smiles, and hands me one of the glasses. 'So why on earth should I agree to do this show?'

I take a belt of the wine. It's the club's house white, nowhere near as good as Chew Hill's Bacchus – I know that, because he showed me how to tell the difference.

'Because it'll be fun?'

'I think you might have to do better than that.'

'I mean it though.' Leaning back, I rotate the glass like he did, holding it up to irradiate the liquid. 'When we first met, you showed me the palate of whites, from pale pinot grigio to rich sauternes. This wine sparkles in the light so that means it's not dense and isn't oak-aged. I really enjoyed that afternoon, and I learned something.'

Suddenly I know what to say, and it isn't a script, it's just what I feel.

'We have the chance to make a show that will look really beautiful, and be really funny, and tell the audience something they don't know. And the kids might get drunk, and throw up on your lawn, but we'll clean it up, and at the end of the series they'll come out with a bit of knowledge that might make them more responsible and interesting people. Who knows, maybe there'll be a future winemaker amongst them. Just because this show won't win a BAFTA doesn't mean it's going to be as bad as Oz's *Would Like to Meat*. There's a middle ground, and I think we can find it.'

For a second, David is silent, looking at the red wine undulating around his glass. 'Do you know why I said yes in the first place?' he asks.

I shrug. 'Because we offered you a fat location fee?'

He smiles, acknowledging the hit. 'Well, yes, I'll admit that was part of it. But I mainly said yes because the producers who've approached me in the past had a well-worn spiel that I could spot a mile off, and you didn't. You looked rather embarrassed, and you stuttered when you spoke, and you made sure your associate here' – he indicates Flora, who's joined us and is talking to Finn – 'had a glass of my wine, and you asked her what she thought about everything. In short,' he smiles, 'you were very genuine. I liked you.'

Oh God, this is awful. I feel like we're on an American talk show. Is he going to sing? Noticing my discomfort, he holds up his palms in contrition. 'Don't worry, I won't compliment you any more. I didn't like you as much this afternoon.'

'Today has been a weird day.'

'Let's see where we are tomorrow, then.'

'Does that mean you're back on?'

'I wouldn't say that.'

'But not off?'

He nods. 'On the fence would be a better way of putting it.'

'On the vertical trellis,' I say, and he laughs.

'I might have to do the show just so I can provide you with better vintages than this,' he says, indicating his red. 'It's abominable.'

'Vince needs people to get leathered so that they're more likely to buy his new format,' I say. 'Talking of which, the screening is starting in five minutes. I'd swerve it if I were you – it might put you off us again.'

'Thanks for the tip.'

Tick. Well, not a tick, but not a cross either. Hearing Vince shouting at people to get a bloody move on, I head towards the screening room, along with the rest of the party, who seem reluctant at the prospect of having to sit still and stop gassing for thirty minutes. We're all going to watch a rough cut of our new show, *Blind Dinner Date*, which Oz executive produced. It's a stupid idea and no doubt Oz has made a hash of it, but it has an easily appreciable concept, and Vince managed to scrape together international funding from Red Eye's parent companies to make a pilot. Channels are sniffing round and everyone has high hopes of selling it around the world. I spot Petroc at the back, and squeeze in next to him, far away from my dressing room demon, who is at the front, being shown to his seat by Vince. The guest of dishonour.

'How are you?' Petroc says.

'Just dandy.'

He laces his fingers through mine. 'Are you ready?'

His nicely shaped nails have mud under them – he's

probably been digging up bodies in his graveyard. 'Do I need to be?'

'Yes.'

I settle back, looking at the black screen as the lights dim. 'Then let's go.'

# 42

When David complimented me, I felt deeply uncomfortable, because I'm not used to it. Obviously, praise from Rose was and is as rare as hen's teeth, and no one else in my family is particularly effusive. Susie is a very supportive friend, but not really the type to applaud. Robbie is more of a doer than a sayer, which I much prefer. When people tell me I've done well, I want to run away, unnerved by the scrutiny, the positive confrontation. I duck my head, sit at the back, wince when my name appears on the credits, happier to be behind the scenes than on screen. With Petroc's hand in mine as the viewing begins, I'm safe in the dark, anonymous, hidden, and I like it that way.

Rough cuts are always pretty . . . well, *rough*, often with time codes left on screen, and if they haven't been through the final online edit, then the picture quality isn't great. This can actually enhance a viewing – commissioners feel they're seeing something raw and new, the first to pluck the coarse diamond from the crust. So we're all used to watching slightly cobbled-together footage and appreciating what it could be rather than what it is. Which is why when the film starts, it takes the audience quite a while to understand that they are *not* watching *Blind Dinner Date*. No; they are watching me.

When I first started at Red Eye, Petroc taught me there's more than one way to skin a cat. Sometimes you have to get sneaky. Sometimes you don't make a scene; you fake it. I knew the dressing room face-off wouldn't go well; these things never do. It was always going to end in denial – he's the villain, but sees himself as a hero, and there was no way my words were going to change anything. But in the end, I didn't need them to. Because in the edit he comes out as a total monster.

The scene is filmed on two cameras, discreetly placed in different positions in the dressing room. We see him snort the line, beckon me over; I back away, shaking my head. There's a cut, and I'm semi-naked, him tugging my dress off me as I try to pull it back. Then he's looming over me, turning my chin this way and that, assessing me. I'm clearly uncomfortable, writhing and wrestling from his grasp, pushing him away: '*Get away from me.*' More dialogue:

'*You said that if I slept with you, I'd get a promotion.*' I'm clutching my dress against my body as protection. There's a gasp in the audience.

'*Well, I'm sure I didn't force you.*' The camera cuts to a close-up of his self-satisfied smirk.

'*I'm sure you think you didn't.*'

Another jump cut and he's pushing me against the door, pressing up against me, my face turned away. '*Please, don't.*'

The cameras – and the cut – are an extremely effective means of conveying exactly how unpleasant the moment was. The edit doesn't tell the *whole* truth, but it does reveal an essential truth; *my* truth – which is that this man is dangerous, and must be stopped. Women in the audience are turning to each other, men shaking their heads, murmuring as they work out who the baddie is, pointing at him, the turned-to-stone man in the front row. I shift in my seat, feeling twitchy and unsettled as various members of the Red Eye staff crane round, eyeing me with curiosity and confusion. This is my moment in the spotlight – I didn't want it and don't enjoy it, but I knew it had to be done, for all the other Clovers who weren't able to make it stop.

'*Put your clothes on before you go out, you might cause a scene. Thanks for the fun times.*'

The final shot is of me thrown against the wall, and sinking against it, my hands over my face. It looks like I'm crying – I wasn't. What does it matter what I was doing? All that matters is how it looks. And it looks very, very bad for this particular CEO of a US conglomerate, who thought everyone would rather listen to him than me. The film finishes with his name on screen, followed by his position, and the company, lest there be any doubt. The nail in the coffin – his kingdom is lost.

The screen fades to black again, and the murmuring

crescendos to an excited clamour, as TV's great and good all pull out their phones to make sure everyone knows what just happened in this room. Nothing's real until someone's put it on social media. As they tap and exclaim to each other, he stands, surveying the room in disgust. His eyes rove around, and eventually they meet mine, locking in on me as he assesses the damage. But there's no way of putting out this fire, and he knows it. And so, I hold his gaze. I want him to know I'm not scared, that he has no power, and that seems like the best way to show it. I stare him down, Petroc still squeezing my hand, and finally he turns, spitting out a curse, and stalks out, the tails of his jacket flapping. I don't think he'll be buying our format.

'Prick,' someone shouts as he exits, and I feel something inside me lift and soar. A true mindful breath. I've done it. I delegated this job to Petroc and he has risen to the occasion, turning around this edit in record time and producing a rough cut that hit its target perfectly. He deserves an award, maybe an Emmy.

'Where did you get the cameras?' I murmur, as we both sit still, ignoring the demented chatter and fussing around us.

'Flora,' he says. 'She was happy to help. And Imogen switched the links so our film played instead. He's been sending her creepy emails.'

'Stars, all of you. Thank you.' My throat feels thick.

'You owe us doughnuts. Me, mainly, for working my filthy fingers to the bone in the world's fastest edit.'

It's true I owe him, big time. 'I was thinking,' I say, 'about your church. Why don't you film it? Make a taster on the perils of religious restoration, pitch it to Channel Four, then you can get some experts in to help you sort it all out.'

'Hmm.' Petroc strokes his chin. 'That's not a bad thought.'

I tap my temple. 'You see, I did have a show idea after all. So it was worth taking the day off.'

He smiles. 'Oh, I'd say it was worth it.'

And we sit together, hand in hand, as Vince stands up looking like he's been hit by a truck, and announces that, following a technical hitch, we will now be watching an episode of *Blind Dinner Date*.

Tick, tick, tick. He was a suspect package but, rather than run away, I blew him up.

See? I *said* I had a plan.

# 43

Afterwards, Vince collars me as I'm collecting Bigwig from the attendant.

'What the fuck was that?' he says, as I ladle the rabbit into his pouch.

I stare at him appraisingly, stroking Bigwig's twitching nose with one finger. 'It was me, getting my own back,' I say, eventually. 'I've been waiting twenty years.'

The attendant staggers out of the cloakroom, lugging Vince's Segway, but he ignores her. 'Well, you could have at least warned me you were going full-on revenge porn. I would have directed it a hell of a lot better. That second camera angle was too wide, and the final jump cut was a fucking travesty. A cross-fade would have been classier.'

I laugh in disbelief. 'Blame Petroc, it was his work.'

'He always was an overhasty editor. Slapdash.' Vince shakes his head sorrowfully.

'Effective though.'

'Sure, sure. Maybe I should give him your raise.'

'*I* still want that.'

'You're going to have to earn it. Particularly now I've lost a buyer.'

'I'm sorry he's not going to take your format.'

Vince shrugs. 'Plenty more fish in the sea. Less slippery ones. By the way, Avon House called again. They've reinstated your membership. You live to pitch on a sunlounger another day.'

I grimace. 'What changed their minds?'

He holds up his phone. 'Apparently you're a superstar Instagrammer now – they don't want you to badmouth them. The manager called me personally to assure me you'll be given special privileges. I don't know what that means but it sounded filthy.'

Permission to be one of Avon House's water baubles. The thought makes me smile. Maybe I'll take them up on it, go and stare at my pearly toes again one day.

'Thanks,' I say. 'I could do with some good news.'

To my surprise, Vince puts his hand on my arm, very briefly. 'You did well,' he says. 'It was a good show.'

Before I can react, he's distracted by a woman collecting her bag. The bag is Hermès, and its owner is the chief executive of ITV.

'So good to see you!' he exclaims. 'If I could just steal one moment of your time before you go . . .' And he bears her off back to the bar, winking at me over his shoulder.

When I emerge from the club, it's finally dark, though the warmth of the day lingers. Many of the Red Eye staff are going on elsewhere to carry on partying, but I can't wait to get a cab home, fall into bed and maybe have that moment of peace I've been chasing, before sleep consumes me. The effects of the booze have long worn off, and I'm left feeling strangely empty and bereft, though buoyed by the comments and hugs from my colleagues as they exit. Caroline embraces me again, clutching my neck and shouting 'You did it, girlfriend!' until I have to gently disengage, track down her fellow crew members and palm her off on them. Flora gives me a shy thumbs up as she departs, and I think what a nice girl she is, how I'd really rather help *her* become a good producer, show her the ropes and set her on her way. Now I've seen off my (de)mentor, it's time I became one myself.

Taking a deep breath of the night air, I wander towards the nearest taxi rank, but am interrupted by the buzz of my phone. Assuming it's Robbie, and wanting news of Hazel, I pluck it out of my pocket, but it's not my husband; it's my sister.

'It's Rose,' she says, her voice unusually sharp and high. 'She says she's going to throw herself off the bridge.'

'*What?*'

Maz sounds tearful. 'The suspension bridge. I've been on the phone to her, trying to talk her down. *Not* down. She's completely hysterical.'

'Why did she call you? Aren't you back in Crediton? Why didn't she call me?'

'She did, apparently. You didn't answer.'

All the missed calls from her today just blended in to another thing I didn't have time for. And I'm not sure I have time for it now. Not for one minute do I think my mother is about to jump off a bridge to her almost-certain death, no crinoline to slow down her fall. She's far too self-satisfied. But it's certainly a deviation from her usual modus operandi. An unexpected narrative twist from Baby Jane. I thought it wasn't the last I'd seen of her tonight, but I didn't expect *this*.

'Is it even possible to jump off the bridge? I mean, aren't there barriers or something?'

'I don't know, but I'm not sure we should leave her there on the off-chance that jumping off is difficult?'

'No, no, of course. I'm on my way. Don't worry, she just wants attention. And Maz?'

'Yes?' I can hear a dog barking in the background. It must be Gawain.

'What you told us today, at dinner. I just wanted to say, I'm really pleased for you. And . . . and proud of you.'

'Thank you. I'm sorry I didn't tell you before. Wasn't sure how.'

'No, I get it. It's just . . . I'd really like to meet Calum, get to know him. But before that, I'd like to meet you. Get to know *you*, Mrs Fraser.'

She laughs, shakily. 'You know me.'

I grip my mobile. 'Not properly. Let's meet and talk, properly.'

There's a pause, and then she says 'The IKEA café is a

good place to talk. I could meet you there.'

'You've got yourself a date.'

'How nice.'

Putting my phone back in my pocket, I sigh. It looks like I'm not going to bed just yet. At least Rose has chosen her location well, since I'm only down the road. Almost as if she planned it that way. Grumbling to myself, I set off briskly in the direction of the suspension bridge, answering another phone call en route. This time it *is* my husband.

'How's Hazel?'

'The Keynsham One is fine, we're on our way home. Just a slap on the wrist, thanks to her lawyer, who also gave her a slap on the wrist.' That's the thing about Robbie, he's like the Kipling poem about keeping your head when all about you are losing theirs. What's it called? I can't remember now. But he's that Man, treating triumph and disaster just the same. Such an even keel.

'Thank God.'

'How was your party?'

'Um . . . It was . . . useful. Professionally, and personally.' I've never lied to Robbie, but I don't want to tell him all this over the phone, particularly when I'm ostensibly on my way to stop my mother chucking herself into the Avon Gorge.

'Good. Are you coming back?'

'Not yet. Bit of a job to do first.' Again, I don't want to alarm anyone, when I'm still convinced Rose is just staging an elaborate 'look at me' moment.

'OK, I'll see you later, midons.'

Midons. He hasn't called me that in years. Early on, at the beginning of our 'courtship', he used to say it, explaining it was an old poetic version of 'my lady'. I liked it; it suited my preference for indirectness. I wonder why he's thought of it now, when we're both middle-aged exhausted parents struggling to balance chaotic home life with demanding careers, wondering if the joint account will stretch to fixing the roof. Once, I was his midons, slim and unlined, ready to be wooed and won. Maybe I will let him book that holiday in Greece, after all, to trawl the ruins. Like a second honeymoon, albeit one with two moaning kids. I smile to myself. It could be fun, the Hendrys hitting Athens, doing our respective things. Robbie can look at his relics, Ethan can find somewhere to hole up, Hazel can visit the Greek salons and I can . . . what can Clover do? Just rest, and think, and be. *Stop*, for a while.

But first, I've got to stop my mother.

# 44

I find Rose standing at the base of the Clifton tower, leaning against the abutment wall, smoking a cigarette, of all things. The bridge behind her is all lit up, the illumination dazzling against the inky night sky; a fittingly climactic backdrop for her continuing emotional meltdown. When she sees me, she lets the cigarette fall to the ground and stamps on it with the toe of her kitten heel.

'Nice of you to drop by.'

'I just happened to be passing. Since when did you take up smoking?'

'Since my daughters publicly disowned me.' She wipes a hand across her face, and I see that she has mascara tracks on her cheeks. The elegant chignon is long gone, her hair straggly around her shoulders.

'Bit of a dramatic way of putting it.'

'Well, how would *you* put it?'

I go to stand beside her, dumping my bag and Bigwig on the ground, grasping the rough sandstone of the wall and staring out over the dark chasm of the gorge. 'I'd probably say that you finally got your comeuppance after years of being a total bitch.'

There's a gasp of shock and outrage. 'How can you say that? When I . . . When I . . .'

'See? You can't even defend yourself against it. When you . . . when you . . . what? What have you done for us? Comforted us when we cried? Praised us, supported us, paid for us, *loved* us? You can't claim you did any of those things, because you didn't. What did you actually do?'

'I *stayed*.' It bursts out of her as a snarl. 'When your father buggered off.'

Biting my lip, my fingers scrape against the wall, eyes probing the darkness, ignoring the light from the bridge. 'But don't you understand why he left?'

Rose takes a shuddering breath. 'You don't know what went on between us, not really. He was always gone. Not ever there, fully. I knew it, and I didn't know what to do. I thought . . . if I kept the house nice, and myself looking nice, and made sure you girls didn't bother him, then . . .' She trails off, turning to face the same way as me, out into the abyss. 'It didn't work, but I tried.'

All that cleaning, and what a mess she made of it. I think about my father, who I never really consider at all – Cousin Jack, a vague presence in my life, on the periphery. For the first time, I realize he really wasn't that great – like Rose, he didn't do any of the things you might expect of a parent but, rather than blame him, I just switched him off, focusing all my attention and ire on my mother, who stayed.

'Can I have one of those?' I gesture to the packet she's clutching. She opens it and offers me one, getting a lighter out of her bag for both of us. We light up, inhale, and exhale into the sweet summer night air. I cough, because the last time I smoked was at university, and I never really enjoyed it, just thought it looked sophisticated when I was in the pub. But now I want to blacken my lungs as a penance, because I'm feeling guilty and wretched and wrong and I'm not quite sure why. Rose slaps me on the back and I think it's one of the most motherly things she's ever done, and my eyes water as I hack and splutter.

'I'm sorry,' I say finally, taking another drag. 'It was probably a bit much, back there in the restaurant, but I've had a difficult day.'

'*You've* had a difficult day? What about *me*? I'm homeless!'

Now I'm coughing and laughing, flicking ash over the wall, watching it float down. 'Again, that's a bit of a dramatic way of putting it. Can't you just stop the sale?'

Her mouth twists into a grimace. 'I've sold the house to Alice Barber's daughter and her new husband. There'll be a terrible to-do if I back out. Is Jack really moving in with you?'

I shake my head, flicking more ash, the particles idly drifting and gliding. 'Of course not. Like he'd give up the cushy expat life.'

'Then why . . .?'

Turning to meet her gaze, I frown in disbelief.

'Are you really asking me why I don't want you to move in? When you've barely ever visited, never bothered with your grandchildren, shown no interest in my family whatsoever? A better question would be: why on earth do you want to live with us? To play the dutiful granny?'

She gives me a bitter smile. 'You know that's never been my style. I like my own life. But . . .'

'But what?'

Rose takes a deep drag, leaning her elbows on the wall and gazing out into the gloom. 'I'm lonely,' she whispers it into the darkness, like the dirtiest confession. 'I've got no one.'

For a second, I'm winded by the admission. 'But . . . you're always so busy, you never have any time . . .'

She nods. 'I fill my time, to avoid thinking about it. But then I sit in that house, on my own, with no one to talk to, and I just . . .'

I picture Dorothy Fletcher, the previous owner of our house. 'What about . . . um . . . one of those retirement village thingies?'

Rose shudders. 'Ghastly.'

I remember I read about the foundations of the bridge we're standing on, how everyone thought they were solid, but then they found immense vaulted chambers beneath, a huge lost space just sitting there, waiting to be discovered. Taking another long pull, this time I don't cough. I'm a smoker now.

'Listen, I'm sorry that you're feeling lonely, but I don't

think moving in with us is the answer. We'd just annoy you, the house would annoy you, and, putting it mildly, you would annoy us.' I stub out the fag and chuck it in the nearby bin. 'But . . .' I can't believe I'm about to say this. 'Why don't you come visit a bit more? I mean, *really* visit? Stay with us, hang out with us, take the kids out? You might find your empty silent house is actually quite nice and peaceful when you get back.'

Rose laughs, wiping her cheeks again. 'Maybe.' She stares at the smouldering tip of her cigarette. 'I . . . Your grandfather – my father . . . He was very strict. I wasn't . . . I didn't . . .' She clutches her neck with her free hand, remembering.

'Grandpa Bill?' He died when I was little. Thinking hard, I can't recall much about him except he had a beard and a Volvo he cleaned every Saturday morning.

'Yes.' Rose lets out a breath. 'He's why Harry is such a mess.' Uncle Harold, always crying at weddings. 'He was such a soft child. I was made of sterner stuff. But . . .' She turns to me, smiling a twisted smile. 'Father liked things neat, quiet. Girls were girls, boys were boys. It stuck.'

'I see.' Poor Rose. Poor Harry.

'Anyway, no point getting all introspective.' Rose stubs out her cigarette. 'But maybe your messy, noisy house would be nice, once in a while.'

'And in the meantime . . .' Having a brainwave, I bend towards my bag. 'Here's a companion to keep you company in the evenings.' Reaching in, I carefully lift out

Bigwig, smoothing his soft fur and kissing his downy head. His whiskers twitch enquiringly.

'What on earth is that?'

'It's a rabbit. I got it for you. You know, as a pet. It's not a cat, so you won't be allergic to it.' I'm sad to let him go, but he's going to a better place. Better, at least, than a boiling hot car. 'I think it's an English Lop.' That's what Danny the taxi driver told me, after googling it on his phone.

'What will I do with a rabbit?' Rose is baffled, but reaches out a tentative finger to stroke Bigwig's long floppy ear.

'Live with him. Look after him, fuss him, talk to him. Show him the sights of Stroud.'

'What will people say?' My mother looks horrified by the prospect.

'They'll say: "Oh, there's Rose Parker and her rabbit. She's such a character."' Leaving no room for argument, I load Bigwig into her arms. To my astonishment, he nuzzles her and settles in the crook of her shoulder. If he *was* a cat he'd be purring. My mother looks confused for a second, but then her expression clears. She's obviously picturing herself out and about, bunny in tow, the talk of the town: '*Yes, it's an English Lop; from a very old family. A pure pedigree.*'

'I'll call her . . . Clover,' she breathes, her face transfixed.

I frown. 'But . . . *I'm* called Clover.'

'Mmm,' returns my mother absently, gazing at her

new offspring dotingly. '*This* Clover will be a true comfort to me.'

'Right.' Picking up my much-lighter bag, I give my alter ego rabbit a farewell pat. Rose clutches her jealously. 'Bring her over to show the kids soon, won't you? They'd like to meet their new . . . aunt.'

She nods distractedly, busy picking up her bag. 'I'll need a cab back to Redcliffe. Can you arrange it?' Rose's crown is restored, she's returning to the palace.

'Sure.' I get out my phone, summon an Uber and add one for myself at the same time. To hell with it; I make mine a Lux. Mum can slum it.

We have another cigarette while we wait, and by the time the first car approaches I'm heady with nicotine, a full-on fag ash Lil. Maybe this will be my thing now; I can learn French and wear sheath dresses and carry a little dog like Lafayette. Except I hate Lafayette. I miss Bigwig, my emotional support animal, who is now my mother's daughter substitute. Maybe I could try to summon Barbara the alpaca again, but feel the moment's passed. There's always Grizelda, waiting at home with a dead mouse and a flicking tail, but she's not exactly comforting – more of a fluffy assassin. I need comforting.

The first car pulls up and I help my mother into it, tucking her Visa card back into her purse before I hand it to her. Rose makes herself comfortable in her carriage, and then my own arrives and her eyes narrow in annoyance when she sees it's a better one. She opens her mouth to complain and suggest we swap.

'Too late now.' I slam her door. She lowers the window.

'What happened to you today, to make you like this?'

I hesitate. 'Robbie put the forks in the dishwasher the wrong way up. Down. It set me off.'

She nods, satisfied. 'Count yourself lucky. Your father never even bought me a dishwasher. My hands were red raw.'

'What a shitbag.'

Rose grins. 'That Spanish woman is welcome to him.'

'*Olé.*' I pat the roof of the car and step back; she waves her vertical hand twist, and they're off, back to the Redcliffe penthouse. Then I get into my own car, which is a gleaming Jaguar, and finally I'm on my way home.

# 45

The driver is a very different beast from Danny. Or maybe I am a different passenger. Taking one look at my face in the rear-view mirror, he switches the radio from Magic to Classic FM.

'You look like you need something soothing,' he murmurs. 'I'm Stanislaw. I'll leave you be.'

It's just too much. I begin to sob loudly, much to his distress. 'There, there,' he says, doing a three-point turn, taking in my bedraggled hair and wild eyes as he cranes round. 'Shall I call someone?'

'Nooooooo,' I wail. 'I'm actually quite happeeeeeeheeeee. I just need to . . .' I give into the paroxysms, relishing the release.

'Ah,' he nods. 'Catharsis.' He passes me a box of ultra-balm tissues. That's what you get with a Lux.

Mumbling my thanks, I put my hands over my face to really go for it. It's pouring out, all the tears, along with the anger and guilt and worry and fear, to the accompaniment of Mozart's 'Queen of the Night' aria. It's pretty frenetic – the station's choices aren't as calming as they might be and

Stanislaw discreetly flicks to Radio Four, which is playing the shipping forecast.

'*North-West Malin . . . losing its identity . . . new high expected . . .*'

'Do you want to talk about it?' asks Stanislaw softly.

'No,' I say, and then proceed to tell him everything. 'I threw food at an old woman and shoplifted a dress and destroyed a priceless artwork – well, it wasn't priceless, but it was worth over five thousand pounds – and I told my daughter to fuck school and she got arrested, and I made my mother throw a brick through a restaurant window, and broke into someone's house, and dealt class A drugs, and drove a lawnmower through a yoga group, and nearly lost a million-pound commission, and oh God, I stole this from an arms dealer.' I pull the golden finger out of my bag and wave it helplessly.

'*. . . thundery showers, occasionally good.*'

'Quite a day,' says Stanislaw.

'Yes,' I say. 'It was.'

All this time I thought what happened on the night of the Beatnik party was my fault. My fault for being feeble and naïve, and my mother's for bringing me up to be that way. I felt it was a mess of my own making, and hers, when of course it wasn't.

It was *his* fault.

His fault, his flaws, his mess. I did nothing wrong. Rose, despite her failings, is not to blame. Just him. Him and his entitlement; his monstrous hubris and casual cruelty. I thought that one thing led to another and everything was connected, but it's not. Sometimes bad things happen, no matter how good you try to be, or how strong you are, or how many times you try to stop it. Sometimes kingdoms are lost, even if every last nail is in place. The realization makes me catch my breath, the most mindful breath I've ever managed.

'*Mainly fair. Good.*'

'I'm better now.' I blow my nose on one tissue, and wipe my eyes with another.

'Good. You rest a while.'

Settling back into my seat, I send my best friend a series of texts.

I'm really sorry, but I took Dubai guy golden finger. An accident.

Not an accident, but I wasn't myself. Will return tomorrow.

Might have a house for SOjourn. Renovated church in Batheaston. Not finished yet, but could be beautiful.

Good bones, like that poem. Can't remember it now.

Soz Sooz. Tx 4 everything. I luv U.

'. . . *Rising slowly. Moderate or poor.*'

I see the dots pulsing, and eventually her reply comes through: Twat. You owe me a tenner.

I think that means we're OK.

\* \* \*

In the cocoon of my cab, I remember a day years ago, when our parents took us to the zoo. No, it wasn't a zoo; it was a wildlife park, in the grounds of a country estate, rhinos roaming around outside a Victorian manor house, all a bit incongruous. We went because Rose had been given free tickets by a friend, and although she had no interest in going, she thought it might be construed as ungrateful and rude if she didn't use them and report back. I would have been about ten, and Maz seven or eight. Dad drove us there, with the intention to send us round the park on our own while they sat in the car, but they must have had an argument or something because we'd barely got past the wallabies when Rose caught up with us, looking out of breath and irritable. She joined us just as we were approaching the reindeer. Maz always says they were alpacas but they weren't because I remember the sign.

'Don't!' was the first thing she said when she saw us. One of the reindeer was rubbing up against the fence, trying to scratch himself, and Maz was reaching out to help him. 'They're dirty.'

'I'll wash my hands,' Maz promised, her little fingers itching away at his thick fur. The reindeer grunted in pleasure. As luck would have it, one of the caretakers arrived with a bucket of feed, and he let us have a handful, so Maz was able to let the animal snuffle at her palm, huffing and grunting as she giggled and squealed. She was enthralled and although my mother disapproved, she didn't like to say so in front of the staff, just watched with slight anxiety as the herd gathered around us, sniffing and nudging. The food was soon gone, and therefore the reindeer, who don't tend to stick around unless there's something in it for them. They turned their attention to the caretaker, who had more of the good stuff. As he bent down to empty the bucket into their trough, one of the biggest reindeer butted him, caught him at a bad angle, and he tumbled, flat into the mud. It had been a rainy summer, and it was a proper pratfall. Rose fell about.

I'd never seen my mother laugh like that. Not her usual tinkly 'how very amusing' titter, but a full-throated guffaw that shook her whole body and flung her head back. We thought it was pretty funny as well, but mainly we were laughing at her; *with* her. Sharing the joke. When she finally stopped, her cheeks were pink and her eyes bright. She took us to the café to wash our hands, and then bought us an ice cream each, ones with a chocolate flake and sprinkles, and when Maz dropped her flake, rather than scold she just said 'Butterfingers!' plucked it from the floor and plonked it straight back in the cone. The laugh seemed to have relaxed her, and she sat with a coffee, listening to us talk about the animals, smiling when Maz said one day she would have her own farm. She even took us to the little park playground, pushed us on the swings, applauded when we came down the slide. I'd never had such a prolonged and focused interaction with her, and it was a revelation. When we got back to the car, she flopped into her seat with a happy sigh and said 'Well, Jack, you missed a treat.' And he grunted like the reindeer and started the engine. By the time we got home she was back to her normal self, tutting, preoccupied, wiping our finger drawings off the windows.

But at bedtime, when we were usually dispatched and left to our own devices, she put her head round the door to quell the chattering.

'Quiet, please! Your father is watching television.'

'That was the best day of my life,' Maz said.

Rose paused, her hand on the light switch. 'Mine too,' she replied, and I saw Maz wriggle in delight just before the room was plunged into darkness.

It wasn't, of course, but I liked that she said it. I didn't have any dreams at all that night. Not a single one.

# 46

It's half one in the morning by the time I arrive home, but there are still lights on inside the house. Robbie will have left a pint of water on the kitchen table – that's what we do for each other when one of us goes out on the lash. I always think it's a very tender form of passive aggression: 'You're drunk, drink this.' Sometimes we leave tablets too, if we know it's going to be a big night, though of course such nights are rare nowadays. I think of the Vicodin I took this morning – surely it will have left my system now? Along with whatever else assailed and fired me today – I can feel it all draining away with every breath. Back to normal. Whatever normal is.

I say goodnight to the lovely Stanislaw, who opens the door and helps me out, an anxious steward. We part by the front gate. He shakes my hand and says '*Co się stało, to się nie odstanie.*'

'What does that mean?'

'Polish saying. What's done is done. How do you say, the phrase about milk?'

'Don't cry over spilled milk?'

'Exactly. *Co z oczu to z serca.* Out of your eyes, out of your heart. Put it behind you.'

We should get this guy on TV; he could be an agony uncle dispensing his wisdom to the masses and make a fortune, instead of driving Ubers. But who am I to say that being a taxi driver isn't just as fulfilling? So I don't get out my business card, I just press his hand and say '*Dziękuję.*' I can say please, thank you and sorry in many, many languages, because I like to be prepared. Some might say that's crazy, but I think it's just polite. You never know. As is being proved, this very moment, at my own front door.

Stanislaw bows and releases me and I walk down the path looking at our lintel, illuminated by the security light Robbie installed. 1680. All the drama that this house has seen. The births and deaths and shouting and laughter and dinners and sex and quiet contemplation. All the spilled milk. Whatever has happened to me today is probably nothing compared to what went before. He's right: what's done is done and it's time to consign it to history.

I let myself in, quietly, bending to stroke Grizelda, who weaves around me miaowing, pretending she hasn't been fed. Actually, she may not have been, because everyone in my household tends to assume someone else has done it, and by someone else, I mean me. Usually, this would pull out a tiny grenade pin, cause a little light fuming as I make myself a cup of tea flavoured with bitterness, but right now I think it's nice to be the lintel in the Hendry family. Without me, they'd crumble. Also, Grizelda loves – well, *tolerates* – me best, so I win.

In the kitchen, there's the pint of water waiting, and Robbie with it, sitting in a dishevelled suit looking exhausted. Instead of tablets, there's the empty Vicodin packet.

He nods towards it. 'Exceptional circumstances?'

'Unprecedented. Bit weird, checking the bin?' Taking a sip of my water, I finger the sharp edges of the foil and plastic.

'Lost my bank card.'

'Why would it be in the bin?'

'Threw it in with the takeaway cartons.' He grins as I roll my eyes.

'I leave you all for five minutes . . .' Flicking the kettle on, I root around for a tea bag.

'Speaking of which . . .' Robbie hands me the milk. 'Would you like to tell me about the "five minutes" you've been gone? Because I've had calls from Petroc, and Maz, who are both worried, and Glynis Johnson from your book group, who thinks you're unwell. Then there's Hazel saying you're insane and she's been arrested because you told her to go on a climate crusade. Nice hair, by the way.' He tweaks one of my curls. 'And the dress.'

'How did you get her out? Was it awful?' I pour hot water over the bag, watching the leaves infuse the liquid, leaving their mark.

'Of course not. She's a sixteen-year-old middle-class white girl and I'm a forty-six-year-old lawyer. Everyone was very polite and apologetic. Unfortunately, Hazel's new boyfriend isn't so lucky. I had to get him out as well. With less politeness, and fewer apologies.'

'Hazel's *boyfriend*?' I can feel myself smirking. He was so handsome and idealistic.

'I'm going to rock on my heels and brandish the shotgun tomorrow. Right now, I'm too tired. But I want to know about you. What happened?'

I sigh, closing my eyes against the tears. I'm tired too. So very tired.

'It was such a long day. Can we do it tomorrow?' Obviously, I'm going to tell him everything. But it feels like too much to go into at nearly two o'clock in the morning – taking the pin out of a much bigger grenade. Also, I suspect a certain disgraced CEO of a US media conglomerate will be on the first flight from Heathrow, and I'd really rather he was out of the country before Robbie is any the wiser, otherwise his shotgun might get some use.

There's a pause as my husband ponders, his urge to know battling his urge to sleep. 'OK,' he says. 'But try not to take any more out-of-date drugs.'

'No, sir. Only fresh narcotics for me from now on.'

He laughs, and kisses me. 'I'm going up. Don't be long.'

I sit for a while sipping my tea, watching the cat, who has curled up for a night-time nap on the draining board of the sink. She takes great pleasure in resting in awkward places, looking hugely attractive while doing so. Grizelda does exactly as she likes, all the time – we can take it or leave it, and of course not only do we take it; we love her for it. But cats can get away with that, day in day out, whereas we humans have to compromise. Maybe not please and thank you and sorry in every language, at every step, but at least general politeness and the occasional apology. Bagels now and then. And that's not being feeble, it's just being nice.

Switching off the lights, I make my way upstairs, to Hazel's room, and gently push the door open. She's asleep on her silken pillow, hair fanning out around her head, all kinked from the plaits. She's smiling, like she's having a pleasant dream, and she looks beautiful, with my mother's cheekbones. Dear, silly, vain, funny, crusading girl. I close the door again and head to Ethan's room.

'Shit.' He's lying on the bed, mid-spliff, too dazed to react quickly enough.

I raise my eyebrows. 'Caught red-handed.'

He moves to stub it out.

'Uh-uh.' I shake my head. 'Give it here.'

His expression is lugubrious, anticipating the destruction of his tenderly rolled creation, and when, instead of grinding it out, I take a pull, he blinks, processing everything very slowly. With the joint still smouldering between my fingers, I sit on his bed.

'Budge up.'

He shifts over, and I lie down next to him, offering him

the roll-up. For a second he just looks at me sideways, still stupefied, then takes it and inhales cautiously.

'Can we agree that if this is the last one you're going to have – and I want it to be – that we may as well enjoy it?'

Because Covid never affected our sense of smell, we've been aware of Ethan's penchant for the occasional spliff, and, after much agonizing, mainly on my part, decided we would kick the cannabis down the road. At least he was doing it in the comfort of his own room and not on street corners, at least it was just hash, at least he wasn't a total stoner, etc. I fretted that it's a gateway drug and that we should really stamp on it straight away, but was wary of doing so, because I worried we would drive it underground, make it temptingly forbidden fruit. How to play it? Now I realize I just have to do it with him to make it ludicrously uncool. It's clear it's working – he's utterly appalled. Dope is no longer dope. Not now he's watched his mother inhale.

'Didn't know you were into this,' he mumbles, scarlet with embarrassment, passing it back.

'I remember my first joint, at a Valentine's school disco in 1992,' I say, breathing in the heady honeyed fumes. 'Afterwards, I snogged a boy called Eustace MacQuoid. It turned out he also snogged my best friend Sophie, so I spent the rest of the evening crying and being sick in the toilets. Not my best night.'

It's all true, although actually I remember the evening quite fondly. But Ethan will never recover from these memories. Joints shall forever be tainted. I am the grim reefer, killing his buzz.

'Then there was the great whitey of 1995,' I continue ruthlessly, taking another hit. At least he's got decent stuff, this is doing the job nicely. I feel like I did in the Red Eye meeting this morning, on a slow waltzer, or after Entonox, swirling gently, like ash flicked off a bridge. 'That was bad – dizziness, cold sweats, with a crowd of people around me chanting "Clover's unlucky." I didn't do it again after that.' Reaching across him, I stub out the roll-up on the plate next to the bed, alongside the crust of a piece of toast.

'You're too good for this, Ethan. What are you doing, smoking a joint at two in the morning?'

He stares up at the ceiling. 'Had a bad dream,' he whispers, and I am undone. Suddenly he's a little boy again, scampering into our bed in the middle of the night, and I'm clutching him to me, feeling the pounding of his tiny heart. I always thought my bad dreams were caused by my childhood, my anxiety festering and infusing my sleep like tea tannins. What does it mean that Ethan is similarly afflicted? That, thanks to me, he's had a bad childhood? Or are they just . . . dreams? Passed down the generations, like cheekbones?

I feel for his hand on the bed. 'Do you want to talk about it?'

He shakes his head, still looking up. 'Maybe tomorrow,' he says. 'When it's gone.'

'OK then,' I reply, squeezing his hand, which is bigger than mine. 'We'll talk about it tomorrow.'

Tomorrow and tomorrow and tomorrow. Some things matter, and this is one of them. My son. My dear, quiet, thoughtful, sensitive, embarrassed boy. Tomorrow we'll sort it. But tonight . . . tonight, we'll just rest here, and think, and be.

So I switch off the light, and we both lie gazing up at the ceiling, which is dotted with old glowing stars from when Ethan was small, which no one can be bothered to prise off. And that's how my day ends, with a celestial vision, that soothes and lulls me, my eyes growing heavy as they contemplate the heavens, light and dark swirling together until I'm dragged down, down, down into a dreamless sleep.

# FRIDAY

# 47

The next day, 17th June, starts like any other. I wake up in my own bed, having somehow transported myself there in the night. Robbie is slumbering beside me, snoring lightly. Grizelda is reposing on the lid of the laundry basket. The house is quiet, apart from birdsong.

I have a headache, which crept up in the night, because yesterday I drank my own bodyweight in booze, and fully deserve the stonking hangover coming my way. Groggily rearing out of bed, I stumble downstairs and begin clearing up last night's detritus, which Robbie no doubt imagines he already dealt with. The table is greasy with curry oil and littered with shards of naan bread – a feast for our resident mice. No one switched on the dishwasher, so it's stacked with dirty plates and cutlery, thrown in every which way. Ditto the washing machine, which has finished a cycle but not been emptied, so it's full of dank clothes.

After dealing with it all, I treat myself to paracetamol washed down with tea, which I drink in the garden, admiring our field of weeds and withered plants. Sitting on the swing Robbie hung from the cedar tree, I sway on the seat in the early morning sunshine, gazing at the boughs above. There's a fresher feel to the air today, sunny but not as sultry, and the slight cool breeze is a balm to my aching head. Ethan and Hazel grew out of this solid honed plank years ago, but we didn't like to take it away because of what it stood for. What it swung for. Our new lives, and new family, and new start. There was a time when this oak slab soared high into those branches above, and perhaps it will again one day. My children seem so young still, and yet soon they'll have moved on, with their own lives and families. Life moves so fast. You have to slow down occasionally, stop it slipping from your grasp.

Back in the kitchen, I look at my Instagram page and see that my following has already plummeted to 30K. 'Falling quickly' as the shipping forecast would say. Ah well, it's still more than an average working mum might expect. I post a photo of Grizelda sitting on the bread bin, then check my emails and find one from Imogen telling me that Vince has called his usual 9 a.m. meeting. He has a streak of sadism which makes this even more likely after parties. Reading on, I see we're being summoned to brainstorm a new documentary format Petroc has devised, called *Get the Church to Me on Time*. It's a renovation show set in a beautiful derelict chapel in Batheaston, exploring the challenges of restoring religious buildings. Vince is describing it as 'God meets *Grand Designs*.' What a good idea.

As I lay out the breakfast things, smiling to myself,

Robbie comes down looking smart in a suit, ready for a breakfast meeting in Bath.

'How are you feeling?'

'Not bad, considering. But I could do with a coffee if you're making it.'

After a strong cup from his cafetière, I take a long shower, regretfully washing out my curls along with the last vestiges of yesterday, emerging a new(ish) woman. The headache has receded to a light thud, easily manageable, and for once I take my time with my make-up, erasing the bags under my eyes, the age spots at my temples, editing my face until it's the glossy online, polished version. Because I'm worth it. In the cold light of day, it's clear my lovely green dress is speckled with shepherd's pie, so I wear a blue skirt with red roses embroidered on it, and a mustard-yellow T-shirt, with my new sandals. Adding a silver clover brooch that Hazel bought me for my fortieth birthday, I study myself in the mirror. Maybe I'm imagining it, but my hair still looks like it has an ounce of bounce. A very slight wave. The outfit has Mrs-Brown-from-*Paddington* vibes, just as I intended. I want to look bright, and fun, and nice, and not boring. You dress as you are, or at least as you'd like to be.

On my way back downstairs, I bang on the twins' doors bellowing 'Time to get up!' and then go down to feed Grizelda. But Robbie is already doing it, and I catch him stroking her, saying 'You is a pretty kitty' in the silly voice he reserves just for her. She gazes at him with disdain, before eating her breakfast with her usual dainty precision.

Hazel comes downstairs with her hair restored to its smooth glossy sheen. Avoiding my eyes, she busies herself eating cereal, scrolling on her phone. Pouring myself another coffee, I casually don my parental gardening gloves.

'Quite a day yesterday, wasn't it?'

She shakes her head, one finger on her phone.

'But a result in the end, no?'

My daughter tips the bowl to get the last of the cornflakes. 'Hmm-mmm.'

'Oh, go on, tell me *something*.'

She looks up, a gleam in her eye. 'It was a good day.'

'Invite him round.'

'Never.'

I laugh, mussing up her perfect hair. 'One day.'

My gloves are still on when Ethan finally appears, but this tender cutting needs to be carefully handled. He shuffles in, sliding into a chair and pulling the packet of Shreddies towards him.

'Thought I might come by the skate park tomorrow, if you're around.' He usually heads there on Saturday mornings.

He glances at me warily, and I hasten to reassure him. 'I won't let anyone see me. But I could treat you to brunch after?'

My son nods, steadily spooning wheat parcels.

'Right, it's a date then.'

He grunts. Job done.

We're all out of the house by eight-fifteen, though I have to go back to check Hazel's hair straighteners, and it's a good thing I do, because she's left them on, and the whole house could have burned down were it not for my scrupulousness. She's not nearly grateful enough, but then we're all scattering in various directions, Robbie catching a lift with a colleague, the twins on the bus pretending they don't know each other, and me heading to the station. Back to the grindstone.

And yet . . . I go slowly, deciding I'll get a later train, enjoy the meander through our little town, relish the feel of the sun on my bare arms, the sense of a day beginning. Tomorrow night, I might suggest Robbie takes me out for dinner – we can leave the kids to their own devices while we check out the new Italian place that's opened near the market. It'll give us a chance to have a proper talk. I've always been the worrier, and Robbie the calmer, but going forward I'll ask him to do a bit more of the panicking, so I can relax occasionally. I think I'm ready to take my foot off the gas, but I'll need someone at the wheel, keeping an eye on the road.

Boarding the train, I instantly spot an unattended rucksack, and swiftly move down the carriage, not away from the threat so much as the fret. Why worry? Why not just move on? Life's too short. Finding an empty seat next to the window, I pick up a discarded local paper.

A headline catches my eye: 'MADWOMAN MOWS DOWN YOGA GROUP', but before I can read the article, my gaze is snagged by another, bigger, story: 'PARK WARDEN APPREHENDS PEEPING TOM'. Seems like there was a lot going on in that park yesterday. Ah well, today's news is tomorrow's fish and chip paper. No point stressing over it.

Putting the paper down, I settle myself, pull my book out of my bag, turn to page 49, and start to read. It's going to be a good day.

# ACKNOWLEDGEMENTS

Hi there. It's that bit of the book where you thank all the people who helped make it happen. I often skip to that bit first, as if it's going to give an extra insight to prepare me for reading. So, if you've done that, here's something to entice you. The first thank you goes to Ferris Bueller, because he was a huge inspiration, both in writing and in life. I wish I could be more like him, but I can't, so I made Clover like him instead. Maybe both of them can persuade the rest of us to take a day off occasionally, to recharge.

Here are the others who deserve my gratitude for their time, generosity and expertise:

From TV Land, I want to thank all the production people I've worked with over the years – I never knew a funnier, more flippant bunch of miscreants. Specifically, I'd like to salute the RDF crew, who were my telly family for so many years – Jim Allen, Mel Bezalel, Jack Bootle, Sam Burr, Alexa Carey, Lynn Sutcliffe, Teresa Watkins, and many others. Thank you for making the job so much fun, and providing so many useful anecdotes. And a huge hat tip to the lovely Jo Scarratt-Jones, for being my Beta(max) reader. A superb TV exec (much better than Clover) and Bristolian, her help and insight were invaluable. I would also like to mention Jo's beloved dad Ron and the wonderful work of the Bristol Royal Infirmary who care for and support so many.

Staying in the West Country, I'd like to thank the Bristol branch of the Price family for responding to random texts like 'what's the poshest golf club down your way?' They were very patient with me, and I owe them a round (of golf or drinks).

Talking of drinks, Clover quaffs an awful lot in this book, and some of what she imbibes is good stuff. I'd like to raise a glass to Frog Stone, who shared her vast wine knowledge with me and indulged a long discussion about coolers. I'm sorry my penchant for prosecco disappoints her.

Once again, I found myself needing to know things about the academic year, school terms, exams etc, and turned to Lydia Aers for teacherly tidbits. An apple for her.

*Dziękuję* to Marta Antończuck for helping me with my Polish phrases – I was amazed I got them right, and now want to use them in real life.

To my fantastic publishing teams at HarperFiction in the UK and Putnam in the US: you're the villages that raise the book-baby. Such hard work, skill and passion goes into the publishing process and I'm in awe of what you do. Sales, marketing, copyediting, proofing, cover designing... the credits go on and on. And my excellent editors, Martha Ashby and Tara Singh Carlson – you're the ones who get the rough cut and have to make something of it. Thank you for working wonders.

All the awards go to my amazing agent, Madeleine Milburn, and her team of agency superstars. We authors can be so needy and insecure, but they're always there to reassure, support, encourage and respond to obscure questions about rights issues.

Taking my cue from Clover, I'd like to thank all the assistants at the above offices, who work so hard behind the scenes to make sure everything runs smoothly. I see you, and you deserve all the Bloom & Wild bunches.

I owe a huge debt of gratitude to booksellers, on the frontline of the industry, championing our books and starting the word-of-mouth ball rolling. I always used to say I wanted to see my book on a shelf in a shop – now I understand that it's better to get it *off* the shelf and into the hands of readers, and it's the booksellers who make that happen.

Finally, to my family. Thank you to my mum and dad for enduring my phone rants, my wonderful boys Wilfred & Edmund for ensuring my to-do list never gets done, to Phoebe for ensuring I'm never without a wipe in my hand. And to Tom, for criminal loading of the dishwasher. It wouldn't be the same without you. x